I0684944

Mars Quake

Copyright © 2015 by
Jon Batson

All rights reserved. No part of this book may
be reproduced in any form or by any
electronic or mechanical means, including
information storage and retrieval systems,
without permission in writing from the
publisher, except by a reviewer who may
quote brief passages in a review.

Second Edition

ISBN-10:098937260X
ISBN-13:978-0-9893726-0-2

Midnight Whistler Publishers
midnightwhistler@gmail.com

Characters and events in this book are
fictitious. Any similarity to real persons,
living or dead, is coincidental and not
intended by the author.

What they're saying about **Mars Quake**:

A breath of fresh air! I've come across a number of books lately that left me uninspired and uninterested, but **Mars Quake** really grabbed my attention and pulled me in. This delightful sci-fi features an attractive everyday Joe who juggles politics and romance as he pulls together pieces from his past lives to better understand recent quakes on Mars and save the world. An all around enjoyable read.

Robin Walls - K'un Health & Healing

When I received this book I was 25% into another. I don't generally read more than one at a time, but out of curiosity, I took a peek at the first chapter. Before I knew it I was five chapters into it and didn't want to put it down. I loved this book so much that I ended up putting the first book aside. It could wait.

James Paddock - Desert Book Shelf

Mars Quake is not just a story about life on Mars and space travel but a journey across the universe of human perception and political secrets. Batson has created a story intriguing enough to propel the mind toward uncharted territory and yet possible enough to defy the limitations of scientific certainty. A book you won't want to put down until the last mind-blowing page.

~ Sandra Carrington-Smith,
award-winning author of The Book of Obeah and Housekeeping for the Soul.

Fast-paced for sure - a good page-turner. Quite satisfying. A fun read.

Steven Garry Schlussel - World Class Entertainer

Mars Quake

by
Jon Batson

Midnight Whistler Publishers – since 1979

1

Dana Wright, Pocatello, ID

Dana Wright put on her fuzzy slippers and her favorite Sponge Bob PJs. She filled her over-sized "The Truth is Out There" mug with coffee and placed a croissant on her napkin. She planned to spend some time with her favorite planet.

Dana picked up her cane and hobbled out the door of her double-wide on the outskirts of Pocatello. At the shack on the other side of the yard, she balanced her cup and croissant, opened the door and slipped inside. She climbed into the jockey-chair and adjusted the telescope to focus on the planet Mars.

Dana had a PhD in Physics. She was the winner of the American Astronomical Society's award for extraordinary service to astronomy, the Alexander von Humboldt Senior Scientist Award, and Newcomb Cleveland Award from the American Association for the Advancement of Science. She was an expert in Martian Studies and a noted advocate for women in science. She was also in line to be the mission manager for the Mars Rover Mission – before the accident, that is.

"Come on, god of war!" she said to herself as she brought the red planet into focus. The Earth and Mars orbits were in alignment. This was the closest she was going to get for a long time to come.

Her father had the fascination before her ever since the first flyby in 1965 with the Mariner 4. He monitored the orbits of the Odyssey and the Express Orbiters. He cried with the fall of the stricken Reconnaissance Orbiter.

Dana took over in 2004 after college, following the adventures of the rovers, Spirit and Opportunity and the lander, Phoenix. There were others: landers, rovers and orbiters. But nothing to produce what everyone hoped for – and against: proof of extraterrestrial life.

Then in 2008, as Dana was lying in a Pocatello hospital recovering from the effects of a drunk driver who mangled her left leg, Mars Phoenix shook enough soil through its fine mesh screen and into its oven to bake up samples in search of water.

Dana sued the driver. The settlement paid for a larger telescope with computerized auto-alignment. The enhanced hardware allowed her to keep a constant eye on the Red Planet.

"Valles Marineris," sang Dana as she set her coffee cup down on the side table. She used both arms to adjust herself in the chair. The Noctis Labyrinthus on the western edge of the Mariner Valley was typical of the kind of ground found at the exit site of a flow of water. That is, water or ice or carbon-dioxide gas.

"Call me crazy," muttered Dana to herself, squinting to get a bead on a wide spot on the surface that might have been caused by flooding. "But this looks just like..."

She watched throughout the night, until Eos and Ganges Chasmata came into view to the West. Mars authorities believed they were carved by flowing water. There stood the irrefutable proof.

It was early in the morning when a tremor went through the shack, causing her coffee to ripple. She remembered the scene from Jurassic Park, when a tremor caused ripples in the coffee.

"But this is not Jurassic Park, it's Idaho!" she told herself. "There are no giant dinosaurs here, nor earthquakes – that's California."

The ground stopped shaking. Dana returned to her telescope, bringing a wide plane into focus.

The shaking was not only on her end, she could see that Mars also experienced some sort of event. There was a three minute lag for the light to get to Earth. She saw the ground shaking, redistributing the red dust. The Eos and Ganges disappeared as the dust rolled over the plains.

As the wrinkles of the Martian landscape smoothed out, other layers rose to create a new surface. She couldn't get a clear image through the clouds of dust.

Mars was not supposed to be tectonic, yet here it was: a Mars-quake, and she was a witness.

Without removing her eye from the scope, Dana picked up the remote and turned on the television on the table.

"...located in the area just off the Eastern Florida coast. We have here pictures sent via cell phone from an unidentified vessel said to be in those waters..."

Dana changed the channel.

"...moments ago. We do have an expert on earthquakes here right now. What? Oh! OK. Ladies and gentlemen, as soon as possible we will bring you..."

She hit the channel button again.

"...of a possible tsunami hitting the Florida coast. There is no way to predict the damage..."

Dana turned off the television. Yes, there had been an event on Earth, but now there was an event on Mars. She couldn't look away, though she couldn't see much through the dust clouds. The trembling had stopped, but far away, car sirens and dogs were both howling at the moon. Then three minutes later, the trembling on Mars stopped. As the dust settled she was able to bring the new Martian landscape into focus.

Dana pressed her face against the eyepiece, first the right, then the left eye. She then sat back, pale and frightened.

"Ho-ly shit!"

2
Tom Matthews at NASA, Washington, D.C.

We all remember where we were when this happened or that happened. When the biggest double earthquake in history occurred, I stood outside of the NASA administration building in Washington, D.C.

Simultaneous underwater quakes occurred off the coasts of the United States and Japan.

All I remember is that the ground began to shake in Washington. It wasn't in Los Angeles, where they're used to it. It was in Washington, where the ground is solid but the politics are not.

I didn't know what was happening at the time, but I was the one who would have to explain it to the Senator.

Not far away, the sound of barking dogs mixed with the car alarms going off in the parking lot. The cacophony of modern security technology and natural reaction was worse than the ground shaking. The dogs thought so too.

My phone went off, playing "Take Me Out to the Ball Game." I hit the button: "Matthews."

"Tom! What the hell was that?" screamed the voice of Senator Hughes, the man I worked for. Senator Hughes was the one heading up the committee that held the purse strings for NASA. He held the financial future of the Space Program in his hands.

"I'm investigating that as we speak, Senator. As soon as I have a cogent response, you'll be the first to know."

"Are you at NASA?"

"Yes, sir. They're coming now to brief me, I have to go."

"Get back to me as soon as..." I disconnected the call. I couldn't hear him over the din of car alarms. He would believe I lost the signal.

"Mr. Matthews?" said the young woman approaching me. She had on a gray skirt, a white blouse and blazer, accented by a dark red scarf emulating a necktie. She was carrying her shoes.

"Yes," I replied, turning my phone completely off. I didn't need the Senator calling while I was getting the tour.

"I suppose you can come with me, though I don't know who will be available. You know we just had what appears to be an earthquake."

"Yes, I was right here when it happened."

The young lady stood looking at me, holding her high heels, as if she hadn't understood what I said. Then she shook her head, as if waking from a bad dream.

"OK! Um, this way, please."

She walked toward the imposing building that was the NASA headquarters in her bare feet. At the front doors, she paused, smiled and placed a hand on my shoulder.

"May I?" she asked, not waiting for an answer. She raised one foot, slipped a shoe onto it.

She repeated the action with the other, using me as her steadying influence – something that hadn't happened in quite some time.

I didn't answer, of course. I just stood still and made sure I was ready to catch her if the ground began to shake again.

"Thanks," she said. "This way, please."

She seemed a foot taller, though it was more like three inches in reality. The click-click-click of her heels across the marble floor caused me to look down as she walked. The effect of the high heels on her legs was notable and distracting, yet I couldn't help but wonder how she could walk in those things.

At the elevator, an armed guard stood, stern faced and grim.

"Sorry, Miss Carlyle, no elevator, not today. We just had an earthquake."

"But it's a long way up, George," she replied.

"Sorry, no can do. Use of the elevator in time of building instability is prohibited." He was no doubt quoting from a company rule book he had tucked in his lunch pail.

My guide, Miss Carlyle, took out a phone. She tapped in a code and did an elaborate step involving a head swirl, freeing her hair from her left ear. She fluttered her eyelashes and held the phone to the side of her head.

"Mr. Jameson? He's here, sir. I would, but the elevator is not working." She looked at me, smiled and winked. "Yes, sir. Thank you, sir."

She put the phone back into her pocket and smiled like an airline flight attendant. "He'll be right down. We can wait over here. Coffee?"

"Yes, please. Does this happen a lot, I mean, quakes?"

"In Washington? Never."

"I haven't been here long."

"So you're new with the Senator," she said, not as a question, more like a guess that I was to confirm.

Several snide responses to Miss Carlyle's observation played in my head, but I let them go by. Social politeness precludes me saying "Duh!" to the person who is showing me to the office of the NASA representative – or in this case, to coffee.

I answered her question with a "Yes."

We stepped up to the coffee station. It was decorated like a wagon, with large, spoke wheels and complete with a girl in a white apron. The girl offered us a weak smile. She just survived an event that never happened in

Washington. She celebrated by pouring us each a cup of coffee.

We stood there, drinking our coffee, while people ran to and fro around us. Alarms went quiet, one by one, and the scurrying slowed as normalcy returned.

A tall man of about forty came trotting down the stairs. He looked to be in good shape, but was out of breath.

"Mr. Matthews?" he said, still trying to regain his composure.

"Mr. Jameson," I replied.

"Whoosh! I run every day, but those stairs..." he said, panting.

"I understand. Maybe we should sit."

"Good idea," he replied.

I set the cup, half finished, on the coffee wagon counter. I followed Jameson to the leatherette covered benches.

"So, what just happened? Did we actually have an earthquake?" I asked, as we sat down. Miss Carlyle sat on the next bench, ready to be of use at need.

"That's what it seems like, though it has never happened before. That is, not in this part of the country, not that I can recall, and I've been here since Pathfinder in '97."

"That's the Mars Pathfinder?" I asked, just to clarify.

"Yes, it was a glorious time. The possibility of Martian

exploration was on everyone's mind."

"It's still on your mind, with two rovers landing in 2004 and the Phoenix in 2008."

"Yeah! We've got orbiters still in operation: Odyssey and Express. Curiosity is measuring temperature and seasonal changes."

"And the possibility of water," I added.

"Oh yes! If they find water, there might be life of some sort. They already found some form of ice and formations in the dust that could only be from water flowing. There could at one time have been life on the Red Planet, and the remnants might still be there. But hell, man, look at the way things are now. They seem to have junked the whole thing for the sake of a war we can't win."

"Is that the belief around here? That we shut the Shuttle down due to the war?"

"After the event in '86, questions began to get raised. No one knows what happened to that one, you know. But we didn't think they'd pull the plug on us. Then this whole thing in the Middle East kicked up and ... Do you know that trillions are going into that thing? Trillions!"

"Yes, I knew that."

"And yet, there you sit, calm and cool and ask me why we aren't going to Mars?" He was hot under the collar now.

"Uh, I didn't ask..." I stammered.

"We're shut down, sir! Tell that to your Senator. Shut

down! There's not enough money to upgrade the coffee, much less send a man into space."

"I just wanted to..."

"You came here to take the temperature of the patient, to see if he was still alive. Well, he is, but just. Next week they'll be looking at our offices to see what else could go in here. It'll be 'the building once known as NASA' before you can say 'Man-in-the-Moon.' You'll find Space Exploration in the basement." Jameson jumped to his feet. I remained sitting.

"Mr. Jameson, I didn't mean to..." I held my hands out wide.

"Tell the Senator, that NASA has done a lot for this country. More than just ball-point pens that write upside down. There's things in your car that came from NASA research. You remember that as you drive back to your grand office on Capitol Hill."

"I uh..." I said to Jameson's back as he stormed away. My awkward stammer echoed in the empty lobby, as everyone had found where they had to be and had gone there.

"Sorry about that," said Miss Carlyle. "He cares about the cuts to NASA's budget."

"I didn't cut his budget. I just took a job. It was this or teach in Nebraska."

"I'll tell him. Goodbye."

I turned and took the extended hand of the young

woman who had shown me in, feeling a small twinge as we touched. We had known each other before, once upon a time, a long, long time ago, in another life. I felt it, she did not. It was a feeling I knew well. I had felt it many times before.

3
Memories

There was a time when I could have touched someone and felt nothing. That was when I was young, before my memories came into focus. I remembered quite a lot. Sometimes whole scenes would play out in an instant inside my head, always with me in the lead role.

The S.E.5 biplane veered out of control as I over-steered. It was a common but sometimes fatal mistake. The horizon began to spin and I couldn't get my bearings; which way was up? At my left a wire snapped and bits of fabric tore from the fragile wings. The wind on my face told me I was going faster than the biplane's design – I was going down. I looked ahead, but didn't see blue sky and white clouds. I saw brown earth. A tree was spinning round and round and it was getting bigger. The propeller had stopped; the smell of oil and smoke filled my nostrils. I grasped the thin roll of leather just below the windscreen in a vain effort to hold the plane back. The sounds of wood splintering to my left and right stopped, as did the spinning tree and the ground that held it. Everything, the whole world, was in suspended animation. It was a training mission; I never saw action. The Vickers and Lewis guns were never fired. I was 19. It was a useless death.

In the Scottish Highlands several men dragged my father and me from our small hut. I was dirty and ragged in only a nightshirt. I didn't know the men who pulled us out into the cold, gray morning, but they were angry and cursing. They took me first and my father cried out. I saw his mouth open, his eyes wild. He froze in mid-scream and the cold and damp were no more. I was 12, I think.

There are more memories.

I remembered a *pistol duel in the snow with an aristocratic gentleman outside of London.*

A blast left me feeling numb as I watched our Yankee Militia charge the Dragoons in silence and without me.

A single hole appeared in my jacket while charging down a gorge in a particularly funny hat.

But why bother? That was then. This is now.

Now I was living this life, meeting new people, the same people. At the interview for my current job, a man walked in looking at my resume. He smiled and looked up at me.

"Mr. Matthews?"

"Yes." I stood.

"Danning. Pleased to meet you." He extended a hand.

"And you." I took the hand. As I did, I felt a flicker, an instantaneous surge of energy across my consciousness. Just as fast, it was gone. I blinked. Then I shook his hand.

Danning smiled. We let go and he went on with the interview as if nothing had happened. To Danning, nothing had.

Early on, when I first felt that flicker, I didn't know what it was. Perhaps carpet static, or a surge in the power, or a brain tumor. Now, of course, all was crystal clear.

He wasn't Danning back then, he was *a pretty nurse who took care of me after the third push toward the line. The nurse didn't seem like the other Germans who ran our Italian unit like slave masters. She was kind and caring. She tucked me in with extra care when incoming fire interrupted us.*

I knew I was going to do well on the job. Danning and I had an inexplicable bond.

"The Senator is looking forward to meeting you, Mr. Matthews. We're happy to have you as part of the team." Danning showed me to the door and the hallway beyond. "We have a desk all set up for you and you can start right away. That is, if you can start right away."

"Oh, yes, I can jump right in."

"Excellent! Then come this way." Danning led me down the hall, chatting up the wonders of the office. The coffee corner is this way, the restrooms are that way. We passed small offices where my co-workers labored. It looked like the whole team was there.

"This is Barkley. She'll cut your checks. Pam Barkley, Tom Matthews."

"Hello, Barkley." I took the slender hand and looked into the soft brown eyes. In an instant, the memory of "Barkley" came up and *bit me on the shoulder. The hard, dark wood of the ship pressed me as I struggled to lower myself even further below the railing. I cowered in the corner next to the gun that "Mate Gurney" and I crewed. The tide of battle had turned against us. Our gun was useless. Gurney looked up at me, managed a slight smile and died.*

"Mr. Matthews, or should I call you Tom?"

Barkley did not remember dying in my arms on board the *HMS Kensington* so many years ago. There was no reason that she should.

"Tom will be fine." I smiled.

In my private word bubble, I said, "Glad to be working with you again." Barkley smiled, as if she heard me.

* * *

The first time I was aware of the memory was in basic training. When I met "Slick," I knew we were buddies. Our arms touched while we juggled our gear to the barracks and I felt the flicker. It wasn't a picture, no sound, no smells, just a flicker of light followed by a warm feeling that I was with a friend.

We weren't a pair that you would have guessed would become friends. I was the country boy from a place with a single gas station, the sandy-haired yokel who was sure to be the first screw-up. Slick was from the inner city, black as night. He danced when he walked and it took me several days to understand anything he said. We became inseparable.

After the Army, I found a job as a waiter. Connie was the hostess, aloof and distant. She would have nothing to do with the serving staff. She brushed me too close one day and the flood gates of my memory opened.

In a drafty monastery high in the Spanish mountains, a young monk looked up at me with questioning eyes.

Connie was not female then, she was male, looking to me for guidance. Then the memory was gone; just a flicker, like a single subliminal frame inserted into real life.

Connie and I dated for the rest of the year. When she left me to marry another fellow, I made it my job to meet him. His name was Brad and he was quite a catch. I didn't blame her, but I still felt hurt.

When I met Brad, he shook my hand with gusto, grinning like he had just scored the winning touchdown. I reached my mind out to hold on to the coming flicker of memory. I soaked it in, looking for a clue that would put this in perspective.

"Slap!" went the hand across the face of the fellow next to me at the bar of the Trotter's Inn. I laughed. The girl who just delivered the open right to the face of my friend was Kate, the innkeeper's daughter. It was she my friend had promised to wed the day before and took to his bed the same night. He failed to mention that we would be sailing for the new world within hours.

The girl was now Brad and my friend who jilted her was now Connie, hanging on his arm as if she would live there forever. Somehow it all came into focus. I smiled back at Brad. He furrowed his brows, as if not understanding the response. "No," I said inside my head, "and it's likely that you never will."

And so it went, as I moved from place to place, time to time, meeting and greeting the team with whom I shared so much history.

The landlady who rented me the Washington apartment used to be *a barmaid in a place so remote, the larder was empty most of the time.*

The memories rolled over me as I followed her middle aged rear end up the stairs, listening to her extol the virtues of the apartment on the second floor.

The mechanic who cares for my car was *a rake and a reckless swordsman at school in England. Though we were friends, he took offense to an off-handed comment and challenged me to a duel. Thinking it a joke, I drew steel and we were at it — only I was playing and he was not. I died looking into his eyes.* Now he had grease on his hands and was telling me I needed a new air filter. Forgive and forget, I say.

4
Meeting Dana Wright

How do we remember? Do we just reach back into time and call up the picture with sounds and smells, feeling the smooth and rough edges? Is it a solid thing a surgeon can remove? Or is it nebulous, like the aura you can measure but not see? That aura present in a living body, but missing from a dead one?

At night, dreams would come. I wouldn't be on a sailing ship, *I would be in a room. But the room would be on a sailing ship.*

I wouldn't be in Portugal, *I would be in a bar. But the bar would be in a port town in Portugal.*

I wouldn't be in Scotland at the time of Robert the Bruce, I *would be in a hut on the side of a hill. But the hill would be in Scotland and I would be waiting for Robert to show up.*

When I met Dana, there was nothing. It surprised me. That hadn't happened before. There was always some flicker of memory.

"Mr. Matthews," said April.

She was the Senator's secretary who I had last seen *over the sights of an Enfield rifle.* "This is Dana Wright, your two o'clock."

I stood up and took Dana's hand, waiting for the rush of memory. It didn't come. I smiled like a six-year-old. "Hello, Miss Wright."

"Mr. Matthews," said Dana, and we continued to hold hands. Dana had a strange look on her face, like I had just said something she did not understand. I noticed the look and let go of her hand, turning red in the process.

"I don't believe we've met before," I said to Dana.

"No, I don't believe we have," she replied.

"And yet, you seem familiar. Perhaps I've seen you, where, on television?" I was hoping for a hint from her.

"It's likely that you have seen a videotaped lecture. I have given several lectures on space travel and the planet Mars. It's the reason for my visit today."

"Strange that you come today, as I just got back from NASA. You know we had an earthquake there this morning."

"Yes, I felt it in Idaho just before I boarded a plane to D.C. In fact, it might have a connection to the reason for my trip."

I indicated a chair and Dana Wright sat down. The obvious thing would have been to ask the reason for her trip. How did it connect to the earthquake felt in D.C.

21

and Idaho. But my mind was still on the fact that we had no previous memory together.

As far back as I could remember, I rambled through my life surrounded by the same people. The same team of colleagues, rearranging ourselves in unique relationships, came along with me. They were different each time, but they were always the same people. Of course, I knew that there were more people in the world than there used to be – after all, at one time, I knew most of them. So I expected that sooner or later, I would meet someone new. I just didn't expect that it would be today.

"Mister Matthews?" said Dana Wright, leaning forward. "Would you like to know what brings me here today, all the way from Idaho?"

"Oh! Yes! Please, tell me. What brings you here today, all the way from Idaho?" I had lapsed into a dream and now felt like an idiot.

She opened a large case designed for carrying art work. From this she produced several giant sheets of paper, rolled. She unrolled a large sheet on my desk, from which I saved my coffee cup just in time. The sheets were photographs of the planet Mars.

"That's interesting, I was just discussing Mars this morning with Mr. Jameson from NASA."

"Yes, I know Jameson. Not the brightest bulb on the tree, but he's passionate."

"That he is." I remembered his tirade in the lobby.

"But you work for the man with the budget in his hand and I am told that you hold the keys to NASA. I need to talk to whoever is over Jameson and whoever is over him. Look at this."

Dana Wright stood up, steadying herself on a cane in her left hand. With her right hand, she pointed to a place on the face of the Red Planet, Mars.

"What do you think that is?"

I peered at the surface of the small planet at what appeared to be writing. It occurred to me that it couldn't be writing.

"It's a joke. A bunch of kids on spring break have gone up there and written 'Drink Mars Cola' in the dust." I looked up at Ms. Wright. She was not smiling.

"In eight mile high letters?" she said.

"OK, no. But that's what it looks like. What do you think it is?"

"I don't know, and I'm the expert. So that's why you are going to take me to NASA."

"NASA in Washington is an administrative building. It's full of bureaucrats and lobbyists. They're money boys, not scientists – well, not these days, anyway."

"Then you'll get me to Palomar Observatory in San Diego so we can have a look at this thing."

"When did you take these?" I asked, looking closer at the pictures.

"This morning, just after the early morning shocks

that rocked Pocatello. They're not used to that up there."

"No, we're not used to it here either."

My gift, my curse, was kicking in. I had not met Dana Wright before. But I felt that I had met the collection of strange lines across the face of the nearest planet. It was familiar territory, though I could not recall specifics.

I looked up at Dana Wright, determination setting into my face. I reached over and pushed a button on the side of my desk. April came in. Ms. Wright looked around at her.

"April. Would you please call Mr. Jameson at NASA and tell him we're coming over with the answer to his question."

5

The Senator

"Care to share, Mr. Matthews?" said the Senator from the door.

We had almost gotten out clean, without the obligatory explanation of our activities. The Senator loved to make people explain what they were doing and why. It made perfect sense to me, as he had been in a position of power for as long as I had known him. He was *my teacher in a one-room school house in Maine and my captain on a frigate out of Boston. He was my colonel in the Great War and again in Korea.* It was no surprise that he was my boss once again.

When the Senator and I first shook hands, hundreds of years of history played through my mind. He, of course, felt nothing. It seemed that the memory was mine and mine alone. I had yet to meet one of the many team member who remembered me. Still it was my team and we kept showing up to share the joys and the sorrows.

I had grown used to recognizing other members of the soap opera that was my life. Meeting Dana Wright was a surprise.

No, let me rephrase. Meeting her was a shock. I didn't know other people existed, only my team. They were my personal group of damaged people.

Now here was *the old sea captain, the teacher, the colonel,* all demanding to know what was going on. Typical!

"Allow me to introduce Dana Wright, sir. Miss Wright, Senator Jason Hughes. Miss Wright is an astronomer with some interesting discoveries concerning Mars. I should bring them to the attention of the folks down at NASA. I think this might be a game changar."

The words hung in the air as Senator Hughes considered them. He then stepped to one side and raised his hand, indicating that we are to come into his office.

"Pleased to meet you, Senator," said Dana. "Doctor Dana Wright."

I winced, having screwed up the introduction and gotten our whole trip off on a wrong foot. Of course, she would be Doctor Wright. How could I have missed that? Meeting someone for the first time threw me.

"The information I have could be time sensitive, so if we could get to NASA..." started Doctor Wright.

"We've cut the funding to NASA," interjected the Senator. "You might find no one there. Perhaps you could show me what you found."

The Senator walked to his desk, sat in his chair and awaited a professional presentation. Doing things at a leisure pace when others were in a hurry was his way of showing how little he thought of the project at hand and the people involved.

Dana looked as if she had considered hitting him over the head with her cane, but must have thought better of it. She walked instead to the globe in the corner.

"Mr. Matthews, a hand if you please."

I got behind the globe, glad to see wheels on the stand, and rolled it into the open space to the left of the Senator's immense desk.

"Thank you. Here off the coast of Florida, along the 35 degree latitude line, lies an area of water known as the Bermuda Triangle. It is an area well known for the unexplained disappearances of both seagoing vessels and airborne craft."

She kept her finger on the place over the Bermuda Triangle, as she rotated the globe, stopping off the coast of China.

"The Devil's Sea, the Dragon's Triangle, is located in the Philippine Sea off China's eastern coast. It is also at 35 degrees latitude, known for vanishing ships and planes like the Bermuda Triangle. Both areas, as you would know if you had monitored the television news stations, have experienced large earthquakes early this morning. Both areas are experiencing tsunami conditions and both are undergoing changes that we could not predict."

She walked to the desk, unrolled one of the large photos she brought and laid it across the items the Senator had on his desktop.

"This point here," she indicated with a finger, showing one end of the string of lines and dots looking like writing, "and this point here," she pointed to the other end of the strange sentence in the red dust, "are exactly the same places on the Martian orb, indicating that deep within the Martian soil, as within Earth's crust, a violent quake has shaken the surface. The quake has revealed, between these two points, this stretch of figures. If you imagine them as occurring between the Bermuda Triangle and the Devil's Triangle, you will get some idea of their size."

Dana left her finger on the photograph, looking at the Senator through her eyebrows. She was making a point and wanted to know if he was following her so far. Her entire composure said, "Are you with me?" Of course, she was quiet. She was like that for a full minute. When she spoke, the old school master was not present. This was beyond his education and experience.

"It's a quake, sir," she said, without moving.

The Senator continued looking at the photograph.

"It's a Mars quake, sir," said Dana Wright.

The Senator looked at her with no light of recognition in his eyes.

"Which has revealed these markings," she said, as if he needed a shove through some unseen door in his mind. "...are straight or curved in even strokes and repetitive. Intelligent life, not nature, created these."

The Senator sat back, looked from her to me, then at the photograph again. Dana had not yet removed her finger from one end of the string of markings. She stood up straight, placed both hands on the edge of the desk and leaned forward.

"Senator. There are rock formations under the Bermuda Triangle so uniform, so straight, they must have been made by man, not by nature. There are formations under the Dragon's Triangle that are also indicative of buildings, temples. We do not find straight lines in nature, nor perfect curved lines. They do not exist. Only man, only intelligent life, makes these. These could only be..."

"Buildings," I said before I knew it was coming out of my mouth.

Both Senator Hughes and Doctor Wright, the knowledgeable astronomer, looked up at me. I looked from her to him and then at the photograph that was between them on the desk.

"Well, I mean, it looks like buildings. It can't be letters. No one would write in letters that big."

"No," added Dr. Wright, still looking up at me. "They would have to be many miles high. So, yes, I suppose it is a line of structures, miles across; big, huge structures."

"Sooo," said the Senator. "We should…"

Dana looked at him. She was wondering how he could have ever have won an election.

"So, we should go up there and see what they are. We should see what is in them and if it is the remnants of an early Martian civilization. Or the site of a current civilization. Who knows, there may be people up there." Dana delivered the ultimatum without emotion or passion.

The Senator's eyes went wide. His face went pale.

"There might be people?"

"Yes! People; not like us, of course, but intelligent. They are playing with the equipment we landed there. They're wondering when we're going to come and get it. This, Senator, is proof that there either was or is intelligent life on Mars."

6
The 35 Degree Latitude Line

At NASA headquarters, Miss Carlyle met us at the door as before, only with her shoes on. She held the door, smiling at Dana Wright as she hobbled into the lobby with her cane.

It was clear that Ms. Wright was not used to this much walking in a day. She had thrown on a traveling suit and boarded a plane to D.C. She took a taxi to my offices. I drove her to the National Aeronautics and Space Administration building.

She didn't speak all the way to NASA. I assumed she was either angry or frightened. Washington traffic can do that to you.

"The Senator's office called that you were on your way. The elevators are working now. Well, actually they were working before, it's just that..." she decided not to go into the explanation. "Right this way."

We followed Miss Carlyle to the elevator. On the way up, she felt the need to entertain us.

"The shaking we experienced earlier was, as it turns out, an earthquake. Isn't that odd? Usually they happen in California."

"It did happen in California," said Dana. "And in Texas and Florida and Idaho and Hawaii and was even felt in Toronto. They felt the quake from the China Sea to the Bermuda Triangle. That's why we're here. Jameson had better be taking us to someone with some real clout or I'm calling the President."

"There may be more than one briefing today."

Dana turned toward me, her eyebrows dark with anger.

"Kee-riste, Matthews! How many people am I going to have to explain this to?"

"A few hundred more, I'm afraid, but I'll try to herd them all together for you."

The elevator doors opened and there stood Jameson, wide-eyed and shaking. He looked as if he had just seen zombies in the halls.

"Come this way, they're waiting."

Jameson trotted down the corridor to a large conference room. There was already a table set up with an overhead projector. Every chair had a body in it and there was a line of people around the room against the walls. As Jameson and I walked in, the rumble of talking subsided. As Doctor Wright entered, somewhat behind due to her bad leg, a murmur ran through the attendees.

She walked to the front of the room and spread her first picture on the overhead projector. She spoke in a strong, commanding voice, a voice that was not afraid of talking over others.

"Along the 35 degree latitude line, lies the Sargasso Sea. It is a sea without shores, within the Bermuda Triangle and surrounded by North Atlantic currents. It is often called the Graveyard of Ships. It is blamed for the unexplained disappearances of hundreds of air and sea vessels.

"On that same line, in the Philippine Sea off China's eastern coast, is the Devil's Sea. In it, the Dragon's Triangle, known for vanishing ships and airplanes as well. Declared it to be a danger zone by the Japanese government in 1952, when the vessel, the Kaio Maru No. 5, sent to investigate the troubled waters, vanished without a trace. Twenty-two crewmen and nine scientists also disappeared.

"Some say extraterrestrials are to blame. Others say lost kingdoms or ancient curses are to blame, with no resolution. The two areas share some magnetic anomalies. Some say undersea volcanoes influence the area's sudden environmental changes, others site UFOs. Both may be right."

A nervous shudder went through the room as heads leaned into other heads to exchange comments.

"Both triangles exist at 35° west and 35° east latitude.

If you were to start in the Bermuda Triangle and travel straight through the center of the earth, you would come out at the Dragon's Triangle. There is a connection."

The murmuring continued. Dana Wright looked up from her notes to see who was listening, if anyone. She decided to raise the ante.

"The two locations are polar opposites. Both have the world's deepest waters and both share the same anomaly. Geographic North and magnetic North are in a line to both of them."

Now the comments grew to a point where she had to speak up. When she did, the place went silent:

"Amelia Earhart went down in the Dragon's Triangle."

Dana Wright stood at the head of the room silent and still. Before her was a room full of NASA bigwigs, also silent and still. She decided that she had their attention.

"This morning, as you saw on your televisions and felt in the seat of your pants, an earthquake occurred. I felt it in Idaho. Others felt it in Hawaii, as in Florida, as in Mexico. I believe it was the result of seismic activity deep within the Earth. Further, I believe the Bermuda Triangle and the Dragon's Triangle were both affected."

Senior staffers gave orders to juniors, others wrote notes. A handful of staffers ran out of the room to take orders to other offices.

"If I may continue," said Dana Wright. The room quieted down. Some who had been standing around the edge pulled out chairs now empty and sat down. All listened, intent on what the visiting doctor was about to say.

"At the same time, there was an event on the planet Mars."

She had their attention now. There wasn't the sound of a breath in or out. Every eye was on her.

"The event was, let us call it for the time being, a Mars quake. The two ends of the event lie on the corresponding points to those on the Earth, the two Triangles. Between these two points is something revealed by the shifting topsoil. Between these two points, there is something new not seen before."

Dana reached down and turned on the overhead projector. She straightened the photograph so that the part of the red planet that showed the change was in the center. There was an audible gasp throughout the room.

"These are not natural, but made by intelligent life. Straight lines, curved lines, parallel lines. They resemble some sort of writing. As if an alien intelligence is attempting to send us a message written on the surface of Mars. If that is the case, these letters would have to be more than eight miles high, each. I prefer to go with another theory I heard just today, that they are buildings. I believe this, ladies and gentlemen, is a city."

The questions flew.

"Where did it come from?"

"How come we're just seeing this now?"

"Who made them?"

"What does this mean?"

And the clincher: "Does this mean the space program will resume?"

At that, there was silence. All eyes looked to me.

Doctor Wright tilted her head, anticipating my answer. Her eyebrows tilted up, her perky blond page-boy fell to one side. Her mouth pursed, as if a little miffed that I was keeping her waiting.

"Well," she said, "Will the space program be resuming or not?"

In truth, I didn't know. I had only been on the job a short time and had no power. I was not the one voted to the Senate by the people. I was a gofer, a well-educated gofer, but a gofer just the same.

"Ah, let me get back to you on that. We will have to prepare something for the Senator and then present a case. We will commission a study, form a committee, address the issue. You know: the usual."

"The usual Capitol Hill bullshit," said one gruff old codger. "slow as molasses and headed in the wrong direction."

"Ladies and gentlemen," said Dana, taking the pressure off of me. "with the prospect of life on Mars, I am pretty sure this will be a priority changar. Remember, there is an election coming up. If this doesn't become an issue, I'll take up knitting."

Conversations picked up. People stood, leaving the room. Several people shoved their cards in Dana's hands. And in my own as staffers and assistants left to rearrange their priorities. Two stayed behind. When they rose from their chairs, it was a sign for the rest that it was time to leave.

"Doctor Wright?" said the first man, a tall, imposing gentleman who towered over Dana and yet bowed as if in subservience. His address surprised me, as no one introduced her as "doctor."

"Doctor Cutler. How nice to see you again. You may not remember, we met in San Diego. It was a conference at the Palomar Observatory."

"Um, oh, yes, of course. Nice to see you as well. Are you getting along all right?" The man looked down at her leg, unable to keep himself from drawing attention to the object of his curiosity.

"Alcohol, I'm afraid, has been my undoing," Dana said, in her flat, matter-of-fact voice. "A drunk driver."

Dana turned away, giving the man her back, gathering her papers. She didn't need him, he needed her.

"My apologies, Doctor Wright. I remember you now. You wore that little black number with sling heels and I fell in love with you immediately. It never occurred to me at the time that you were a leader in your field. If you will excuse my clumsiness, it will be an honor to work with you."

Dana stopped gathering papers for a moment. She turned to Doctor Cutler.

"Thank you, Doctor. We should be working together. But since there is life on Mars, it would be best that we put our attention on the work and not on the 'little black number.' Don't you think?"

Dana turned back around and continued gathering notes. She didn't fear this man or his power. Doctor Cutler made a resolute face with a glance at his colleague. He sucked in a large volume of air and walked around the overhead projector. He looked Dana in the face.

"My apologies again, Doctor. You're right, of course."

Cutler waved another man over to the circle. He was another executive type in a striped suit and wire glasses.

"Allow me to introduce Doctor Bronson, who holds the keys to the Palomar. You and he should have a few things in common."

Dana turned to regard Doctor Bronson, a short, middle-aged man.

I stood back, away from the group but still part of it. I wanted to be in the middle of this, wherever that might lead. It wasn't that I longed to be near power, as some people might. With me, it was Dana, a new team member, one who had not been in my company before. I wanted to know where she would take me.

7
Washington in the Rain

The skies grew dark and foreboding, as if announcing the coming of doom, but all that came was rain. The already humid days of summer in Washington were only made worse by rain.

I stood at the window of the fourth floor conference room. It occurred to me that I had never been there before today. Yet I had been there twice.

The glass showed my face to be that of an average man in his mid-thirties, with brown hair, blue eyes. At one time, I considered that face somewhat handsome. But then, I shaved it every day and was rather tired of it.

Beyond my own reflection was that of Doctor Wright talking with the two PhDs from NASA. They were the ones I didn't want to meet yet. They were powerful men, rulers of the organizations that held sway over outer space. One was the top man in NASA, the administration at least. The other was the man to talk to if you want to look at the heavens through the Palomar telescope.

Such men tended to be such men lifetime to lifetime. The captain is rarely the cook unless he is under cover or taking a lifetime off. The cook is never the captain unless he is a total incompetent put there by family money. More often the captains of industry were unmistakable from one century to the next. Whoever these men had been in the past, I had said "Yes, sir!" to them.

Walking through the halls of Washington power, I had brushed old allies and adversaries from centuries ago. The smell of old parchment and mead more than once filled my nostrils. The clanking of chain-mail had resonated in my ears by the mere brushing of someone in the NASA hallways. We were old associates, comrades, brothers-in-arms and enemies. The workings of lifetime-to-lifetime were something I was still figuring out. Still it seemed clear to me that we didn't stray too far from our old crews. We went from the battlefield to the sandbox with ease.

As fast as the weather changes in Washington, I felt a change inside me. I now wanted to meet these men, to learn who they are new and who they had been. Not that it mattered in the long run, but it was of curious interest to me.

Past life experience or character, I had learned, had little bearing on present day. Some people tended to end up in leadership positions no matter what. A screw-up is a screw-up down through the ages. Yet, I had proven bad at guessing who would be a friend and who would be an adversary.

The face of my ex-wife, Helen, came into my head unbidden. She was an excellent example of bad judgment. We had betrayed each other so many times that it was love at first sight. We couldn't let go of each other. Friends thought destiny chose us to hold the record, that we would be together forever. Little did they know that we already had been.

The marriage lasted three years. The joy lasted for three weeks. The rest of the three years was an argument that covered three states. She later moved to Seattle, where she met and fell in love with another old adversary. Better him than me. I pushed memories of Helen out of my head.

I caught the eye of one of the men standing with Dana, girded myself for the confrontation and moved forward.

"Doctor Cutler? Tom Matthews, from Senator Hughes' office."

The big man reached out a hand and I knew I was in for it. Here stood a Walter Raleigh, a Thomas Jefferson, a John Adams. Here would be the man in charge wherever he went. He would lord over the playground, claim class president and rule the frat house. His hand took mine and I looked him square in the eye.

In a rush, the windy ramparts of a castle threatened to blow me from my feet. The lord of the castle grabbed me by the tunic, pulling me to him, his grizzled face set in determination.

"We have them now, m'lord! Draw sword and follow me to hell! Get a little blood on ya, it'll put a willow up that spine!"

"Pleased to meet you, Mr. Matthews. Are you assisting Doctor Wright?"

The winds abated, the smell of horses and stale hay went with them. I stood in the conference room at NASA, gripping the hand of Doctor Cutler, the man who at any minute would ask me for money to go to Mars.

"This is all rather new, Doctor. This morning when we both got up, we didn't know we would be standing here with a tsunami about to hit."

"Oh, yeah. That. Well, we should find out about that, shouldn't we. Let's find a television and see if we're going to get wet." Cutler turned to Bronson and called out.

"Bronson. Gather the good doctor and come to my office. There's a television there and we can find out what is happening here on Earth before we decide about Mars."

8
Doctor Bronson of Palomar Observatory

When I shook the hand of Doctor Bronson, I found a friend; I had not seen him in centuries. *Professor Wilbur was the old man of the university. He was sharp as a whip and just as quick to sting a young student caught unawares.*

"You have not the time for fancies and frivolities, young man," I heard him say. "Some walk these halls with ease, but you must run, skip, jump and burn the late night oil if you are to keep up."

In an instant, the professor was gone. Brusk Doctor Bronson stood there instead, pumping my hand as if I had just given him a prize.

"It's good to meet you, Mister Matthews. I don't know where we'd be without the money people financing our endeavors."

"Out of money, I expect." I don't know why I said it. I suppose I had to say something. Bronson laughed. He let go of my hand and slapped me on the shoulder like an old frat buddy.

"Say, you're all right, Matthews."

"Thank you, doctor. So you're the one we see about putting an eye to the Palomar telescope?"

"Yes, and under the circumstances, it would be best if we do just that as soon as possible. That is, if Palomar is not under water."

We all turned toward the television screens. There were five of them in Doctor Cutler's office. They were set to Fox, CNN and the three major networks.

The talking heads were having a field day. There had been an earthquake far underground that had shaken the whole world. They felt the tremors in Australia, China and Canada. The anticipated tsunami shook out and the expected mile-high wave never happened.

Water rose on the Outer Banks and there was some flooding in the Florida Keys. The death toll was at sixty-seven and rising. Many had lost boats and property destroyed by quake and flood, but not the millions we were expecting.

Off the coast of China, in the Devil Sea, another quake and tsunami had occurred. And just as strange, the expected disaster had been smaller than anticipated. The waves had abated. The death toll in Asia was eighty-four, though some areas were unreachable for a count.

Reports were still coming in. Hoards of people stormed the markets for water, food and Pampers.

There was looting going on in many areas. Snatches of footage showed people running from electronics stores with giant TV screens.

In an emergency where you are certain to lose your life, you must have more Pampers and a larger television. The Pampers helped those who knew if the tsunami came the last thing they wanted to do was soil themselves. Rather thoughtful, when you consider it.

"Gentlemen," said Doctor Wright, turning to the three of us. "There is nothing we can do about this. We are not going to have to evacuate D.C. Let's find out if we can get a flight to San Diego. If it is still there, we can go and have a look at Mars."

Doctor Cutler nodded with agreement. He produced a cell phone and punched in a number. He began speaking to someone in hushed tones, as if it was top secret.

Doctor Bronson looked at me, and I thought for a moment there was a spark of recognition. But his face broke into a smile, one of those social smiles you keep ready for when you don't know what else to do. He took out a phone and tapped it twice.

"Darcy? Are you still alive out there? Good! I want you to do a few things for me. First, sort me out a few hotel rooms, we're bringing guests. Then, get the scope warmed up and point it at Mars. That's right, Mars. We'll be on the next flight. Tell my wife, I'll be late for dinner. In fact, tell her I'll be late for everything for a while."

Doctor Bronson closed the phone, looked at me and then at Doctor Wright.

"This is going to be fun!"

9
Senator Hughes

"April, get me Tom Matthews."

Senator Jason Hughes stood in the middle of his office, his eyes on five television screens of his own. They were set to the same channels, ABC, CBS, NBC, Fox and CNN.

The same talking heads were giving the same news of death, destruction and coincidence. But not the amount of death and destruction expected of a disaster of this magnitude.

There was property damage in the millions and deaths, of course. There were injuries and the occasional heart-warming story. But the extent of the damage was minimal compared to what a tsunami could do if unleashed. Couple that with an earthquake felt around the world, and you have the makings for a real catastrophe.

The extent, or lack of extent, was not lost on Senator Hughes. Better for him if the death toll was high. Better that the destruction of private and public property be immense. A national disaster of epic proportions would suit him just fine right now. In fact, keeping this page-one would be perfect.

They could rush money to the areas affected. They could step up research into global warming and other programs. The shuttle to and from the proposed International Space Station would be further cut. It would then be easier to hail a taxi to the moon than take a NASA shuttle.

"The death toll in Asia has risen to 89..." said a voice on CNN.

"Come on! Come on!" whispered Senator Hughes.

April had not called back with Matthews on the line. He had gone off to NASA with that woman, the astronomer with the cane, doctor what's-her-name. If she stirred things up at NASA, it wouldn't look good. President Statler cut the funding and Congress backed him up. What's done can't be undone. He had relegated space exploration to the private sector.

"See if they can make a profit on it!" Hughes said to himself.

NASA prepared to spend eighteen billion a year on replacement shuttles. Each shuttle retired after five missions. And the construction of an orbiting International Space Station at $100 billion. Both were a waste of time and money to the Senator. Matthews' trip to NASA was a waste of time and money. The Senator wondered which was the bigger folly, Doctor Wright or the Orion project.

Already nine billion had gone down the drain on Constellation, the moon program. Many wanted to delay the program. Senator Hughes was working on canceling it altogether.

There were, after all, expensive wars going on in the Middle East. There were research projects involving robotics and global warming. A fact-finding trip to the Bahamas was coming up. A Congressional research study in Hawaii and three weeks in Bora Bora as well. He had already promised April she could go. April had already shopped. In other words, things were already in motion and money spent, so something had to go. It was either three weeks with April or funding to NASA. To Hughes, it was a no-brainer.

A former head of NASA said the U.S. would abandon its leadership of the space frontier if it halted funding. China or Russia would take the lead. To Hughes, that was just fine. He couldn't think of anything of less value than the leadership of the space frontier. Let Russia and China have it.

Space research sucked the American taxpayers dry. It was time to send it to the private sector.

The economy needed a shot in the arm. The commercial space flight industry was just what it needed.

Thousands of hi-tech jobs, especially in Florida, would bring it back to life.

Florida had been bitching of late, due to the loss of jobs in the aerospace industry. A colleague quoted Senator Hughes as saying, "Let 'em work. There's just no money to pay 'em." There was laughter all around on Capitol Hill.

10
California or Bust

"Tom Matthews is on line one," cooed April over the intercom.

"At last!" gasped Hughes as he walked around his desk to the big chair he considered to be his birthright. He picked up the phone.

"Matthews? What the hell? You were going to take her to NASA and come back, weren't you? You aren't going to stay to help them decipher the writing on Mars, are you?"

"Well, it got more complicated than that, Senator. The boys here at NASA are excited. The marks on Mars, ridges and indentations, the writing, as you put it, could be buildings. A whole complex, planet-wide, a city if you will. It means there has been or is now life on Mars."

"You're not buying into this, are you? Tom, we have work to do right here. Let Ms. Wright play with NASA. The quake and flood disaster is not as bad as expected, but there are still things to do. Stop messing around down there and get back to the Hill."

"Senator, I think I should go to California, to the Palomar Observatory there. I think I should stick with Doctor Wright. There's something to this Mars thing and I believe we should be on top of it, not underneath as it rolls on by. When the news breaks, it will be a priority changar."

Senator Hughes picked up the travel brochure for Bora Bora and dropped it into the trash can by his desk.

"OK, OK, you go to California. Keep me informed. Let me know if there is flooding in San Diego. All these do-gooders on television are saying is that there are a few dead and minor property damage. What happened to my disaster? I want regular updates!"

The Senator hung up the phone. Before the receiver rested in the cradle, I heard him say, "Damn!" I couldn't help but smile. Doctor Dana Wright looked up and saw me smile.

"Good news?" she said, gathering herself to stand up. Standing up was a matter of getting her cane on the floor, getting the angle right and using it to hoist the rest of her into an upright position. She used chair arms, tables and anyone who happened to be standing by. She didn't have this much trouble getting around on an average day. This was a long, hard day, with taxis, airplanes, car trips and meetings with Senators and NASA.

"We're going to California," I replied.

"I should have thought that was a given," she said.

"Oh, not without the Senator's blessing. Cutler may hold the keys to NASA and Bronson the keys to Palomar, but it's Hughes who holds the purse strings. Nobody gets far without money, it's the slime upon which the slug of life moves itself along." I tapped a number into my phone and held it to my ear.

"Whatever," muttered Dana. "Are you getting the tickets, then?"

"As long as I still have an expense account, I might as well use it."

Doctor Bronson was going with us to Palomar. After a brief stop at my apartment, we drove to Dulles and took the flight to San Diego. A car and driver were waiting for us with orders to take us to our hotel, but we would insist on the observatory. A look at the red planet would be our first priority. Dana had to make sure the writings were still there. I, of course, knew that they were still there, and that it was not writing at all. I was beginning to remember.

11
First Class and Cocktails

The girl at the door of the plane touched my hand as she looked at my ticket. The uniform and eyes were blue, her hair was blond. But I remembered her with *eyes of brown and uniform to match. The hair was also brown, tucked under a steel helmet. She wasn't taking my ticket then, she was reassuring me that everything would be all right. I died looking into those eyes.*

"First Class, this way," she said, smiling. I hoped I wouldn't die looking into her eyes again.

"First Class?" said Dana Wright, once we had settled in. "Now I know why my taxes are so high."

"What? The Senator's office sprung for First Class tickets instead of back with the chickens and goats! That's why!"

"Because you seem far too comfortable in these seats. Government spending is out of control and here we are in First Class."

"The flight attendant seems to like me; I'm sure I can

get you switched to Coach if you prefer. We'll both get to San Diego at the same time, I assure you."

Dana settled back, unwilling to move to Coach. She was still angered by the concept of government spending. Or perhaps it was because I am a man. *How dare I? The nerve!*

"So! You married?" she asked.

As if on cue, the engines started up and the plane began to back out of the gate.

"Here we go!" I said to myself. "The banter has begun." We would dance around each other for a while and end up in a draw, no winners, no losers. I had done the dance before, my unfavoritest thing.

"No, not currently married," I said.

I wondered what sort of team Dana had been used to working with. Who, if she had my gift, could she touch and recognize from the past. I seemed to have my team all around me, from the flight attendant to Doctor Bronson in the seat behind us to the Senator. Random people who came together time after time to interact with each other. Each time different; each time the same. Who would Dana remember? Who had been on her team? Is the reason I didn't remember her at all because she was out of her realm? Was her team somewhere else? Or had she lived and worked through countless lives without a team, all alone? Or was she new?

New? The concept itself was new to me. To me,

nothing seemed new, no one was new. Before this, I had known everyone from my first grade teacher to Doctor Bronson. And Bronson was a completely random attendee to a NASA briefing. He didn't even live in D.C. He had flown in from San Diego for one briefing and was going to leave the next day. Instead, he got a completely different briefing and is taking two people with him, one of them an old team player. He didn't know it, of course. To him, we had just met. Dana Wright was new. I looked at her. New! It was so strange!

"Not currently? So you were married before?" she asked.

"Yes. At one point I was married. It was a bad idea."

"Again!" I added in my head. Marrying Helen was something I had done more than once across the ages and to the same result. It seemed like a good idea at the time. It always seemed like a good idea. You'd think I'd learn, but no! I never learned. Of course, this current lifetime was the only one that I remembered keeping track of everyone.

But I didn't keep track of them, I reminded myself. The memories came unbidden, flowing over me for a second, just enough to register, then gone. The flight attendant had tended me for a moment, and then I died. It's not like we had a lot to reminisce about.

"Have you got a girl?" asked Dana, once more waking me out of my reflections.

"What? Oh, you mean 'girlfriend?' No. No girlfriend. I'm a senator's aide. It means I have no life. With a leased car, a leased apartment and even I'm leased. How about you?"

"Is that why you're trying so hard to impress me?" she asked, ignoring my question.

"I am trying for a civil working relationship. Impressing you is neither on my agenda nor in my skill-set. But there is a question on the table. Allow me to rephrase. Are you married?"

"You do that a lot."

"What?"

"Rephrase." Dana turned her head to me, as if the statement demanded an explanation.

"And you avoid the question. So I must assume that you have avoided other questions directed to you and are not married. Or, let me rephrase. You are also not seeing anyone. Am I correct in that assumption? That you have no one in your life?"

Dana looked at me for a moment. She pulled her lips in like a school girl and sat back in her seat, looking straight forward. I had done it. I had left her speechless.

"I win!" I said inside my head. Of course, I had won nothing but her contempt. That I was, or at least could be right was beside the point. Yes, she was single. That was obvious. And yes, she lived alone, perhaps with a cat. One could deduce that to put it like that, "no one in your life," was mean. I had been mean. I was wrong.

Now what do I do? The flight attendant saved me.

"Cocktail?" she said, her blue eyes fluttering.

"Absolutely! And please, one for my friend here. She doesn't like to fly."

"I love to fly! And make mine a double." Dana's eyes flashed at me. How dare I?

The flight attendant raised her eyebrows and left to get us drinks.

"Look," I said, lowering my voice to seem less threatening. "I am not sure how I got into such hot water so fast, but somehow I managed, so let me be clear. One, I like you. You're smart, pretty and interesting. Two, I respect you. You're a PhD, top of your field and you know stuff. I'm a school boy in your presence. Three, this is an exciting adventure. I mean, the twin earthquakes, the same thing on Mars and then.... Well, all in all, I have the best seat in the house and I appreciate it."

"Then why insult me?"

"You found my sore spot and dug in hard with your first touch. Yes, I am divorced. Yes, I have no life. Thank you for pointing that out. I had forgotten until this minute. Now could we be civil again?"

The attendant came with the drinks. She put them down.

"There you are. Enjoy!" she said, touching my shoulder as she went by me. A small rush of memory flickered through my mind. *A young boy playing Phaedra in a wig with ringlets and garish red dots on his cheeks, his lips painted like a doll.*

The image faded, but left me with a smile.

"What?" cried Dana. "You're enjoying making me miserable, aren't you?"

"Doctor Wright, I assure you, I am not. But you have to admit, you are a bit on edge. What have I done?"

"All right! Yes! I have no one in my life. This," she held her cane up, "seems to be a deal breaker with men. But I don't miss it, because I have yet to know anyone who made my life better."

Aha! I thought. That's why no team. She's a loner. I wondered if I was right, or was she new to the planet?

"And," she continued, whether I liked it or not. "If I ever meet someone who makes my life better, not worse, it will be the biggest surprise thus far. So my solitude is a choice, not a default position. Anything else?"

"No, that about covers it. Thank you for making it so clear."

"You're welcome!" she snapped. "Let's just get to Palomar and take a look at this city in the dust."

"Complex," I said without thinking.

"What?" asked Dana, snapping her head around.

"It's a complex, a single complex." I opened my drink and poured it over the ice.

"No, it goes halfway around the planet, it has to be ... I

mean, hundreds, maybe thousands of structures, all in a line. Perhaps because of climate or perhaps because that's where the water was. But there was a reason they built there."

"A single building complex, with a single purpose."

"No! But what could you possible know about it? It is ..."

She stopped, looking at me as if for the first time.

"What?" she said. She was asking what I knew that she didn't. I wasn't at all sure that I knew myself, much less that I could articulate it. What did I know? I knew it wasn't writing but buildings. I knew there was a single purpose to those buildings. They were a single complex. But I had told her that already. What else was there? Then I knew what to say.

"Because I've been there."

12
Buh-Bye!

The flight was quiet after I blurted out a pronouncement that I had been to Mars. The possibility that I had visited the strange complex of buildings was too much for Dana. She had nothing further to say to me. She was certain that she was traveling with a crazy person.

Had I told her everything, she would have called for men in white coats. The more I said, the crazier I sounded.

I had yet to tell a single living soul what I knew. I never mentioned that I had lived before and so had everyone around me. I remembered them. We had been lovers, friends, strangers, comrades in arms and enemies together. It was good to see them again. But I never said any of that.

Only Dana was new. When I said to her that we had never met, I meant it. It was a casual, social greeting to her, but I meant it: *throughout the ages*. We had, for the first time in my life, never met. Ever!

The plane landed. It was as if a total stranger was sitting beside me, one who did not want to meet me, to know me. Strangers will talk to you. They'll tell you things they would not tell friends because they'll never see you again. But this stranger didn't want to talk.

The doors opened. The attendant stood at the doors telling everyone, "Buh-bye!" She spoke with a honeyed smile. Se had developed it over years of wishing everyone well on their continued journey.

Dana had difficulty getting up. I reached a hand to help her, but she pulled her arm away. I stepped back to give her room. She staggered up, teetering on her legs and cane, as if neither were enough.

She had only had one drink. It was a double, sure, but not enough to make her drunk. She faltered again. I reached out to catch her before she fell. She grabbed onto the back of the seat, took her hand and pressed it against my chest.

"Get away from me!" she said, her voice in a deep growl.

She reached out and took the arm of Doctor Bronson. He stood wide-eyed by his seat, watching this unexpected exchange.

Bronson had napped most of the trip and had missed our earlier conversations. He didn't understand why Doctor Wright held such animosity toward me. It took him completely by surprise. I have to say, I was a bit shocked as well.

But the die was cast. There was no going back. I would have to follow along and gather what I could, then return to the Senator and report what I had learned. I would just give Doctor Wright a wide berth until then. I was sure I could avoid interaction for a day or so. But the trip to the observatory would be cheek to jowl. Oh, goodie!

13
Palomar Observatory

I'd heard of the Palomar. It was owned by the California Institute of Technology, home to five telescopes. The telescopes are in constant use, each on a different project. Management is by Caltech's faculty, post-doctoral students and researchers at Caltech's collaborating institutions. One of their bigwigs was in the car with me, Doctor Bronson. He sat next to me, bored with the drive he had taken a hundred times before.

Doctor Dana Wright, the guest genius on this trip, sat sulking in the front seat. She insisted on that seat on account of her leg. It was a cop-out. She didn't want to sit next to me and she didn't want Doctor Bronson on one side and me on the other. In fact, she didn't want anything to do with me. And yet here I was and here I would stay. This thing was bigger than the hurt feelings of an astronomical diva.

We had come to press Doctor Wright's educated eye against the eyepiece of the 200 inch Hale telescope. We hoped to peek into the window of one of those buildings on Mars. At least, I knew they were buildings. No one else did. To them they were still some form of writing in the sand.

The Hale was the largest in the continental U.S. To get something larger, we would have to go to Hawaii. I was willing, but that's another five hours by plane and the Hale was enough.

We arrived at the giant tourist attraction at dusk, having gained time in the flight west. It was just over twelve hours since the twin earthquakes shook the planet. We went to the observatory first. Arriving at night was perfect. According to Doctor Bronson, that's when you look at stars and planets. I felt pretty stupid when he said that, because until he said it, I didn't know it. Once he said it, it made perfect sense, but still...

"Welcome to Palomar!" said the cute-as-a-bug's-ear graduate student in a white lab-coat. She had large, black plastic glasses and her hair done up in twin pony-tails out to the side. Under the white coat, she wore a plaid jumper and black-and-white tennis shoes. The shoes looked like what I wore when I was a kid in gym class. When she looked at me, her eyes seemed to glaze over. When she smiled, I expected to see braces, but she was in the 24-26 range - I'd say 24 going on 14.

"Thank you, Carrie," said Doctor Bronson. "Perhaps you can show our guest around while I take Doctor

Wright to the Hale."

"Of course, Doctor. Whatever you say!" Carrie giggled as she took my arm and began a tour of the facility. On the way, she talked about the Mars Science Laboratory, Curiosity. The lab was tasked to look for evidence of microbial life on the red planet. In light of recent events, that made me giggle as well.

"Did I say something funny?" asked Carrie.

"Well, the concept of microbial life on Mars seems a bit silly in light of the events of today."

"Why? What happened today?"

I looked at Carrie. She blinked. She was serious.

"You don't know about the quakes?"

"Oh, yeah, there was an earthquake way early this morning. I was just getting to bed. We get 'em all the time here. This is, you know, California."

We had arrived at the coffee bar. I was ready for coffee. It had been a long flight, a long drive from the airport; a long day all in all and I was beginning to drift.

"Yes, I know what state I am in, but the quake rippled across the country and in fact, all around the world. They felt it on the Great Wall of China; they felt it at the Pyramids. You don't watch TV around here, do you?"

"No!" she said with a smirk. "Why would we do that?" There was a taunting, sing-song tone in her voice, as if watching TV were like watching paint dry or grass grow. They had important things to do.

"Because there was an earthquake... The resultant tsunami effect could extend inland to... Because, there was... Have you not looked at Mars yet?"

"No, I've finished my project. I'm just volunteering now."

"Commendable! There were similar quakes on the Martian surface. The ground shook the sand down to reveal structures made by intelligent beings."

"No way!" she blurted, her eyes wide.

"Yes! That's why we flew out here from Washington. Doctor Wright flew to Washington from Idaho, then to here. All so she could get a look at Mars through your telescope."

"Why didn't she just come here?" asked Carrie, matter-of-factly.

"Good question. If she ever speaks to me again, I'll be sure to bring that up."

"Didja screw up?" asked Carrie, dropping a coffee pod into the coffee maker.

"Big time!" I replied with the obligatory roll of the eyes.

"What'ja say?" she sang.

"To tell the truth, I don't remember. I'm not even sure I know. It wasn't anything I recognized as obvious."

I avoided any mention of having been to Mars. That would go over less here than in D.C., as they know it's not possible here. In D.C. it could be possible depending on what you have been smoking or sniffing. Carrie and I

67

watched the coffee brew, unimpressed by the technological wonder that was the coffee maker.

"You'll have to buy her flowers. Girls like flowers. Or so I've heard."

"I think we're beyond flowers. But it doesn't matter. I'll be out of here soon. I have to report back to the Senator."

"Oh! You work for a senator?" My job impressed Carrie. Some women like to be close to power.

"Yeah, but it's not that big a deal. Lots of times I show people around and get them coffee."

"Like me," said Carrie.

"Only I'm not as cute as you are."

Carrie giggled.

Over the course of an hour, I learned that Mars has a thin atmosphere and impact craters like the moon. Also, Carrie doesn't have a boyfriend. Mars had deserts, volcanoes, valleys and polar caps like Earth. Its rotational period and seasonal cycles are like Earth and Carrie hadn't been out on a date in more than a year. Early astronomers explained the famous lines away as optical illusions. There are two moons and if I wanted, I could get Carrie assigned to me during my stay. She seemed to be particularly eager to make that happen. I was eager to find out what was happening on Mars.

"Could we find Doctor Bronson? I am anxious to find out what is going on up there."

"Oh! No prob. This way."

I followed Carrie back the way we came until the big Hale telescope was in sight. I waved to Doctor Bronson. He noted my wave and turned back to looking inside the chamber without acknowledgment. Perhaps I had insulted him as well.

"Anything, Doctor?" I asked.

"Nothing to report to your senator, Mister Matthews. We're still getting a bead on the Red Planet. It's the closest it's been in years, but still illusive."

"It's been a long day for me, so I believe I'll go to the hotel and catch up with you in the morning."

Bronson took several hotel card key envelopes out of his pocket. Each held two keys. He took one and handed it to me.

"That's a good idea. This will do you. We'll call you if there's anything. Make sure Carrie has your number."

"Um, yes. That's what I'll do. I'll make sure she has my number." I turned around to find Carrie behind me, grinning. "Point me to the car," I said.

"And you're to give me your number, you know, in case anything comes up."

"Got it!" I replied. I left before anything came up.

14
Everyone's A Comedian!

The driver didn't need instructions; he had them already. He took me to the hotel and turned around to return to the observatory. Once in the room, I didn't need instructions either. I ordered a sandwich and turned on the television.

Word of the "writing on Mars" had already found its way to the comedians. Late night talk show host Pat Murphy said several groups had deciphered the writings. He had the top ten possible translations. Number ten was "Grampa loves it - Burma Shave."

I changed to another channel. The movie was *War of the Worlds* with Tom Cruise.

I hit the channel button again.

Funny man Glen Rogers told the audience the writings said "This Space for Rent" and all the candidates were bidding for it.

"Great!" I said to the television. "Everyone's a comedian."

Finally I found a movie that was not Martian in nature: Danny Kaye in *The Inspector General*.

While I watched, the sandwich came. It was a typical club sandwich. I hadn't eaten, so I devoured the whole thing, pickle and all.

Just as Danny Kaye was kissing the girl, signifying the movie's end, my lids began to droop. It was time for bed. The problem was that I felt sticky after such a long day. I went into the bathroom and started the shower.

Hours had gone by and there was no word. I wondered what was going on back at the observatory. I was doing my boss no good here. But if I didn't get some sleep, I would be no good to anyone. I got into the shower and felt better.

After all, I decided, they would call me when there was something to report. There would be no reason not to. I had better be ready to go when they call, because it will be hand-off-the-ball time.

I turned off the light and climbed into bed.

I seem to recall some other thought that drifted halfway through my mind at the time. But the pillow felt good and cool, the blankets were heavy on my legs and I drifted off to sleep.

Deep in the night, enveloped by darkness, I felt another body climb beneath the covers and press next to me.

A faint scent of flowers stirred me. The softness of the

skin that form fitted itself to me said that a woman had climbed in. It had not been so long for me to have forgotten that unmistakable touch.

I turned over and wrapped my arms around the nude body next to me. She moaned, noticing that her presence moved me. In fact, my appreciation was obvious.

"You were right," said Doctor Wright, her voice low and slow, as if someone might hear, just above a whisper. "They are a long, single complex of buildings."

Doctor Dana Wright disappeared beneath the covers to further inspect my appreciation.

15
Knock Knock

Knock knock!

Someone was at the door. I sat up and looked around, trying to remember where I was, when it was and who I was. Doctor Dana Wright was lying next to me fast asleep.

She was beautiful: in her mid-thirties, with pink lips and sandy-blond hair. Her hair was cut short to keep it out of her way. She also had soft, smooth shoulders that longed for kisses. I leaned down and kissed her on the shoulder. She moved beneath the covers, uttering a small moan. She liked that. So did I.

A thought ran through my head: perhaps if I just slip down under the covers, whoever is at the door will go away and we...

Knock knock!

"Mister Matthews?" said a tiny voice. It was Carrie.

I got up, pulled the cover from the floor and wrapped it around me. I didn't want another earthquake jiggle the door open. And I didn't want to embarrass Carrie. When I opened the door, she was standing there looking much as she did a few hours earlier.

"Um, we can't find Doctor Wright."

"I'm here," said a sleepy voice behind me.

Carrie looked at me, her eyebrows high above wide eyes. There was no going back now. I smiled and opened the door a little more.

Dana came up behind me, a sheet wrapped around her. She leaned out with just one eye open and looked at the girl standing in the hall.

"Ummm, Doctor Bronson says you have to come back, people are arriving."

"Please tell Doctor Bronson we will be there after we have showered and had breakfast.

"But..." began Carrie.

"Young lady," interrupted Dana. "Mars has been there for a long time, it's not going anywhere. Shower! Breakfast! Shut the door, Mister Matthews."

I smiled at Carrie, tilting my head, "You heard the lady," and I closed the door.

Dana was already in the bathroom opening up a small, blue bag. She dropped the sheet the door and stood by the sink naked. I dropped the bed cover on the sheet and walked, also naked, into the bathroom.

She stood favoring her left leg, which had blue scars from mid-calf to the hip. There were suture scars on either side. There were other marks showing that she had had pins at one time. The recovery process must have been extreme. In fact, it was still going on.

But, the leg had a smooth curve up to the buttocks and dimples at the small of her back. She was small-breasted with an attractive belly. She would look wonderful in an evening dress. She was a good looking woman; that was for sure.

Standing there, nude and staring at her, was not the best idea, so I took a mental snap-shot and moved on.

"Can I call you Dana, now? You can call me Tom if you like."

"You can call me Dana in the bathroom. You can call me Dana in bed. If we happen to be watching TV over a sandwich in this room, you can call me Dana."

"Right! That is, whenever we're elsewhere, it's Doctor Wright."

"Yes. And if you were going to make any jokes about 'meeting Miss Right' or some such, I've heard them. They weren't funny then, they're not funny now."

"Right! That is, got it."

"I'll call you Mister Matthews. In ten minutes everyone at the observatory will know where I slept. Still, we'll be professional on the job."

"Understood. And I hope you will be joining me again. I mean it would save on hotel rooms. You were so concerned over the budget, is the only reason I bring it up."

"Budget?" Dana turned to me.

"OK, I don't care about the budget, I just want you to sleep with me again. I liked it."

"Don't crowd me, Tom. We've got a lot to do. Take a shower."

"Yes, ma'am." I got into the shower, telling myself to behave and be amiable if I wanted another late night visit.

Dana climbed into the shower with me and wrapped her arms around me. She was not one for a lot of chit-chat. I held her arms and let out a deep sigh. I didn't know the language, but I would learn it.

When we got out, I went to dress, giving Dana the bathroom. Halfway through the put-on-shoe-cycle, the phone rang.

"Matthews," I said into the receiver.

"Mister Matthews, what will you be having for breakfast?" said a female voice.

I held the phone to my chest.

"Preferences for breakfast?" I yelled at the bathroom.

"Standard lumberjack: eggs, bacon, toast, potatoes, coffee, OJ," came the answer.

"That's eggs, bacon, and toast, potatoes, coffee and orange juice for two. We'll come down."

"We'll have it ready." The phone clicked off.

"I'm guessing ten minutes. Is that real?" I asked.

"Wish I could say otherwise, but yes, that's real." She was telling me that she, too, would rather stay in the room. My guess is that it had been a while for her as well.

When Dana came out of the bathroom, I went in to let her dress in private while I finished getting ready for the day. My take was that it would be a long and exciting day.

"Ready!" said Dana as I walked out of the bathroom.

"OK. For the record, Dana: I'm glad you came in last night."

"For the record, Tom, me too. And now, Mister Matthews, will you escort me to breakfast?"

16
Breakfast

The waitress poured the coffee as soon as we got out of the elevator. The rest of the food arrived as we were sitting down. At nearby tables, heads were turning, wondering who we were that we got such royal treatment.

"Once we got the Red Planet in focus, the surface showed much more detail than I was able to get on my home telescope."

I didn't respond. It would have been snide. It would have been something about her home telescope not being 200 inches. Ha ha. I chewed something and took a sip of coffee instead.

"For one thing, the quake looks like a sympathetic quake. The epicenters appear in the same relative positions as those on Earth. If you mark the two triangles on a globe, Bermuda and Dragon, you'll see corresponding triangles on Mars. Thus I believe, as here on Earth, the Martian quakes originated deep within the planet. They were due to proximity and alignment, not volcanic activity. That may be the reason that there were tremors felt but only small tsunami events. Well, smaller than anticipated, anyway. It could have been catastrophic."

"And the other thing?" I asked, wanting to get to her utterance of last night. I didn't want to stop what we were doing to discuss it, but it was on my mind to hear about the giant complex on Mars.

"Oh! The Other Thing!" She lowered her voice. "We're going to have to wait until we are at the observatory to discuss *The Other Thing*. It's not something I want let out yet, and walls have ears."

And so we ate in silence after that. She didn't want to talk about what she said last night or discuss our feelings. It seemed like such a girl-thing to do and yet I was the one who wanted to talk about "us."

Of course, she was right, we couldn't go blabbing in public about Mars or about staying over last night. In the first place, it was just not done in polite society and in the second, we had decorum to keep. I represented Congress. She represented the Scientific Community. While it made perfect sense that we should be "in bed together," the fact that we were actually in bed together would raise eyebrows.

The one thing I had learned on Capitol Hill was how to keep a secret. If we had a dollar for every secret kept on the Hill, we could wipe out the National Debt. Also, funding NASA wouldn't be a problem.

As the last sip of coffee went down, the driver appeared at the door. He nodded and stood there. I returned the nod, tapped Dana on the arm and indicated the driver. She took the time to lift the napkin to her mouth, stand and raise her head to me. She looked at me and sighed.

"Mister Matthews, thank you for a lovely, um, breakfast. Now, I believe we should go."

"After you, Doctor Wright."

All the way to the observatory, we looked at the scenery out of our separate windows. Dana reached over and took my hand and we sat for the duration of the trip in silence, holding hands. At the observatory, we walked in the picture of two professionals, about to do the most important thing of their careers.

I had a thought.

"It occurs to me, Doctor Wright, that we name asteroids after the scientist who first discovered them. Once we find out what we are dealing with, I'm going to push for naming it after you. Does that seem right and proper?"

"Oh, by all means, Mister Matthews, let us do what is right and proper." She was being snide. Her natural defenses were coming online.

It was natural that she would have a hard exterior.

Doctor Wright was short, slender and pale. That would have been enough to earn her a hard time among the male scientific community. But she also had a bum leg and walked with a cane. I was sure that the recovery process was ongoing and the cane would not be a permanent fixture. Still, for the moment, that's the way things were. I made a decision to throw any weight I could wield behind her.

"Where are we, Doctor?" she said to Bronson.

"They've been waiting for you, looking over the photographs. The blowups, I'm afraid, show less than we'd hoped."

"Then let's not hope so much, let's just take a look at what we have."

17
Late-night Comedians and the Hollywood Sign

"Gentlemen," said Doctor Wright, walking into a large conference room. At the end of the table, five men and two women poured over a series of photographs with magnifying glasses.

"Ladies," continued Dana, upon noticing that there were two women among the team.

"Doctor Wright, did you make this discovery?"

"Yes, I did." Dana began walking around the table toward the busy end. "I first saw it on my scope in Pocatello. I then brought the news to Washington. Mister Matthews suggested viewing it through the scope here. It was Mister Matthews who first suggested that we are looking at structures. He has been invaluable."

"We can't see here that they are structures. Why would you think they are structures?"

Dana shot a sideways glance at me. She was not about to say what I had told her on the plane. She would be risking her career. Yet, somehow, she believed me.

"If they were letters, as the late-night comedians suggest, they would be miles high. Even the Hollywood sign isn't that tall. Let us move ahead and see what the evidence tells us. There will be speculation enough without us adding to it."

A small chuckle rippled through the seven scientists. They had come to find out what the foremost of them had discovered on Mars after the shakeup. She believed that the quake on Earth had somehow caused the quake on Mars, but there was a time factor. The twin earthquakes had happened at more or less 4:00 am, California time, or 5:00 am in Idaho. The quakes on Mars were simultaneous, though they appeared to be several minutes apart. There would be no way one could affect the other. Only light travels that fast.

One scientist mentioned Neutrinos traveling faster than light, quoting recent experiments with faster-than-light particles. Others said it was all experimental and not grounded in good solid science. The argument went back and forth.

Someone brought up the possibility of tapping into the functional orbiting spacecraft: Mars Express. We could see what it was seeing, if anything. Several surface craft already on Mars either failed or completed their missions, but were still there. There were inert landers and rovers at several places on the planet. Perhaps we could hack into one of them at a distance.

When the conversation soared above my head, I backed out of the room and went to find the coffee machine. There was no sign of Carrie. My guess was that after seeing Dana and I together, she decided that she had volunteered enough. One can only sacrifice so much for science. After a while you go home to eat chocolates and watch *Traveling Pants* in your PJs. I pictured Carrie doing just that.

A click-click-click behind me said that someone had left the room. By the sound, I guessed a woman and by the stride, a tall one.

"Mister Matthews?" said an alto voice, strong and sure. I turned around.

"Yes," I replied. I was right. She was tall and she was walking up to me.

She wore a business suit, medium gray. Matching heels added another three inches to her height. She wore her hair in a tight French curl. In any other place, I would have made an evaluation about her, I would have said lesbian. In this setting, professional would be closer to the mark.

"Doctor McClellan," she said. "Megan McClellan. May I walk with you?"

"If you like, Doctor. I was just searching for the coffee," I replied. "Come along, we'll find it together."

"Thank you. The biggest hurdle in getting the gear we sent to Mars to work was the temperature and pressure.

It's not like here on Earth. Mars could support life, but you don't just step out and start your day. For one thing, only 13% of the air is oxygen. The biggest part is carbon dioxide."

"I'm learning more and more about Mars as time goes on," I admitted. Luckily, I saw the coffee station up ahead. I needed a distraction so that I would not be the center of her attention. What could she be getting to?

"The new 'Curiosity' is up there, you know. There's 'Spirit' and 'Opportunity,' still in operation and capable of sending back pictures. I have requests out now to find out where they are on the surface and to have them re-tasked."

"Sounds like a good idea. Coffee?" I asked.

"Tea, please," she replied, then continued. "The thing is, just as when we dig in the ground somewhere, we come up with layers of life of centuries before. The Martian soil could hold similar treasures, if there had indeed been life there."

"But here on earth, what we have is plants and trees creating layers of dirt over old ruins. As time goes on, it covers up evidence of previous civilizations."

"Exactly!" nodded Doctor McClellan.

"And on Mars, there are no trees, no plants; just dirt. For the dirt to cover a civilization, that civilization must have sunk into the surface. Either that..."

I stopped, as if in mid-air. Doctor McClellan looked at

me. I was holding a tea bag over hot water, about to drop it in when the thought struck me.

Doctor McClellan touched my hand, bringing me out of my trance. At the same time, a flicker of memory went through me. *A woman in uniform, a white uniform with a short, navy shawl, walked by me. I was looking up, as if from a seated or lying position. She looked down and walked past me. The last thing I saw was white stockings with seams.* Doctor McClellan was also a small part of my team. We had been together before and as today, in passing.

"Mister Matthews?" asked Doctor McClellan.

"Either that or the structures were buried on purpose, hidden. They weren't meant for us to find. We have to get back."

I set off in a run back toward the conference room. I had remembered something. We weren't meant to find these.

18
Hide & Seek

In the conference room Doctor Wright and the other scientists were going over the photos at the table. I burst in with Doctor McClellan right behind me. Doctor Wright looked up, a little surprised to see me running in followed by McClellan. We were both out of breath. "We aren't supposed to find them," I blurted. All heads turned my way.

"Something to add, Mister Matthews?" said Doctor Wright. Her tone was sharp, her voice adversarial. It put me on guard.

"Uh, I mean... Hi. I'm Tom Matthews, from Senator Hughes' office. And it, uh, just occurred to me that... You know, I was thinking about these, uh, buildings, I think they are, and I think they got buried on purpose."

I turned one of the photographs around and looked at the markings across the face of Mars.

"Yeah! You see, this is just as I thought. If you take a

look, it's pretty clear. These didn't get buried in the ground over time, like ancient ruins. No, they buried these on purpose so they would stay buried. Yeah, this is a mistake. We weren't supposed to find these."

I stood there leaning on the table. My tie draped across the photograph of Mars and my new-found lady-friend looked at me like I was crazy. I wondered why I have this tendency to blurt things out without thinking. It seemed there was a good reason for her to be looking at me like that. It was true: I was crazy. How was I going to explain this, when I didn't understand it myself?

"Mister Matthews," said a balding gentleman with wire-rimmed glasses and a cardigan sweater. "Why do you believe that we were not meant to find these ruins? That is, more than any other ruins that we unearth on our own planet?"

I didn't have an answer. In fact, I didn't have any kind of response. I stood there with eight sets of eyes on me, all expecting me to be brilliant.

"I'm sorry, and you are...?" I said, playing for time.

"Doctor Davenport of the Smithsonian. I also serve on the board of directors for this observatory. I am interested in just what these are and you seem to have the inside track on that. Please be so kind to share with us."

"Aha! Doctor Davenport. You've met Doctor McClellan, I suppose."

Davenport tilted his head, inspecting me as he would an insect he had just discovered.

"And you know Doctor Wright." Several heads turned toward Dana. She continued to look at me, unable to look away, as with a bad accident.

"In fact, I bet I'm the only one here who is not a doctor. Isn't that something? Yes. Um, well! To tell the truth, I don't know why I would say that, except that it seems right. You know when you dig in a desert on Earth, or in the hills of England or just about anywhere, you find layers from the past? And the further down you go, the earlier the remnants turn up. Archaeologists uncovered a whole village under an English estate house last year. And under that was an earlier one. I saw it in the History Channel."

Dana's head tilted to the side, coming into the same degree of tilt as Doctor Davenport. Doctor McClellan was looking at me the same way. It was an epidemic!

"You see, the trees and plants, old animals, years of dead leaves and what have you, build up over time. Nature has a proclivity to reclaim its territory, so they cover such ruins over. A few hundred thousand years and you can hardly recognize the place."

It was as if we were in suspended animation, like there was a scratch in the DVD, and all motion just stopped. I continued.

"But on Mars, there are no trees, no plants, no

animals, no rivers to change course. There could have been at one time, but that was long ago. And there wouldn't be straight and curved lines, like new buildings. Jagged lines, ruins. But there aren't any. There are straight lines. These buildings are not that old, not millions of years. Perhaps a few hundred thousand years, but not millions."

Nothing registered on a single face. There was no understanding for what I was saying.

"These – these buildings, this complex of structures, was buried under the Martian soil on purpose, hidden. It was a freak accident that wiped away enough of the dirt that we are seeing the rooftops. You see?" I pointed to one of the photos. All heads looked at my finger. "There is no depth to the lines and circles. It is, for all intents and purposes, two-dimensional. In fact, these buildings could go down several hundred feet to the ground floor. It must have been an immense undertaking to cover them. A huge outlay of ... Well, it's the biggest game of hide-and-seek ever!"

I looked at Doctors Wright, McClellan, Davenport and the rest, and they looked back at me. It was as if someone threw us in the air and we had reached our apex. Preparing to fall back down, but still in that momentary suspension, weightless and still.

The room exploded with conversation. In the tumult they all forgot about me. Some pulled cell phones out, others shuffled the photos and drew attention to this one or that one. McClellan stepped around me and into the mix, pointing and shouting. In the middle was Dana, looking at me with a peculiar look. It was a cross between not understanding a word I was saying and loving me for saying it. There was admiration in those eyes, though there was much she did not understand.

The noise level grew as one authority beat down the contradictions of another. Several pulled out their phones and briefed their associates. Soon the conversation involved think tanks from Main to California.

From the middle of the pack, Dana walked past me, pulling me out into the hall by the lapel. "Call your Senator. Tell him that priorities have changed. We're going to Mars. We'll re-task the existing equipment, the rovers and satellites. They'll send back photos and take samples from the area. Then we're going to have to send someone out there. This is too big to worry about a few trillion bucks! This is perhaps the biggest news of this or any other century and you are smack-dab in the middle of it. Fasten your seat belt, mister! It's gonna be a bumpy ride!"

Dana kissed me on the cheek and went back into the conference room. I stood there completely unaware of what I had done to deserve that kiss but glad I did it.

19

A Call to the Senator

I called the Senator. April put me through. I smiled to think that she had actually picked up a telephone. It occurred to me that she's going to want a raise for all the work she's doing.

"Matthews! What the hell is going on? Is there writing on Mars or not?"

"Not writing, Senator, the letters would have to be pretty large. No, they're edifices, buildings. They're buried in the red Martian ground. The earthquake, I mean, Mars quake, shook the ground loose."

"What are they for?" asked the Senator.

"We don't know that yet. We're going to use the rovers up there to take a look, and the satellites to take photos. There are a couple of them up there and they can take photos a lot closer than we can from here."

"Is that going to cost a lot?"

"Not much. The real costs will occur when we go and take a look."

"Go-and-take-a-look?" repeated the Senator. The strain was telling on him.

"Yes, Senator. The only way we can tell for real if these are offices or warehouses or hangars or barracks is to go up there and take a look. Someone is going to have to go to Mars."

"Why? Go to Mars and do what?" asked the Senator, screaming now. "Pat Murphy says it's writing. Now you tell me it's not?"

"Well, I hate to contradict late night talk show host Pat Murphy, but he will be the first to admit that he doesn't know a lot about Mars. I mean, apart from what he hears from comedian Glen Rogers. The thing is, the people here are smarter than most folks on TV and they are looking through a really big telescope. We'll know more when we get the snaps back from Mars. I'll keep you informed."

"Call me with the least little development. Don't leave me out here in the cold. I need information. People are starting to ask questions."

"Tell them that whatever it is on Mars, intelligent life forms made it."

"You have proof of that?" he asked.

"Yes! It's a game-changar, isn't it?" I hung up with the Senator, knowing that I had not given him what he wanted. He wanted a nice, quiet resolution to the whole thing and me back in the office showing people around and getting coffee.

There was a disturbance outside. Through the glass doors I could see bodies moving. A low rumble grew in strength and there was a vibration beneath my feet. For a moment, I thought it might be another earthquake. Was it an aftershock from the previous morning?

Doctor Bronson ran by me to the doors, stopped, looked out and rolled his head back. Then, girding himself, he pushed the door open and went out. I seized the opportunity to slip out a side door, about 30 feet to the left.

Outside, press vans were pulling up. Cameramen put cameras on their shoulders. News anchormen, the talking heads of prepackaged news, got a final powder-puff. When they saw Bronson, they ran to him, all shouting questions.

"Doctor Bronson! Is there proof of intelligent life on Mars?"

"Will we be making contact?"

"Will there be an invasion?"

"Will you be going on the Space Shuttle?"

Bronson did what I expected him to do. He raised his hands, lowered his eyelids to half and spoke as if to first year students.

"People, people! We are still discussing the events of yesterday and the unverified markings on Mars. Just as the famous canals turned out to be an optical illusion, these new markings could be the same thing. We will no doubt learn that a change in the atmosphere or some seasonal anomaly created these lines. They're just like the canals."

"Then why have the heads of seven different agencies assembled here?" one reporter asked. Six different reporters shoved their microphones an inch closer to get the answer.

"Because we wanted the best and we met where the biggest telescope is. We are monitoring the situation. In fact, we have been collecting data all night."

That got them going again. "What did you learn?"

"Were the findings conclusive?"

"Will this rejuvenate the Space Shuttle program?"

"Is there life on Mars?"

Again Bronson held up his hands, looking all the more bored, and spoke even softer. "The findings are inconclusive. We will not know more until the satellites orbiting the planet fly overhead and take photos. There is so much potential distortion. The lines could be anything, including a trick of the light."

"Is it writing, Doctor? Are the Martians trying to send us a message?" asked the eager reporter. The rest leaned forward. Bronson rolled his eyes and said the ridiculous.

"Yes. It says, 'Have a Nice Day.'"

The questions flew before Bronson could say he was kidding.

"Will we be responding?"

"Is the message in English?"

"Is it a Martian dialect or code?"

"How long did it take to decrypt it?"

"Will you be going to Mars?"

Bronson held up both hands, this time at full arms' length. "Don't be ridiculous! How could Martians send us a message by writing in ten-mile-high letters? Like I said before, it is most likely an optical illusion. There is no writing, no message, no Martians. When I know something, I'll let you know. In the meantime, don't call me, I'll call you."

Bronson turned around and walked back into the observatory. Two security guards, the only two on duty, stepped in front of the door. I had a thought that Bronson might have gone back in to call for more security guards.

The reporters turned to their cameras to recap. The one nearest me was already spinning the information. "So there you have it: the scientists are still analyzing the Martian writing. We have no confirmation at this time of the Martians sending us a message. There is no word as to whether the Space Shuttle program will be reinstated. Scientists here at Palomar are hopeful. Back to you, Ted."

"And we're out!" said the cameraman. The lady reporter turned around and saw me. She made a motion to her cameraman and scurried over to me, trying to look non-threatening.

"Are you from the Observatory? Are you part of the scientific team?"

"No, I'm just an observer. Nothing to do with it."

"Charlotte Stansfield, Channel 8 News. And you are?"

"Me, I'm nobody. Just a driver. I go back and forth, careful not to listen to what's going on in the back seat."

"No, you're not. We just interviewed the driver. Come on, let me in on the big secret. Who are you and what do you have to do with this? I'll treat it with kid gloves. Honest."

"Please, I'm just a friend, here for moral support. I don't know anything about Mars."

Before she could ask another question, I turned around and went to the door. The locked door wouldn't budge. I picked up my step to the main door, swept past the two guards and scurried inside. I turned and looked out the window.

I had gone past the guards without them stopping me, asking who I was or even reacting. The fact was not lost on Ms. Stansfield of Channel 8 News. She whispered to the cameraman and looked back at the building.

Several other journalists were wrapping up their live, on-the-scene stories. It looked like they were packing up to go home. I almost breathed a sigh of relief. But when the first truck pulled up to the curb and shut off its engine, I knew they were just settling in.

My phone went off. "This can't be good," I said to

myself. It was the Senator. "Matthews," I said.

"Matthews! What the hell is going on? There was an interview where a spokesman told reporters the Martians are sending us a message. Are you on top of this or not?"

"They're reporters. You remember the campaign, you would say 'icepick' and they would report 'corkscrew.' There's no writing, no message, no Martians, that's what the man said, that's the truth. Tell your committee that, and you'll be right. I have to get back."

"I want hourly updates from here on out!"

The Senator had said his last. He clicked off without a polite goodbye.

"Hourly updates," I said to the phone. "that's what he wants? Hell, that's what I want! Good luck!" I put the phone in my pocket, hoping it would not see the light of day for another hour at least.

Outside, news vans lined up in the red zone, camping out for the next wrinkle in the story. In a side office, the scientists had collected several televisions to track the news. Without Doctor Bronson, the news teams reported whatever they could. That included the weather, the angle of the telescope and a description of anyone coming or going. Volunteer staff arrived in carpools, everyone wanting to get in on the action.

"Now do you want me to be your personal volunteer?" said a voice behind me.

There stood Carrie, arms folded, a scolding look on her

face, as if I had misbehaved.

"I don't know what you mean," I said, turning back to the television.

"I know, she's pretty, smart and at the apex of this sudden turn of events. I understand and I don't blame you. So let's start again. I'm a volunteer and pretty smart myself. In fact, I'm a few semesters from my master degree, heading for my doctorate. You need someone to be your assistant; you're a central player, whether you like it or not."

"I'm a Washington gofer. I'm in this by accident. I'm a side-car. In fact, I don't need to be here at all."

"Mister Matthews," Carrie reached out and took my hand, holding it in both of hers.

In an instant, a picture flashed. *I was in a grand bedroom, high in a mansion. In a narrow bed placed by the window, a pale young girl in ringlets smiled up at me. My sister was dying and there was nothing I could do about it. Her lips were moving. I leaned in closer, to hear.*

"Don't worry," she said. "We'll be together again." A tear formed in my eye.

"I'll always remember," I said to her.

I sucked in a mouthful of air, looking into Carrie's eyes.

"Oh, did I shock you? Sometimes we get static electricity here. Sorry about that. But what I meant to say was that while you're here, you need someone to take care of you. Someone to run errands for you, and get you a cup of coffee. Would you like a cup of coffee?"

"Yes, please."

Carrie smiled and let go of my hand. She skipped down the hall to the coffee bar, humming to herself.

"So my sister was right," I thought. "We're together again."

20
April

"Not now, April!" came the shout from the office.

April returned to the phone call. "Uh, the Senator is not available for comment. OK, I will." April Wills hung up the phone. It was the fifteenth media call and Senator Hughes was taking none of them.

Things had been so simple a mere day and a half ago. NASA funding was all but dead. The money was going to needed programs. Programs like her trip to the Islands, her raise, her bonus and her new car. Senator Hughes was not in the news, so it was easy going here and there, even together. People stared, but so what? They were jealous is all; because she found herself a rich and powerful man and he found himself a young, hot girl. They each had what every man and every woman wanted.

But now everything had changed. Now they were interviewing the Senator, waiting for him at his car, at his house, at his club. They were interviewing his wife and his kids. Soon it would be impossible to sneak away for a long weekend.

It was not as if what they were doing was wrong. In fact, it helped the country. She allowed him to relax so he could make the big decisions. Decisions such as whether to continue to fund the NASA program or continue to fund the war. Well, actually, wars. There were three of them going on and they were all expensive. Throwing money away on space travel seemed insignificant compared to funding the war effort. She was, after all, a patriot.

Mrs. Hughes had given up on the Senator long ago, so even if he went home to her, he would be sleeping in a separate room. If he's going to sleep elsewhere, it might as well be with...

Rinnnnng!

"Senator Hughes' Office. Yes, Beth, I can make it for lunch. The Senator has meetings all day. Since they found writing on Mars, nobody'll leave him alone. I know! But they seem to think he's got his eye in the telescope himself. OK, see you at 11:45. Bye."

Message in the Dust! The headline on the paper at the edge of April's desk shouted. No one knew if it was a message, or if it was dust or dirt or clay, but lots of people bought the paper that day. Not a lot of people bought newspapers anymore. Whatever gets folks to buy them is good for business - at least if you're a newspaper.

"April, come in, please," said the Senator over the intercom.

April stood up, smoothed her skirt, puffed up her breasts and turned to go into the office.

The Senator was at his desk, back to the door. He was holding a book, something from the bookshelf. High on the shelf, there was a space. The books were the exact number to fill up the extensive shelves. There had never been a space before. No book could lean over, not even the distance of a book-width.

"Mars, April! Damned Mars! Cancel the upcoming trip. Believe it: no one wants to do that less than me, but cancel it. Cancel everything, cancel everyone. It's all changed now, upside-down. It's damned Biblical, that's what it is."

"Biblical, sir?" asked April.

"The first shall be last and the last shall be first, April. Biblical. The lion will lie down with the friggin' lamb and no one will know enough to write the book on it. But everyone will write a book anyway and they will all get publishing deals and movies made about them."

"Movies?" April was wishing it was two days ago.

"No one can see us together, not leaving, not arriving, not at the place in Virginia. I'm going back to my wife and you're taking a different route home each night."

"Yes, sir. I will." She was beginning to get the idea. The days of wine and roses were over.

"And don't go to the suite. If they find out about that, we're sunk."

"I have stuff at the suite, stuff I need," April protested.

"Do without, or I'll give you money to buy new stuff, just until this blows over." The Senator rolled his eyes. "Until this blows over!" he thought. It was like President Lincoln saying, "until this blows over!" about the Civil War.

"Writing on Mars! What was Matthews thinking? A double earthquake wasn't enough for him, he had to find writing on Mars!" He blamed Matthews for this. It was his fault.

"Can I get you something, sir?" asked April.

"Get on the phone and cancel my entire upcoming calendar. I don't want to speak to anyone; not anyone. And put Tom Matthews' phone number on my cell, give it a shortcut. And a distinctive ring, so I'll know it's him calling."

Being Senator used to be a walk in the park. Show up for a vote now and then, attend a meeting, sit in a board room. He was smart. He'd been to college. He was a damned lawyer, for Pete's sake! The ability to read someone's half-baked bill, attach a rider or two and then slide it through Congress was child's play for him. He could do it with fast talk when most men would be too confused to push it through. There were things he could get past Congress that would make the average man shrivel and die. He had skills!

But now, they just wanted comment, so he could misquote about something new. It was more than just the comics now, it was *Markings on Mars Mean Intelligent Life!* all over the news. They wanted to know if he was going to Mars! Did they think a trip to Mars would do for a fact-finding mission?

The Senator looked back at the book. It was an encyclopedia, the M's for Mars. He read the paragraph again:

Mars has a thin atmosphere composed of the tiny amount of remaining carbon dioxide (95.3%) plus nitrogen (2.7%), argon (1.6%) and traces of oxygen (0.15%) and water (0.03%). The average pressure on the surface of Mars is only about 7 millibars (less than 1% of Earth's), but it varies with altitude from almost 9 millibars in the deepest basins to about 1 millibar at the top of Olympus Mons.

It didn't make any more sense now than it did a minute ago. He was going to have to pack more than a spare suit if he was going to Mars.

The Senator shut the book and threw it on the desk. He turned around. April was still standing there.

"Now would be better than later!" he glared at her.

April ran back to her desk. She sat down, steadied herself and turned to her computer. The first order of business was to Tweet this.

21
Juggernaut

"Pack!" said Dana. "We're going to Houston."

"What's in Houston?" I asked.

Doctor McClellan, Doctor Bronson and the rest of the growing multitude followed Dana. Volunteers scattered before the juggernaut of scientists. Drivers came alive. Many of them had sought refuge inside the dome from the onslaught of reporters.

"NASA Control Center. You remember, 'Houston, we have a problem!' You can be 'Major Tom.' We're going to reprogram the rovers. That's where you do stuff like that. A handful will stay here and keep track of Mars, but I've learned all I need from the Hale. It's time to go see what the Mars Orbiter has to show us."

She moved pretty fast for a small woman with a cane, I had to skip to catch up.

We went to the back of the building and got into a red Ford Explorer with a child's car seat in the back. Dana sat on one side, I sat on the other. Doctor Bronson got into the front seat. A woman of about 25 was driving, one of the volunteers.

Bronson turned around as the driver put on her seat belt.

"When our drivers pull the cars around to the front, the media will be all over them. We'll be long gone by then." He looked at the woman driving. "The hotel, please," then back to us, "We have a flight set up out of here to Houston. They're waiting for us at Control. They're waking up the scientists and engineers as we speak."

"You think they're asleep?" asked Dana.

"Doctor Wright, we've all been asleep," he replied. Doctor Bronson turned back around. The line of personal vehicles drove off in different directions. Some contained volunteers, driving off to lead the media away. Carrie was in one of those cars. I felt a twinge of loss. I had wanted to spend more time with her. I thought of requesting her as an assistant, but it might be misunderstood. I didn't need to muddy the waters at this point, I needed things crystal clear.

"They're calling it the Wright Complex," said Dana, over the child's seat.

"See? I told you: they always name it after the discoverer."

"Well, I wish they'd name it something else. It sounds like a diagnosis by a shrink."

"It's a compliment – you have the Wright Stuff!"

"Not funny!" sang Dana.

"You've been Wright all along," I said, wanting to poke her in the side, but deciding not to.

"Not funny then, not funny now."

"OK, OK, I'm Wright with ya."

Dana sucked in a breath, held it and let it out, pulling her lips in and furrowing her brow. If she could have thought of another way to show how pissed she was, she would have.

"Wright Complex. That's rich!" I chuckled.

The woman driving the car looked at me in the rear view mirror. Her eyes said I should quit while I was only a little behind.

"So, Doctor Bronson. Houston. Do you think they can tell these things to go and do what we need them to do?" I asked him.

Doctor Bronson turned in his seat.

"That's one of the brightest minds in the world sitting beside you, Mister Matthews, G.E.D. If she says she can reprogram Spirit and Opportunity to drive over to the Wright Complex and look around, you had better buckle up."

He turned back around in his seat. I looked at the rear view mirror. The driver was smiling, I could see it in her eyes. "And what about the orbiters? Are you going to move them too?" I asked.

"It will take more to reprogram the orbiters, but we can do it. In fact, they might be sending us the first images. After all, they are in flight, looking down and in orbit. Spirit and Opportunity are on the surface. They might be hundreds of miles away. They probably are, in fact."

"What about Phoenix?" I asked, trying to show that I was not completely stupid on the subject.

"Phoenix is a lander," said Dana, looking out the window. "It's stationary. Unless it has already landed on top of a roof, it's not likely to see anything." The response was not even worth delivering to me. It was just said to the air and whoever wanted to hear it could take it from the air. The eyes in the mirror were still smiling at me. It was not a jovial, good-natured smile. It was a "gotcha!" smile.

We arrived at the hotel before the media could overtake us. The driver of the red Explorer pulled around to the back in anticipation of a hasty retreat.

In the hotel room, we threw clean and soiled clothing into suitcases without regard.

"You know I was just ribbing you. Good, clean fun."

No response from Dana.

"I have the utmost respect for you, as a scientist and as a person."

Still nothing.

"Please don't do this. Don't shut me out. I only..."

Dana grabbed me, stood on tiptoe and pressed her mouth against mine. Soon her tongue slid between my lips and we were off to the races. She pulled her face away from mine long enough to say, "Shut up!" then kissed me again.

We fell back on the bed and Dana rolled me over so she was on top. She got me completely worked up, ready to throw my clothes off and do the deed then and there. That's when she stopped.

"I'm a woman of few words. I hope I've made myself clear. Now let's get packed. We've got places to go, and I don't mean Houston. That's just a pit-stop."

She pulled up the extending handle on her luggage and put her shoulder bag on top. She was heading to the door while I was still on the bed wondering what just happened.

"OK, so this is how it's played," I thought. "That works for me."

I got up, straightened and adjusted my clothing, closed my bag and ran to follow her to the elevator. Waiting for the doors to open, she looked at me sideways and I looked at her sideways. We said nothing. It was a volume, a tome, a complete works in a glance.

It was clear that she had gotten to me. I had it bad. I had the Wright Complex. I stifled a smile, deciding not to say that out loud.

22
Mars Explorer

We threw our bags into the red Ford Explorer and jumped into the same seats we had on the ride from Palomar.

"Next stop, the airport," said our driver.

"Making the trip today, the Red Mars Explorer," I said, hoping to throw some levity into the trip. It wasn't working. There was silence.

"Oh," said Doctor Bronson, "Mars Explorer, red. I get it."

The driver started the engine and we departed for the airport.

"Here they come," said the driver. We all looked.

Behind us and coming fast was a caravan of media vans. Fox News was in the lead, headed for the hotel. There were eleven possible hotels where we might have been staying. Somebody given them the name.

"There's a leak," I said. Doctor Bronson turned in his seat, not only to look at me but also to see the gang of reporters chasing us.

"What do you mean?" he asked.

"There's someone who has been leaking this stuff to the press, they have been a step behind us from the start. I can feel their breath on my neck."

"You mean someone at the observatory?" Bronson's eyes were wide with sheer terror. In his innocence he could not believe that someone within our circle could betray the project.

"Yes, Doctor, I'm afraid it is someone at the observatory." I replied.

"Could it be your little friend?" asked Dana, turning her head toward me.

"Don't be mean. And no, it couldn't be Carrie. She wanted to be my assistant. She sees a value in me. She wouldn't turn us in. I haven't known her long, but I know her well. It's someone else." I looked at Dana. I wanted to say that I cared for her and also for Carrie but not the same way, it was different. I wanted to tell her that Carrie was the sister I had lost so many lifetimes ago. I wanted to say that we had history and that we shared a bond. I pictured that going over like a lead hippopotamus in a cold-air balloon, so I decided to not say anything. It was a language we shared.

"Doctor Bronson, who in our immediate group has recently suffered a setback?" asked Dana.

Bronson turned his head, thinking. He pursed his lips

and gave a little shake of his head, then stopped, raised his eyebrows and sighed.

"The institute passed Doctor McClellan over for several grants last year. That left her studies in the dust I'm afraid, just not relevant enough. Mineral Composition is her area, what composes dirt. Her interest is in the soil around the Complex, not the structures themselves."

"So she might have reason to have the press show up and put her in the spotlight as one of the scientists involved?" I asked, just to make things clear.

"Oh, yes. She would need something to jump-start her career. She has no projects in progress. Jupiter is still years off. The Moon and Mars are on back burners. She has nothing to analyze. If some planet doesn't get investigated soon, she'll have to get a job."

I pictured Doctor McClellan saying, "You want fries with that?"

"Well, I think if you check her phone, you'll find CBS, NBC and ABC on her fast dial," said Dana.

"Don't forget Fox and CNN," added Bronson.

"So that's..." I said, more to myself than anyone else. I was not even sure I had said it out loud.

"What?" said Dana.

"She was talking to me in the hallway," I said, as if in a dream. I remembered touching her, seeing the flash of memory. It had been at a hospital, she had been wearing a nurse's uniform. But she was so clean. All the other nurses were blood-spattered and sweaty. Why was she so *clean*? And why did she walk by me with a glance, without stopping?

"What are you saying, Tom?" Dana calling me by my first name shook me out of my thoughts. To do that in front of Bronson was breaking protocol. I turned toward her.

"She was talking to me in the hallway, trying to get some information from me. She was saying that on Earth, civilizations get buried by the years and we find them by digging. That's when I realized that these were not buried by time but by someone who didn't want them found."

"That's when you came in and said that," said Doctor Bronson.

"Yes, but what was she going for? Was she trying to get close to me to get more information? Was she looking for an *in*?"

"Or was she trying to get close to you hoping you would say something unguarded at some later hour, say, in bed?" asked Dana. She had an edge to her when she used that tone. She saw in McClellan a bit of the adversary.

"It didn't occur to me at the time," I said. "But looking back, it's a possibility she could have been using wiles on me."

"What?" asked Bronson.

"Wiles! Feminine wiles. Trying to trick me, to seduce me."

"Hmm." Bronson turned back around.

"Well, it's possible," I said to Dana.

"Yeah. Possible," she said.

Dana turned back to regard the media behind us, who had stopped at the hotel. Our little caravan continued on to the airport.

"It won't be long before they're on the move again," said Doctor Bronson, looking back.

"Our destination would not be hard to guess. And McClellan knows we're going to Houston." Dana was putting it together and Doctor McClellan was coming out as the villain.

"There might be people waiting at the airport," said Bronson.

"Then I suggest you arrive at a different location," said the woman behind the wheel.

23
Houston

At a small private runway, a two-engine jet was waiting. We exited the Explorer, took our bags and got into the airplane. It was like a plush van with wings. The pilot was already in the cockpit and was soon joined by the woman who drove us from the observatory. We chose seats and buckled in, along with four other members of the scientific team. Doctor McClellan was not among them.

With smiles and nods all around, the others buckled themselves in for takeoff. The older woman to my left leaned across the aisle.

"This is exciting! I've never flown before!"

The movement of the plane cut off whatever it was I was about to say to reassure her. Unlike larger craft, this one needed no long, drawn-out taxi down the runway. The plane leaped into the air like a frightened goose. The storm that had been threatening to rain on us for the past day buffeted us around until we got above it. Once above the clouds, it was blue skies and smooth sailing. The woman next to me was looking from window to window like a kid in a candy store.

"What can we do about doctor..." I began.

"Shhh! Let's keep that to ourselves for now," whispered Dana.

I nodded. I was searching for something to discuss with her. I had to find some bit of information not yet transmitted to make things easier. There was nothing. But then, Dana's language didn't contain lots of conversation. Her concepts were transmitted without bothersome words.

I slipped my hand over hers on the arm rest. She didn't move her hand. She allowed mine to rest on top of hers. It was a statement of gargantuan proportions.

"Here we go!" said a voice over the intercom, and the plane began its descent.

At a private runway outside of Houston, several personal vehicles assembled as we rolled up to a hangar. Bronson leaned over to us.

"There's a line of limousines at the airport and a throng of press making it impossible for anyone to move. They are going to be disappointed."

"Where's McClellan?" asked Dana.

"I don't know. We'll have to keep track of her."

"She might not be the only one," I added. "In fact, it might not be her at all. We don't know that for sure."

"Oh, yes," said the woman across the aisle. "It is."

We all looked to her.

"Doctor Elizabeth Strayer, Caltech. It was Doctor McClellan who I heard on her phone calling in to the media. She has a contact at each of the networks. She made the call from the ladies' room at the observatory."

It was a revelation. It was also confirmation, something unfamiliar to most of us.

"Thank you. That's good to know," I said.

"Just because I've never flown, doesn't mean I grew up in a vat, young man. Doctor McClellan has a serious need to be in the limelight. My advice would be to give it to her, but cut her out of the information stream."

"So, keep her in the limelight, but keep her in the dark," I echoed.

"You're not as dumb as you look," she said, with a wink.

The plane rolled up to the line of cars and we got out. We got into yet another Explorer, this one dark green and driven by a young man, an undergrad.

"Do you know where we're going?" asked Doctor Bronson.

"Oh, yes, sir. Houston Space Lab, Control Central. Yes, sir!"

Bronson extended his hand forward and spoke.

"Make it so."

The caravan was on the move.

24
Command Central

The room was huge, with lines of desks and computers everywhere. Headphones abounded. Giant screens lined the walls. When the lights went on, there were loud clunks for each bank of lights. A chill went through me. I was standing in the room that was the command center of every flight into space.

Dana and Doctor Bronson followed their guide to the main room while I went to the press room. There were refreshments in the press room and a page, an assistant to fulfill my every need. His name was Steve.

As I looked out the window at the small group of scientists in the main room, my phone went off. I hoped it wasn't the Senator. "Matthews," I said into the phone.

"Mister Matthews, I got myself assigned to the logistics team and I am getting onto a plane on the way to you as we speak." It was Carrie and I had to admit, my heart did a little jump.

"Carrie, what are you doing? You can't come all the

way..."

"Don't worry about it. I have you and Doctor Wright booked in at Best Western Heritage. It has a high rating, lots of stars, and you'll have complete comfort. The coordinators are working together. When you break at the end of the day, you can continue meeting over dinner. Listen, gotta go, they're telling me to put my phone away. See ya soon."

"Carrie? Uh, Carrie?"

She had hung up. I looked into the air, thinking about Carrie. Dana was looking up at me from the floor of the main room. Her head tilted up with that curious puppy look she often gave me. I held up a thumbs-up and grinned at her.

Carrie had already booked *us* into the Heritage. My guess was that she had come to grips with Dana and I being a couple and was greasing the rails for us. An ally! I had a friend, but better still, I had an ally. "The best sister a guy could have!" I said to myself.

For an hour, I sat pondering the ramifications of meeting the reincarnation of my sister. Carrie was a graduate student at Caltech. I worked in Washington and was out here by sheer chance. The odds were, pardon the pun, astronomical.

I looked over at Steve, sitting across the room, ready to leap up to get me whatever I desired, and wondered who he was. Was he part of my team? Had I come across him at some time? I considered walking over and touching him. I could brush some crumb off of his wrist and in the process find out just who I was dealing with.

On any given day, there are people here and people way over there. Centuries ago, people rarely moved more than twenty miles from where they were born. The idea of travel never occurred to them. It was either war or famine that made people move. So people who were on my team in America and Europe would be different from those on other teams in other parts of the globe.

Then there was the fact that there are more people now. There are people who were not here earlier and so on nobody's team before. They are new, like Dana.

I thought of Dana. When I touched her, and there was touching, nothing happened. That is, nothing with prior memory involved.

In the past, I limited my contact with women. Why? I would meet a woman at a benefit and find out that we had *frozen together on a battlefield in France*. Or I'd meet a lovely lady at the opera. I would shake her hand and learn that she had *knifed me for three pieces of gold on a lonely road in Northern England*. With Helen, my ex, it took six months before I cold touch her without a disastrous encounter showing up.

There were times I would remember someone but they weren't there. They were somewhere else. Like the fellow who sold me a paper and touched me when he handed me the change. We had met once *at a small field in the snow. I was in blue, looking over the stone fence at the line of gray uniformed soldiers and he was looking back. Then some idiot yelled, "Fire!" and we never did get introduced.*

After a while, I got used to it, even to the point of watching the other person to see if they recognized me. They never did. It seemed to me that I was the only one; the only one to remember who I was before and who I had been playing with.

It's amazing how many people you meet in a lifetime. It's even more amazing how many of them show up again later, in a different form. My sister died. I cried at the burial. But she reappeared as Carrie and was now booking me into a hotel room along with my new lover. She cared for me, just like before. She was an ally of many lifetimes and didn't even know it.

People, I had decided, remained at their level. Doctor Cutler had been the lord of the castle. Doctor McClellan had been the haughty nurse who didn't get her uniform dirty. So Carrie was a kind and loving sister.

It was common among those who claimed to remember past lives to say they were someone important. It was usually someone completely unimportant who developed such delusions of grandeur. It was exactly that, of course. They didn't remember at all. They were nothing in this life, so they see a picture of Katherine the Great and they like that. So they think, "Gee, I must have been Katherine the Great! Watch the boys at school scrape and bow now!"

Of course, no one scrapes or bows to them.

As I was in this life, I was usually near greatness in my past lives. Someone would shoot at the Emperor and hit me, or they'd go to poison the King and I'd get the cup by mistake. It's never good to stand next to greatness; you always get something nasty on you.

I was pretty sure that at some point Senator Hughes would get investigated. Somehow, it would come out that it was all his aide's fault. There I'd be, with some reporter saying to me, "Well, of course, you would deny it. Who wants to go to jail for that?"

But there's no escaping destiny. I went for a nice, quiet job and got recommended to the Capitol. Before I knew it, I was standing next to a Senator, holding his coat and keeping his secrets. I didn't mind secrets. I had been keeping my own since I discovered that I wasn't crazy. Of course, I realized right away that if I told anyone what I knew, men in white coats would haul me away in a van.

So I kept it to myself. After all, I didn't care if Steve knew who we had been to one another in a past life. It was likely that Steve didn't care. So there you are.

"Mister Matthews?" said a voice.

"Thank goodness," I thought. "I am bored to tears sitting here."

"I'm Matthews." I almost laughed. Did he think the pimple-faced boy in the blue blazer and red tie was Matthews of Senator Hughes' office?

There stood a man in shirt sleeves and a security tag around his neck. He was bald and wore wire rimmed glasses. His chest and shoulders filled the shirt like he worked out. He could press the Explorer we came in with one hand. He had a worried look.

"You'd better come with me."

25
The Senator's Ear

In a large conference room, Dana and seven other scientists sat and stood around the table. There was a phone in the center. As I walked in with the man with the security badge, everyone looked up at me. It was Bronson who spoke first.

"What the hell, Matthews? What are you trying to pull?"

"Me? I'm not trying to pull anything. I came as fast as I could; what's happened?"

The urgency conveyed made me think it was an emergency. I expected to see bloodied faces and broken bones, but everyone appeared to be fine. Still, something had happened and it seemed I was to blame.

"We're shot out of the water, that's what!" said Dana, glaring.

"OK, enough with the skirting the issue thing. What is going on?" I demanded, tired of the games.

Bronson was at his tether's end. He brought himself to

full height like a grisly bear and yelled at me, his face red with anger.

"We were about to see about reprogramming the Martian satellites. We heard that we didn't have funding. Congress cut all funding. Only existing projects can continue. That is until funding runs out, which could be any minute. And it was from your office. So what's the story?"

"Well, I don't have an office. I work for Senator Hughes. He sits on the committee, not me."

"But you have the Senator's ear," suggested Bronson.

"Sure!" I replied, taking out my phone and waving it. "got it right here!"

"Well, get on it!" said Bronson. "What are you waiting for?"

"Yeah. Right on it."

I left while I had the chance and called the office.

"Senator Hughes' office," said April.

"April, Tom Matthews. Let me speak to the Senator."

"He's not here, Tom. I don't know when he'll be back."

"Sure, you do, April. The only time he's out of touch is when he's with you. Is he with you?"

"Shut up!" spat April.

"Look, I've got a bunch of scientists here trying to see what's up with Mars and they don't have the change to put in the machine."

"And I've got a war to finance. I win!"

"You're not on the subcommittee, April."

"Neither are you!"

"No, I'm the guy they're blaming because this is not going to happen until... Just give me Jason!"

"Jason only lets me call him that and he is not here. You can't talk to him."

"April!" Click! The phone went quiet. I looked at the screen. Call terminated. Figures!

"Problem?" said a familiar voice. I turned around.

"Doctor Elizabeth Strayer, of Caltech. How are you?"

"Better than you! Trouble in paradise?"

"Not in mine. But I don't get it. The Senator is on a committee, they make a decision about NASA, but it doesn't take hold for months. It's not like the bank will stop honoring their checks. How can we be operating one moment and not the next?"

"Come on, kid. I'll treat ya to a cup of coffee. You look like you could use some coffee. Me, I could too, but what I'd really go for is a shot of Jim Beam over ice. This way looks good."

I followed Doctor Elizabeth Strayer down the hall. In an alcove was a coffee machine, the kind with the little pods that makes a cup at a time.

"Preference?"

"Uh... Strong, dark roast."

"My favorite too. What did she say?"

"That the war is more important than Mars."

"She's right. Mars will be there. The war might end and then where would we be? Never get between a politician and a good war. You sleeping with her?"

"April? No, the Senator is, and he's welcome."

"Not your cup of tea, eh?"

"Not even close."

"You like 'em a little smarter, up for a challenge?" Doctor Strayer looked at me from the side, her mouth in a crooked smile. The little old lady from the plane was not so little, not that old and not so much a lady.

"Let's not stray from the subject. How does this go from funded to not funded in a matter of minutes?"

"Somebody picks up a phone and tells somebody else if they want to stay in business, the shop next door has to close. Simple as that. We've just experienced McClellan picking up a phone and turning the media's heads. She put herself in the spotlight. You notice she's not in the group you just left."

"Yeah, I noticed that."

"We gave her driver different instructions. She went to the wrong airport. There were no reservations. The emergency number goes to a voice-mail box that's full. She's caught in a loop."

"Doctor Strayer, you're a genius."

"Please, call me Liz. I'll call you Tom. That'll make things easier."

"Doctor Wright won't let me call her Dana in public."

"Yeah, she's wrapped a little tight for me. I can see you like her, though. Here, gimme your phone."

I handed my phone over to Liz, my new friend. I was careful not to touch her, as direct contact would free up a memory and I wanted to know her as she is, not as she was.

Liz dialed and held the phone to her ear.

"Yeah, Speaker of the House, please."

Liz winked at me while she waited. Her coffee finished pouring. I pointed to the cream. Liz shook her head. Then I pointed to the sugar. She nodded. I fixed it for her and put it close to her on the counter, then started on a second one for me.

"Hello, Bob? Liz. Listen, Senator Hughes is on the committee overseeing the budget for NASA. Well, he's kicking them in the ribs. It's not just killing the space program that's the issue, something's happened. Yeah, I saw the Rogers show. Funny guy! But it's more than that. It's proof of intelligent, extraterrestrial life, Bob. Look, we busted a gut to get to the moon where we knew nobody was. What do you think is going to happen with proof of life on Mars? If we're behind on this, it's going to be a black eye on you. Go kick Hughes in the butt and get him to loosen up the funds. Someone called down here and told them the fun house has closed and their tickets are no good."

Liz took a sip of the coffee, still listening.

"You can? Great, Bob. I appreciate it. I will, and you say 'Hi' to Grace as well. Thanks, Bob."

Liz gave my phone back. She climbed onto a stool by the counter and pulled her coffee close to her. She patted another stool.

"Put it right there, Tom. Take a load off."

"You just call up the Speaker of the House?"

"Nothing like going right to the top. Bob and I go way back."

"I've yet to see this sort of thing in action."

"Happens all the time. Someone like your Senator gets on a committee. He funnels a bunch of money from a program like the NASA Space Program into a slush fund labeled 'War Chest' or 'Orphan's Fund' or some such. Then he spends it on pet projects. Some of the money is going to finance the war effort. He can't run off with all the money or someone notices. Then when he wants some money, he looks around and sees what he can cut. He sure isn't going to cut his secretary's abortion or his annual bonus. And his bonus is enough to feed a small country."

"He gutted the Space Program for someone's bonus?"

"Or kid's braces, wife's Mercedes, pet project in a home state. Stuff takes money. Money is the blood it runs on. One vampire in among the virgins and everything gets sucked dry. In this case, Senator Hughes is your vampire."

"Well, I know he completely lacks ethics, but a vampire?"

"Sucking the virgins dry!" said Liz, enunciating every word.

"He sabotaged the NASA Space Program?" I gasped. "That's unconscionable!"

"And yet, there it is. Hughes got onto the line just after he spoke with you. He told a couple of people if they allowed this to go through, he would take the funding from their project."

"Do you know who he called?"

"No. But that's not important. We have to get him to make another call to the same person. We'll give Bob a few minutes to do his stuff."

26

Tales Untold

Liz took another sip of her coffee, slow and with obvious enjoyment. She looked like my grandmother, with gray-and-white hair pulled back in a bun. She dressed for travel, in a J. Peterman t-shirt with jeans and a denim throw-over shirt. She wore leather walking shoes that looked like she used them for gardening. Liz wore no makeup, as there no one she was trying to impress. She wasn't trolling for a man, so war paint wasn't necessary.

A feeling came over me, one of intense trust and comradeship. It occurred to me that I had knowledge; knowledge that would put this all in perspective. And all it would take was letting down my guard and baring my unprotected belly to the world.

"Do you believe in past lives?" I asked her out of the blue.

I didn't even know why I asked that. Perhaps as a way to ease into the topic. Of course, there's no way to ease into the topic. You either believe in past lives or you do not. Have you lived before, had other names, other adventures? It seemed impossible that anyone would believe otherwise, and yet everyone but me did.

Liz flashed me a crooked smile, regarding me as one would a crackpot who was none-the-less one of the family.

"I keep my options open. Why do you ask?"

"I'd like to touch you," I said.

"Ha! You and half the student body! Get in line, buster!"

"No, I mean, just... oh, give me your hand."

I reached over and took her hand and Bang! There it was! A *military wedding with crossed swords over the steps down from the cathedral. The bride in white, a carriage waiting with four white horses. Then horsemen broke into the square with swords drawn. They cut down the attending friends and family of the bride and groom. Shots rang out and the bride faltered and fell into my arms. She looked up into my eyes and died. At her side and mine, my best friend, Edmond, knelt and touched my shoulder. He looked up, fire in his eyes. "To arms, brother," he said to me.* Then the memory was gone.

I looked up at Liz.

"Anything?" she said.

"Yes," I replied. "Yes, much. We have been friends, close. Comrades in arms."

"Sounds right. I'm willing to be that to you. So you get it when you touch someone, eh?"

"Yeah, I recently ran into my sister from a lifetime in which family was important to me. It was good to see her again. In fact, she should be landing soon."

"Does she know?"

"No. No one knows. I'll let you in on a secret: you are the first person I have ever told about this, ever."

"Hm! I'm honored. You've never told anyone?"

"No one. They would have had me committed. This is more out-there than 'I-see-dead-people.' I'm not sure why I told you. It seems relevant somehow."

"How does it work? When did you first notice?"

"It started in the Army. I touched the arm of a buddy and zing! Something happened. We became close friends. Later I began to isolate and recognize the memory hit. When I went back to school after the service, I got better at it. I began to notice that people were hanging around together. I was working with the same crew, lifetime to lifetime."

"Long distance travel is a recent thing. Until lately, people pretty much stayed in the same place. So you touch, for example, my hand like you did, and the memory flows. Is that it?"

"More like flashes," I said. It was strange talking about it with someone. She was the first!

"Flashes, OK."

"And times of stress come up more than others. I guess they stick in the memory."

"Stress. You mean danger, death?" asked Liz.

"Exactly, a scene will pop up. There's the other person. Then the scene stops, usually just before the rain of bullets. Or the big explosion or before we fall off the cliff together."

"Hm! Action packed drama, the stuff that makes for good movies. And then it's gone?"

"Yup."

We sat there for a moment. I could tell she was thinking of what to ask. I thought of something to say first. "People generally stay in their strata one life to the next, that's one thing I've noticed."

"So you still can't trust Benedict Arnold with a secret?" asked Liz.

"That's right, and John Hancock still has a big ego."

"Good to know there are some constants in the universe. You know, of course, that this raises more questions than it answers."

"That's why I don't ask a lot of questions. I just sit back and watch the memories roll."

"How do you account for it?" asked Liz.

"Well, I don't know. I think sometime I may have..."

I stopped mid-sentence, much as I had several times in the past few days. One more piece of the puzzle fell into place.

It was the fact that I began to remember. That was the whole thing, wasn't it? It was all about memory. Not just my memory, but the memory. The Wright Complex wasn't supposed to turn up and I wasn't supposed to remember. This wasn't supposed to be happening. Not only that, but the funding from Washington was not supposed to be flowing.

But sometimes things happen whether they're supposed to or not. After all, it depends on who is making the rules. Who was making these rules?

In Washington society, we ask, "Who benefits?" The answer to the question is usually the "who" behind the changes going down. If you follow the money, you will see who is behind the scenes, and sometimes it is hard to follow the money.

In this case, Hughes benefited. McClellan benefited from the exposure to the press. Everyone in the room benefited if the funding flowed, because otherwise they would be out of a job. Even Liz benefited if this went on, as she was not likely to see many grants in the future. She was facing retirement and was not happy about it.

But who benefits from the buildings staying under the dirt, from no one ever finding them? Who was behind the marks on the face of Mars. I had a feeling I knew who it was.

"You just remembered something, didn't you?" asked Liz, looking at me with child-like wonder. She saw a look in my eye, a flush on my face that she had not seen on any face in a long, long time.

"Yes, Liz, I just remembered something. I think I know why I remember so much."

"Tell me!" said Liz, leaning forward.

"Oh, you're never gonna believe this!" I replied. There was a quiver in my voice that I could not control. For the first time since the beginning of this strange ordeal, I was afraid.

27
The Speaker of the House

"Senator Hughes," called Bob Cartwright, Speaker of the House, striding up beside him.

"What is it, Cartwright?" said Jason Hughes. His brain swung into high gear to come up with something he was going to be late for, so he could be short with the Speaker. But the Speaker was walking too fast for him.

"It comes to me that there are folks at NASA who have stopped short on a project of growing concern. You have anything to do with that?"

"Don't know anything about it. Now, if you'll excuse me..."

"No, I can't do that, Jason. We have just found the tip end of a thread in this sweater and we have pulled it. We're committed now. Until we have a handful of yarn, we're not going to be happy. You catching my drift? Make a call. Turn on the tap again. I want this rag-tag little project funded."

"You can't tell me to do that, Bob," said the Senator,

backing up a step. He didn't like doing that, but it was automatic when threatened, a tick left over from childhood. The Speaker stepped forward two steps and put a finger against the Senator's chest.

"Then listen up! The funding, the research will go on, the satellites and rovers will do whatever it is they do and man will go to Mars. We will find out what this is all about. When the media applauds those who stepped up and decries those who stood in the way, guess where you'll be. If you don't want to sit out the dance, you had better step to the music. There's a Mars trip in our future. Get on board!"

Speaker Cartwright spun around and stalked down the marble-lined hall of the Capitol building. He left Senator Hughes standing by the bust of a past statesman he did not recognize.

Hughes had taken one of the junior senators aside and put a bug in his ear. Within the hour, Congress pulled funding from all NASA projects. NASA was already invested in some projects. On those, funding continued to the conclusion. Whereas new projects, untried, untested and not invested had no funding. Such new projects got relegated to the trash heap before they began. This included the investigations into the alleged writing on Mars. They had already cost the taxpayers several airplane tickets and some hotel rooms. This madcap spending had to stop!

NASA's administration building in Washington placed an immediate call to NASA's Houston Control Center. Planning meetings and activities of Mars would immediately stop. If continued, would be without budget. The purse strings doubled as curtain sashes, ending the show. Within a span of three hours, the entire project of the discoveries on Mars ended. All personnel had orders to stop.

Jason Hughes pictured someone saying, "Everyone can please go home now." He relished the thought.

He would welcome Tom Matthews back with open arms. The stack of work on his desk would keep him occupied and out of everyone's hair for the rest of the term. Next term, Hughes would find a suitable replacement. All staff hand in their resignation at the end of a term and the start of a new one. The Senator would accept Tom's and there would be nothing more said about it.

What happened to the man sent to investigate the new formations on Mars? He later resigned. Matthews would be a footnote to history. They would classify the lines on Mars as an optical illusion, just as the canals had been.

But now that dream faded. He had new marching orders. Matthews would relish this, he knew it. He hated what he was about to do and yet he knew he had to do it.

"This is Hughes," he said into his phone. "Remember that thing about the NASA budget? Well, something's come up. Upon reconsideration, there might be something to that Mars thing after all." He listened for a minute. Then, "That's right, reverse it. I know, I know, but it was a mistake. Do you want to go down as the man who cut funding to the greatest discovery of the decade? Then go in there and argue just as hard to get it funded."

There was loud swearing coming from the phone and the Senator held it away from his head, wincing. There was a moment of silence.

"Thank you, Milton, that was the right decision," said the Senator.

"The things I have to do!" muttered Hughes as he put his phone in his pocket. He tried to remember where he was going when the interruption came. Oh, yes, to his office, then Happy Hour.

At the other end of the corridor, Bob Cartwright was dialing a number on his phone. He put it to his ear and looked out the window to the gathering gloom of a cloudy Washington afternoon. It had been threatening rain all day and he wished it would just hurry up and get on with it. Of course, he wished that about everything in this town, and in this building. Right now he wished that about this phone call.

"Pick up, Liz! Come on, pick up... Liz!"

He smiled, as if she could see his smile. The Speaker was a campaigner, every inch. "I have spoken with the Senator and he now realizes the gravity of the situation.

Go and have lunch. By the time you get back, the funding should be back as well. And tell Matthews if the Senator lets him go, I have room in my office for him. OK, I will. Hi to Frank."

Speaker Cartwright closed the phone and sighed a satisfied sigh. It was a good day. He had done something.

His composure darkened. He would have to keep an eye on that ferret, Hughes. As soon as he's out of direct sight line, he gets up to mischief. He had a thought that made him look back down the corridor. Perhaps he might just go and look in on the committee and see how they are coming along.

Speaker of the House Robert Cartwright strode down the corridor toward the meeting rooms. Small groups of men gathered there to spend the money of the country's taxpayers.

"Already the most overburdened on Earth," he thought. "Soon, they will also be the most burdened taxpayers on Mars as well."

He didn't mind the cost. Great things have a great price tag. In the end history will applaud him as the man who won the Mars race. This could, spun by the right man; it could lead to a presidency.

"I wonder," he thought, "if Matthews will want to work at the White House?"

28
Press Briefing

Doctor Megan McClellan stood fuming in the San Diego airport. She was there alone. No one was standing with her. No one was there with the luggage, the tickets, the chits for drinks in the clubhouse. There were no reservations made. None of the carriers she checked had tickets for her to Houston. No one was taking care of the details and no one was responding to her calls. She had been completely abandoned.

Well, not completely. The press was outside, armed with battery packs and microphones. They would take her down the moment she said the wrong thing.

She angled for press coverage at every step of the journey. Since she first heard about the markings across the face of the Red Planet. Early on someone said that the marks were writing. But it was she who put her face in front of a camera and proclaimed that there was "A message in the red dust of Mars!" Later, of course, she had to go back and refute it. "Upon further investigation, we believe them to be some sort of edifice. These alien-made structures constitute proof of intelligent life on Mars."

It was her face in front of the cameras whenever they rolled on this story. She saw to that. She was fast becoming the spokesperson to quote for the Mars story.

Her credentials were a weak in a few areas, but that was unimportant in the bright light of the public's need to know. She would guest on the top talk shows, interviewed by recognizable names. She would push her book: *Cities of Mars*. She was still working on the title.

But now, she was standing in the middle of the airport alone. The car that brought her had left. It was a small Mercedes, which was only proper, and couldn't hold more than two in back. She was, as it turned out, the only passenger. When she got out, she thanked the driver, a young man from Caltech. She tried to remember his name. He said it when she got into the car, but who pays attention to these things? He was a driver, for heaven's sake.

Now he was gone. Where was her luggage? Someone should be seeing to that. Where was her reservation, her ticket and boarding pass? Where were the rest of the scientists? Had she beat them all here? Are they just pulling up to the curb now? Or did she miss them? Did that wretched boy drive too slow? Did he allow everyone to arrive and leave again before she could catch up? She was the leader of the group; how could they leave her behind?

The press people outside looked in every direction, searching for the scientists. This was the one time she didn't want to talk to them. What would she say? "Well, yes, I am the leader of this contingency and the main scientist among them. And yes, they flew off without me and left me behind like a child's cast-off jacket."

No, that wouldn't do.

She looked around. The private club? Members only! But she didn't have the reservation, ticket or boarding pass. She didn't even have the membership card. Someone else had that. Where was that horrible child, who didn't even have a degree and yet was her assistant? Where was her assistant now?

She saw the ladies room and in an instant she made a decision. She was not too proud to hide out in the restroom. But just as she had decided, activity outside caught her attention. One of the news crew was pointing at her.

Well groomed women in business suits and running shoes closed the distance. Each one wielded a microphone. Cameramen hoisted cameras on their shoulders. A mass of news people rushed the revolving doors.

Dashing into the restroom was out of the question. The ladies could follow her in there for an interview in a tinny echo chamber reminiscent of high school. Trapped!

Before she could think straight, media spokespeople surrounded her. Cameras crowded her. Microphones threatened her. Questions struck her all at once.

"Has there been a development?"

"Where is the investigation leading?"

"Is there new evidence of life on other planets?"

"Are you going to Mars?"

"Please, please," she said. She held up her hands and lowered her eyelids to half, a tactic to defuse an electric situation.

"There are too many factors to this problem for a simple resolution. The doctors have removed themselves to their home turfs for further rumination. I have the honor of remaining here, at Palomar Observatory, to monitor the situation on Mars. Now that I have seen the rest off on their respective journeys, I will return to Palomar. There I will continue the observation of the Red Planet. Somehow, the student assigned to me had an emergency. Is anyone going back to the observatory?"

There was a moment when it seemed that time had stopped. Then the questions came hot and heavy once more.

"What do you expect to see on the Martian surface?"

"Is there any truth to the rumor that men are already on Mars?"

"Is it writing or could it be something else?"

"Could it be just an optical illusion?"

"Will you be going to Mars?"

Once more Doctor McClellan raised her hands, shutting her eyes completely this time.

"And I will be happy to answer all your questions. First, I must return to Palomar Observatory. I have to confer with my colleagues on the latest developments. Excuse me, please."

She turned and grabbed the youngest and least known of the women reporters, the one with a van sitting just outside by the curb. She continued walking, holding the woman by the elbow. "There's an exclusive in it for you if you will drive me back to the observatory."

"Right this way, Doctor McClellan," said the woman.

29

Palomar Observatory

"Are they off?" asked Doctor Cutler to his assistant.

Doctor Eli Cutler walked down the hall toward the meeting room he had chosen as his headquarters. Several stacks of folders sat on the table. Close by, a dozen photographs of Mars and a collection of reference books from the library. In the center of this array lay his laptop, open and running. On the right were flash drives, all color coded, and a digital mouse on the left. His assistant, undergraduate Sara Cannon, was walking by his side.

"Yes, sir. It took three private planes, but they got off OK. The press is at the main airport."

"And Doctor McClellan?"

"Stranded at the airport. She'll find a way to get back here, I'm afraid. She's not stupid."

"Did she bring an assistant?"

"No, she insisted we assign one to her."

"Who did we assign?"

"Lester Lyons, a junior."

"An idiot!" spat Doctor Cutler.

"Yes, sir, he's an idiot, but he was eager to serve. Willingness must account for something."

Cutler sighed. "Yes, it does. Willingness accounts for quite a lot. Have Lyons standing by when she arrives. Give him some story."

"Can I have her assigned, sir?"

"Yes, by all means, assign her. Find a telescope that's not in use and put her on it. Say its top priority and we want nightly reports. If anything turns up, she should let us know immediately. It's of utmost importance."

"Yes, sir," said Sara. "Where should I have the telescope focused?"

"Doesn't matter. Have it focused on Las Vegas for all I care. Just keep her out of my hair."

"Yes, sir!"

Sara stopped at the door to the conference room, thought for a moment, then turned around. She heading for the dome where the Samuel Oschin 48 inch robotic telescope stood. The telescope scanned the skies nightly and the data collected sent by microwave to astronomers for analysis.

Doctor Cutler knew his instruction was in good hands. They would keep McClellan watching the heavens and the media would grow tired of her in no time. He turned his mind to a more important subject, the 200 inch Hale Telescope.

He walked out and looked up at the telescope's Cassegrain cage. Here they had gathered data for more than 45 years. The telescope boasted a large format camera and a wide-field infrared camera. It was a joint venture between Caltech, Cornell and the Jet Propulsion Laboratory, operated by NASA. If they could keep the interest in outer space up, they could keep the money flowing.

"How can they cut us off?" he asked aloud to the giant telescope.

A commotion outside distracted his attention. The news vans were rolling up. With them, to his surprise, was Doctor McClellan.

McClellan had done some good work early in her career. She was soon overshadowed by younger and more inquisitive colleagues. Lately, she had become a media hound. She thrived in the bright lights, sucking up the attention as if she had a dog in her purse.

"Any second she's going to change her name to Kardashian just for the coverage." Doctor Cutler realized he spoke to the double-glass doors.

He had hoped the diversion would last longer. She added nothing to the investigation. She would come up with an idea now and again. Heads would rise up and look at her, then go back to work as if nothing had happened. She was the extra cook that was spoiling the broth.

Doctor McClellan got out of the van and straightened herself as if having endured an ordeal. She stalked toward the observatory with an angry look on her face. The small entourage following in her wake. Doctor Cutler braced himself to withstand a blast from the dragon.

Doctor Cutler was the senior member. Being angry at him would not be in her best interests. But Doctor McClellan did not always act in her best interests. She often put her foot in her mouth with senior colleagues. She had a tendency to blurt out what she was thinking. It was a prelude to obscurity. You do that long enough and pretty soon you get left at an airport, standing all alone, with the press running at you.

"Doctor Cutler!" yelled Doctor McClellan, sinking the first nail in her coffin.

"Doctor McClellan, ready to begin?"

"Begin?" asked McClellan, taken by surprise.

"Yes! I don't know why you thought it your task to see everyone off. But now that you're back, we'll find your assistant, Mister Lyons, and get you started. There is important work to do, as you well know. There's no time to waste traipsing around the countryside or hobnobbing with the press."

"Uh, of course. Naturally! Um. Well, where is that assistant anyway? Is he not here, awaiting my return?"

"Might be in the boys' room. We'll send someone to check."

"Where can we set up?" asked the diminutive lady commentator from the local station. Doctor McClellan turned to Doctor Cutler.

"I promised this young lady an exclusive. Where would it be best to film it?"

"Wonderful! Always willing to accommodate the working press. Right this way, miss..."

"Sheldon, Andrea Sheldon."

"Miss Sheldon. We'll do this in front of the largest telescope on the continent, the Hale Telescope, 200 inches." This impressed Miss Sheldon. With that many inches, it must be grand indeed!

Doctor Cutler stood in front of the Cassegrain cage and pointed to the floor. "You stand there, young man," he said to the cameraman. "You and I can stand here, Miss Sheldon. Perhaps you can give me an idea of what you are looking for."

"Um, I understood Doctor McClellan to be the head of this investigation."

"Doctor McClellan has been of invaluable aide to us in this project. She will continue to keep track of the situation, not only on Mars but the entire solar system and parts of the Milky Way. Is that what you wanted to talk about? The assignment of one of our junior members?"

"Not at all, Doctor. So you are in charge of the investigation?"

"Here at Palomar, yes. Others, of course, will take the lead in Houston. We have a representative from Washington with that group as well. He works with the senator who oversees the budget for space projects. Nothing moves without the money, you know."

"Yes, I do. All right. If you'll stand there, we'll roll and I'll ask you about the Mars project, what you have found and where it is going."

"All right, ready when you are."

The young woman turned toward the camera and waited. The cameraman gave her a signal, three fingers, then two, then one, then pointed to her.

"This is Andrea Sheldon with an exclusive. We are here at the Palomar Observatory with Doctor Cutler, the head of the investigatory team..."

As she continued, Doctor Cutler looked up to see Doctor McClellan standing by the door. You could have fried an egg on her forehead! Cutler smiled. "That'll teach her," he thought.

"... which could change the way we view outer space. Isn't that so, Doctor?"

"Yes, Andrea, the events of the past two days have been game changing in the way we look at Mars, and thus all planets. What we are seeing..."

McClellan stood by the doors, fuming, as a lad with a

cowlick came up to her.

"Doctor McClellan?" he said, his voice cracking.

"Yes," she snapped at him.

"Lester Lyons, Doctor. I'm assigned to you. You can call me Les."

"Oh, I will," said Doctor McClellan. "I will."

30
Dana & Liz

"There's been a break!" yelled Doctor Bronson. He burst into the conference room of the Houston Control Center at NASA.

Doctors Wright, Strayer and Foster poured over the existing photographs of Mars. Those photographs were all they were likely to get unless they found funding fast. All heads raised to regard Doctor Bronson, who came running in and around the center table.

"We've received a call. They've approved funding. I don't know who was behind the decision to remove it, or to return it, but I am grateful to them. Where's Matthews? I believe he had a hand in this and I want to shake it."

"Yes, I believe he did," said Doctor Strayer.

"How much do we have, Doctor?" asked Doctor Dana Wright. Doctor Strayer looked at her, smiling. She felt closer to Doctor Wright since her conversation with young Matthews. Matthews said Dana was the first person he had never known before, not in his many years on Earth.

"We have enough to reprogram and to continue our investigations on the ground. If we leave the atmosphere, we're going to need more."

"Then let's get to it," said Doctor Wright. She glanced over to regard Doctor Strayer with some curiosity.

They walked out of the conference room together. Doctor Strayer came along side of Doctor Wright and took her briefcase. "Let me help you with that, dear. I'm not carrying anything."

"Thank you, Doctor," said Dana.

"Oh, please, dear, call me Liz. I feel as if we're old friends."

"Thank you, Liz. And I feel as though we have just met, but you can call me Dana."

"Thank you, Dana. I have been talking to that nice Mister Matthews. He has the sweetest things to say about you."

Dana's eyebrows gave her away. "What has he been saying?" she thought. Memories of their brief time together in his room flashed through her mind. Liz saw her surprise and guessed what might be swimming through her brain.

"Oh, nothing bad, dear. In fact, he is quite professional, in fact, complimentary. It's plain to see he likes you."

Liz touched her arm, bare at the wrist. She let their skin make contact, just so see if she got a small twinge of memory. She didn't. She looked at Dana and smiled.

It made Dana uneasy. The sudden interest and admiration put her on guard. What could she want? Dana pulled her arm away, not too fast. No need to be rude.

"You know, Dana. I always feel better on these assignments if I have a friend, someone to talk with. You are so nice, I like you. I hope we can be friends. I promise, I won't make a pest of myself. But perhaps we can have lunch together."

"We did miss lunch," said Dana. "I'm pretty sure now that the budget is back, we can order in. A working lunch is a good idea, so we can catch up on the project."

"That'll be nice," said Liz. "Perhaps Tom Matthews will join us."

"Yes, that will be nice."

"Cutler's on the news!" yelled a voice. It was the voice of Doctor Caroline Foster. She was the head of the Astronomy Department at the University of Arizona. She was leaning out of an office off to one side and was excited.

Dana and Liz had fallen behind, partly due to their conversation and partly to Dana's slower pace. As a result, the shortest women of the group were squeezing into the back of the room. On the television set in the front was Doctor Cutler with a local reporter, one Andrea Sheldon.

"It's a repeat of a local broadcast from California," said Foster.

"...and we are hoping thereby to get a closer look at these formations to see if they are natural or made by intelligent life. If they are proof of intelligent life on Mars, it will change our direction with regards to the exploration of space."

"Thank you, Doctor Cutler. This is Andrea Sheldon for..."

Doctor Foster turned the sound down. "It was rebroadcast from earlier. She had an exclusive. Why would he give her an exclusive? Wouldn't he tell that to everyone?"

"He had a reason," said Doctor Bronson. "Cutler doesn't do anything without a good reason."

"Hungry!" said Liz. "When are we going to get food in here?" General agreement followed, complete with votes on what to get.

As Liz and Dana left the room, Bronson pulled alongside. "Where's your friend, Matthews? I want him here."

"I don't know where he went," said Dana.

"When I left him," said Liz, "we were at the coffee bar. We had just had a most enlightening conversation, and then he got a look on his face, and ran off. I couldn't keep up, so I came looking for the rest."

"I know that look. He's on to something," said Dana.

"Then let's find him fast," said Bronson.

31

Not Like the Other

I pored over the few photographs of Mars that we had brought with us and a few older ones that the NASA boys had around. There was even a Mars globe that I was able to bring into the office where I had set up a temporary headquarters. Several offices were empty, so I had taken the most secluded and pitched my tent.

"One of these things is not like the other," I sang. I was looking at the older photos and the newer ones taken on the big camera of the Hale telescope in California.

Sure enough, the earlier pictures showed a flat plain, pitted and pockmarked. There ran a ravine here and there, but otherwise, just flat. The newer images showed a long line of ridges, some straight, some curved. At quick glance, it could be writing, but the letters would be larger than the Great Wall of China. I tried to imagine what it might say, "Ask your doctor if *Marztonyx* is right for you!" I chuckled to myself.

If it was a series of structures, which I believed it to be, it was a lot of them, all connected.

I opened my laptop. I typed in "Mars Spirit." Up came the NASA website.

"Oh, that's funny!" I said to myself out loud. "I'm sitting in NASA, in Houston, and looking up their website."

"Talking to yourself will get you a Section Eight!" said a voice behind me. I turned around. It was Liz. Dana was with her. I was happy to see both of them and yet, wanted to figure this out on my own.

"Don't let us interrupt you. We'll just sit here like flies on the wall and let you work," said Liz. She pulled out a chair and sat down, looking around as if she was taking inventory.

Dana came up and put an arm through mine, kissing me on the cheek. I supposed the pretense of innocence was over. "What are you up to?" she asked, looking at the photographs I had laid out across the table.

"I remembered something, but I'm not sure what," I replied.

"You remembered?" asked Dana. Her eyes were wide. She was not used to talking in these terms. It was something new to her.

"Quite a memory on that boy. If I were you, I'd listen to what he has to say," said Liz, backing me up all the way. It was good to have another ally on the team.

"I don't know what I'm talking about. It's just that there's something here. Look!" I moved over to the other pictures. "These show nothing. Flat, uncluttered, nothing. OK, these," I shuffled the photos, "show the markings we saw. At first we thought writing, because we were looking at something a couple of inches long. We forgot it was across the face of a planet pretty far away."

Dana looked at the photos. Liz nodded at me.

"These are buildings. And if you look at them, they're straight and curved. The curved ones all go either this or that direction, but all in the same general direction down the line. You see?" I waited. No response. I needed to say more.

"OK. So they designed these to move a particle along from one end to the other," I said. It was obvious to me, not as clear to them.

"Like an assembly line," said Dana.

"Right!" I replied.

"Like Henry Ford's plant," said Liz.

"Exactly!" I said, deciding to stay away from *right*. "At the beginning, they gather the item. Then move the item down the line, changing it along the way and at the end, finished."

"Then what?" asked Dana, still looking at the marks on Mars.

"Then I don't know. But these are structures, buildings. And they buried the whole complex in the dirt, not just covered over by time. They hid them on purpose, hoping no one would find them. That I know."

"Because you've been there." said Dana. She remembered what I had said, something against everything that she knew for certain.

I looked at Liz. After what I had told her and the way she just accepted it, I thought she received this information in the same way. She just nodded, her mouth scrunched up. She seemed to agree.

"Not lately," I said.

Dana looked at me. Silence hung in the air like Spanish moss.

At last, Dana stood up. She put her hands on her hips.

"We're in uncharted territory here. Until we know more about what we're dealing with, until we have something substantial, we are keeping this conversation in this room. You don't tell your theories to anyone else. Understood?"

"Understood," I said, trying not to sound nine years old.

"And we," she indicated Liz and herself, "who you have taken into your confidence, are going to proceed with caution. We need a line of investigation that will lead us to a conclusion that we can hang a hat on. In the meantime, you will keep us apprised of any future revelations."

"Gotcha!" I said.

"Sounds good to me," said Liz, standing up.

"Now, what about these rovers?" I asked.

"Let's find someone and ask them," replied Dana.

32
The Mars Rovers

"Brad, Mike and Ed can't be with us today," said Marsha Wooten. She was an assistant, a graduate student, assigned to answer our questions. Brad Larson, Mike Kivelle and Edward Hidalgo should have been available. They didn't consider our project important. Writing on Mars was the stuff of science fiction.

"Have you told them about our investigations?" I asked.

"No. Sorry. They're really busy. But I know everything there is to know. Go ahead. Ask me."

You had to give Miss Wooten points for enthusiasm.

"OK, what's the status of the Rover Spirit?" asked Dana.

"Spirit is not responding. Spirit received more than 1,300 commands as part of the recovery effort. We've received no communication from Spirit since March 22, 2010. The Spirit recovery project concluded its efforts on

May 25. The remaining, pre-sequenced ultra-high frequency relay passes scheduled for Spirit on board the Odyssey orbiter completed on June 8, 2011."

We stared at each other for a moment without comment.

"So it's not moving," confirmed Liz.

"That is correct," said Marsha.

I looked at Dana and Liz, they looked back. Dana took in a breath.

"Can I sit down? My leg is..."

"Oh, sure. I didn't mean to not offer you..." Marsha pointed to several office chairs, large and expensive. We pulled them up and continued.

"What is the condition of 'Opportunity'?" asked Dana.

"It's moving along the north end of Cape York, on the rim of the Endeavor Crater. It has a northern tilt that is better for the solar array. They're looking for light-toned material."

The three of us looked at each other. Liz moved to the map of Mars on the wall. "I'm guessing – um, 45 kilometers to the west."

"Uh, the Opportunity odometer only has 34.2 kilometers showing. Forty-five is more than it has traveled in its lifetime," said Marsha, looking from Liz to Dana.

"How fast is it?" I asked. Marsha looked at me as if I had just appeared.

"Hel-lo! It's not a race car!" she sang, as if she were in a cheerleader movie.

"The warranty ran out a while back," said Liz.

"How far can it see?" I asked again, hoping for more than just a valley girl response.

"A few feet to a few miles depending on what's in the way," said Marsha, now wondering what was going on.

I spoke to Dana and Liz. "We'll have to go with the others, the satellites. That's too close to the ground. It'll take forever to get there and perhaps not be able to see anything."

"Orbiters," said Marsha.

"What?" I asked.

"Orbiters, not satellites. Not my bailiwick. You'll have to find someone who has Orbiters."

"I want another expert," I said.

"I want lunch," said Liz.

"I want a scooter," said Dana.

33
The Mars Orbiters

"Right this way, ladies, sir," said the young man with an obvious attraction for Dana and a just-as-obvious disdain for me.

It was "Young Buck" syndrome. When a young buck wanders into an area with several does, he starts wooing. This continues until he meets the established buck. He begins to parade and puff, starting a fight, showing how tough he is.

This young buck just ran into an established buck with two does. He began immediately to show the older buck he's not afraid by showing disdain. He's polite and courteous to the females. He shows interest by his stance and facial expressions.

Naturally, I wanted to rip his throat out.

He took us into a small conference room, enough for a dozen around an oval table. On the wall were pictures of satellites in space, all artist renderings. I had seen them at NASA in Washington.

"How can I help you ladies?" said the young buck.

"We," I began, "would like a rundown on the orbiters currently circling Mars." I sat, crossed my legs and smiled at the young man.

"Uh, well. Currently circling Mars..."

"I'm sorry," I cut in. "Your name is...?"

"Curtis. Curtis Mahony."

"Thank you, continue."

"May I ask your name, sir?" he said.

"Certainly! I am Tom Matthews. I represent Congress in this matter and am thus responsible for your entire budget. What is your position here, Mister Mahony?"

"I am special assistant to C. L. Reese, the chief engineer in charge of orbital information."

"Orbital information. Yes. That means that he is in charge of receiving the data and putting it on a flash drive. You help him out with that by holding the top to the flash drive. Could we speak to someone in charge, please?"

"Now, Mister Matthews," drawled Liz Strayer. "No need to be difficult. The boy is trying his best. Look here, son. Doctor Wright here has discovered something on Mars. I'm Doctor Elizabeth Strayer, of Caltech. We have come here to find out more about it. The sooner you get out of our way, the better it will be not only for your career, but how you update your employment status on Facebook."

Liz looked at the boy with an innocent grin that I was sure she had practiced for hours and hours. The boy looked at her, looked at me and without looking at Dana, ran from the room.

"What did I say?" said Liz.

"Someone will be by in a minute. I'll just have a seat while we wait." Dana smiled and sat down.

Liz also sat down, looking around at the pretty artist renderings. Sure enough, a man came in, huffing and puffing.

"Reggie Stanes, more or less in charge. More if you consider who's actually here today, less if you count everyone. How can I help you?"

Liz took the lead.

"Reggie, we found something on Mars. We just came from Palomar where we looked through the Hale. We want a closer look. What can you do for us?"

Reggie tugged at his tie, pulled a chair out and sat down.

He was wearing a short sleeved shirt, yellow with a faint pattern. The tie was violet and gray stripes. He wore this with jeans and tennis shoes. Reggie sported a crew cut and horn-rimmed glasses.

"Well, there's the Odyssey, went up in 2001. But in oh-nine, it registered a memory error and went into safe-mode, limiting operations. Not gonna get a lot outta that. Then there's Mars Reconnaissance Orbiter, MRO.

Buuuuut, it's been experiencing technical problems as well – it burned up in the atmosphere. That leaves the Mars Express, which relays data great. But has an elongated orbit, reducing the data relay rate by a factor of four."

Reggie relayed this data complete with hand motions in the air, making it crystal clear.

"That's it? Express?" I asked.

Reggie thought for a minute, looking into the air off to the side.

"Yup." He extended the fingers on his left hand and used his right as a pointer. "There's Phoenix, a lander. There's two rovers, two probes in '99, Polar lander – lost on arrival, climate orbiter – lost on arrival, Nozomi – lost in orbit... You want me to go on?"

"No, we're good. Can we get photos from Express?"

"You bet! C'mon."

Reggie got up, followed by the three of us out into the hall. Reggie talked to us all the way down the hallway.

"Express launched in June of oh-three, arrived in December, oh-three. It was a joint-mission of the European Space Agency and the Italian Space Agency, to explore the atmosphere and surface of Mars from a polar orbit. The mission's main objective is to search for sub-surface water from orbit. Scientific instruments on-board conduct rigorous investigations. There's geology, atmosphere, surface environment, history of water, and potential for life on Mars. The Beagle lander proved to be a bust. Win some, lose some."

Reggie turned into a room with a large light-table in the center. There was only one chair in the room. Reggie immediately rolled it over to Dana, who was having some trouble keeping up. Her leg must have been bothering her from so much walking. Dana sat down with a nod of thanks. Liz and I leaned on the light table.

Around the room hung artist renderings of the Mars Express and photos of the Martian surface. I went to the actual photos. I marveled at the technology.

"The detail on these is fantastic!"

"Yeah, the ol' Express does OK," said Reggie.

"Mister Stanes," began Dana.

"Please, call me Reggie. Mister Stanes was my father."

"OK, Reggie. Can we in fact change the orbit of the Express?"

"Not without a lot of work. It's pretty much set, and like I said, it is a wide oval, so it's not like it goes round and round. You can see that some of these are the complete planet and some are close-ups, details. That's not because we're artsy-fartsy. When the Express is far away, it takes these, when its close, it takes those. We pick and choose which we like. I usually get a wallet-size to take home with me."

"Excuse me, this moon isn't round," I said, pointing at one photo.

"No, but it hopes to be someday," said Reggie. He didn't laugh at his own joke, but immediately shifted his attention to Liz and Dana. This, I noticed, was not Young Buck Syndrome, but the fact that they were doctors, whereas I was only a mister. "What next?" he asked, ready to be of help.

"Anything from yesterday or today?" asked Dana.

"We can get 'em," answered Reggie.

"You're my man! Get 'em. Where should we wait?"

"Right here. I'll be back in a flash."

"Great. That's good. Reggie, one more thing," said Dana.

"Shoot," said Reggie.

"How soon can we get up there?"

Reggie looked at Dana wide-eyed and dumbfounded. It cold have been the first time in his life he was struck speechless.

34
Team Players

While the photo of the odd-shaped moon held my attention, my phone went off. I knew who it was. I had not called the Senator in several hours and was in violation of my last instruction. I had orders to report to him on a schedule. "Matthews," I said, walking out to the hallway. I pointed to the phone at my ear as I went by Liz, who nodded.

"Where's my update, Mister Matthews?" said the voice of Senator Hughes.

"Things are moving along pretty quick here, sir. I was hoping for a breather so I could report, but so far, no joy."

"No break at all, eh?"

"There was a time when we were dead in the water, but that's passed now and we're rolling again."

"Yes. That's good. Rolling again. What does that mean?"

I filled the Senator in on events, leaving out my

suspicions and how I came by them. The Senator wouldn't understand. "The main thing at this point is that we have to keep the spigot open as far as the financing. If we get a shutoff, it's going to look bad. I have a feeling that the Space Race is back on as of yesterday."

"How important are you there? Can't they get along without you?"

Liz stuck her head out of the door.

"Well, I'm part of the discovery team. I've been able to provide some input."

"But your job is back here. You were just supposed to find out what they knew out there, not help them learn more."

Liz walked up to me and motioned for me to give her the phone. I made the introductions. "Senator, this is Doctor Elizabeth Strayer of Caltech. Doctor, Senator Hughes." I handed her the phone.

"Look, Senator, this boy is a vital part of our investigatory team. If you pull him now, it's going to hinder the fact-finding process. I know you need him there, he's valuable. But let someone else alphabetize the files for a while. He's doing good work here."

She stood listening, looked at me, winked and then looked pleased. "That's great, Senator. And that way you're guaranteed a direct conduit for information. Have a good day, Senator. Here's Tom." Liz handed me the phone. "Lunch is soon, keep it short."

I took the phone and held it to my ear. "Yes, Senator?"

"OK, Matthews. Stay for a while, but keep me informed. It was me who pulled the strings to keep you in the budget. Don't make me regret that. In fact, I'm expecting to be the man who saved the day, so keep that in mind and make me look good."

"That's my job, Senator."

A decided click told me that the Senator had ended the call. I breathed a sigh of relief. The last thing in the world I wanted to do was to go back to Washington and have to read about this story in the paper. I had tasted being on the bleeding edge of the action and it was a heady narcotic. It had me hooked.

I walked back into the photo room with its glass light-table and looked at the other reason I had for staying. Doctor Dana Wright was sitting in the only chair, looking up at me as if I was the answer to a prayer.

The events of the night before came back to me, bringing a flush to my face. Whatever limitations she had while walking around, she had none in bed. Between the covers, she was not handicapped at all. In fact, she presented me with a challenge that tested my endurance. She was another taste I had acquired and wanted to keep tasting. I wanted to say so, but that was not the language we shared. Instead, I walked over to her and stroked her head, smiling down at her.

"You order lunch?" said a voice. It was Doctor

Bronson. "It got delivered to the conference room. Can Doctor Foster join us? Doctor Foster, why don't we eat in here?"

Doctor Foster peered into the room, smiling as she saw that Dana, Liz and I were already there. Bronson pushed a wheeled cart into the room. On the cart were sandwiches, drinks and bags of chips. As if we didn't have enough to ponder, colored paper bags closed with paperclips sat on the table. On top of them, I had mysteries of my own.

The one I was chewing on was the current team. Bronson: the reincarnation of my old professor. Liz Strayer: the friend who fought shoulder-to-shoulder with me in uncertain times. Dana Wright was my fascination. She was the newcomer, who had not sparked even a moment of memory, though we were in close contact all night. I wondered who Doctor Foster had been.

The head of the University of Arizona Astronomy Department was no shrinking violet. When we found ridges on Mars, she took the next flight to San Diego to look through the Palomar eyepiece. Now she was one of a tight-knit little group keeping the flame alive beneath what could become a short-lived joke for late-night television. It was time to find out who the unknown player was. I reached out a hand. "Tom Matthews, Doctor Foster."

"Pleased to meet you, Mister Matthews."

Doctor Foster took my hand and gave it a firm shake. It was an act that established that she was capable of being bold and not intimidated by my size or gender.

At the same time, *the drafty halls of a great hall with vaulted ceilings surrounded me. The tapestries hung on the stone walls billowed as the winds found tiny openings and invaded without mercy. A chill of another kind ran through me as the lady of the hall came out of the bed chamber of the great lord. She had just filled his ear with the details of the decision he would announce later that day. It was clear to me who ran things.*

"M'lord," said the lady in passing. "M'lady," I replied, bowing.

The wind picked up, the cold made me shiver and the vision was gone. Doctor Foster was a force of her own. She would prove a valuable addition to our little group.

I smiled at her and she returned the smile. "M'lord," she seemed to say. "M'lady," I wanted to answer. Instead we released our grip on one another and reached for sandwiches.

Across the rolling cart, also reaching for a sandwich, stood Doctor Strayer. Liz looked at me with knowing eyes and a satisfied smile. She knew that I had just checked Doctor Foster's credentials. That I didn't look disappointed was good news. She picked up a can of root beer and a bag of chips. Then she strolled toward me.

"I trust the doctor has met with your approval?" said

Liz, under her breath.

"A good ally, but don't cross her. She has the ear of the king."

"Oh! I will keep on her good side."

"A wise move." We drifted to different corners of the room.

Dana looked at me with questioning eyes. What could Liz and I be sharing, like teenagers with a secret code? I gave her a reassuring smile.

Reggie appeared at the door, panting for breath. "Oh, good! You got food! That's good! Now! We will have new photos within half an hour. We are focusing on the stretch of Mars with the new markings. We'll be able to see them at intervals, all angles from horizon to horizon. We'll see them at a slant, from overhead, but closer than your photos. We'll see the other slant as Express moves on in its orbit. It'll be in the main room, on the big screen. We'll be recording as well, so you can look at them later. Make it in 20 minutes. Don't want to be late."

Reggie disappeared, no doubt with things to do. I got the impression that he wanted to be in the thick of things and had yet to see an opportunity. Now a strange collection of people arrives with a story about Martian structures. All are depending on him. He was not going to let the opportunity go by without making the most of it.

"Who's he?" whispered Liz, asking about Reggie's secret identity.

"Haven't a clue. Haven't gotten near him. But it doesn't matter who he was, it's who he is now that counts and now he is the man who is eagerly giving us whatever we want. Whoever he was, I forgive him."

"So it's not that much insight into people." Liz spoke between bites. She was searching for data, information to make our earlier conversation understandable.

"Let's say confirmation. Strong people are strong, smart people seek knowledge and leaders will rise to lead the charge sooner or later. Who they were in the past is of mild interest, no more."

Liz looked let down. She was no doubt hoping for some edge my memory might give us. Perhaps she needed a way to tell if people were going to come through or let us down. Knowing who to trust is good in any arena. She had already figured out that my memory was what we were running on, and little else.

We had no proof of what was on Mars. It could be an optical illusion. It could be clouds, or space waves, or sun spots. Who knows? Anything was possible. It was as Dana had said, we're in uncharted territory.

Outside in the hall, people passed by walking fast, then running, then more people. The crowd grew and they were getting faster. Reggie poked his head in, urgency written across his face.

"Grab your drinks and chips, time to get a seat before they are all gone."

35
Command Central

We got to Command Central to find it packed. Reggie showed us to large office chairs placed on the floor up front. Reggie had reserved seating for us with two of his companions guarding them.

"Thanks, Reggie," I said, slapping him on the shoulder. A flicker showed me *an eager young lieutenant, new to the front, anxious to prove himself.* It was over as fast as it began.

On the screen was an image of Mars. Nothing showed that was out of the ordinary. Mars was growing larger though, and each successive image showed more of the Red Planet. Other screens around the room showed different views. The odd-shaped moon was in view on one screen. Another looked out into space, as if watching for a sneak attack.

"We're coming up now," said Reggie. He had brought a rolling office chair from one of the computer stations. He put it beside Doctor Bronson on the end. Liz sat next to

Bronson, then Foster, Dana and me, being the other bookend. Dana reached over and took my hand, squeezing hard. This could be the validation we needed.

The photos flicked by as Mars Express grew closer to the planet. Nothing out of the ordinary came into view. This could be another optical illusion.

Then the planet grew larger as Express continued on. A corner of something in the distance made everyone in the room lean forward. No one made a sound.

Click - Click - Click, the pictures came in and appeared on the screen. A piece of a mountain off on the edge brought some gasps. It was nothing new, just a surprise. Several craters appeared. Then a small ravine, ragged and running across the screen as the camera clicked away. A mountain, a volcano, long dead; a few bumps in the landscape. Then we saw a corner. It was a corner with a straight edge.

It was on the frame of the picture, but it was definitely a corner and an edge. The edge was buried in the red Martian dust on one end. As Express continued to click away, the long edge moved toward the center of the screen. It was as if Express were traversing the complex at a sideways angle.

My mouth fell open and I had to remember to breathe. I reminded myself that this is real, not something created in CGI by a graphic artist.

Liz stood up, grabbed her chair and whirled it around

in front of me. She pulled it close to the other side of mine, so she was sitting next to me. She leaned in and whispered.

"Is this what you remembered? Is this what you saw?"

"No," I replied. "I've never seen this before."

"So it's not familiar at all?" she asked. Dana looked at me. She was the only one to have heard what Liz said. She wanted in on the conversation. She looked back at the screen but her ear was with Liz and me.

"This is the first time I've seen it," I said. I paused, and then added, "from the outside."

Liz and Dana looked at me with concerned and disbelieving looks. It was the kind of disbelief that you have when you know something is true but wish it weren't. They returned their gaze to the screen. With an outside, there had to be an inside, and if they ever got in there, I would be the one to show them around.

As Express continued on its journey, the line disappeared beneath the Martian surface. Then another appeared in the center of the screen. It was long and straight with regular ridges set at precise intervals. The room was silent. Express moved across the line of gargantuan structures buried up to their roofs in the reddish-brown dust.

The second building also disappeared in the dust. Another appeared towards the bottom of the screen, circular and dome-shaped. It was difficult to gauge the size because there was nothing else in the picture that was a known size. We watched transfixed, perhaps eighty of us squeezed into NASA's Control Central.

The dome passed out of screen and another square shape came up. This was the fourth building in a row. Everyone in the room saw it. We all gaped, transfixed on the screen.

Then the camera on Express flickered. It faltered and distorted, then burnt out completely, leaving the screen black.

A mutual protest rose from the crowd, followed by questions and demands. Some offered suggestions and not in the best language.

"Be right back," said Reggie. He ran across me and up the side stairs, out of the room. Technicians left, running. People opened phones and closed them again. There was no signal. "At least the Senator can't reach me," I thought.

"I'm going to find out what's going on," said Bronson, bolting from his seat and out the door.

"I'm coming too," said Foster, chasing after him.

"What's happening, Tom?" asked Liz.

"I don't know, but remember, I said we're not meant to find these things."

The three of us looked at the screen. The screens around the room were blank; no further signal was coming from Express. The connection was dead.

We sat looking anyway, as if the projectionist would splice the film and start the reel again. Technicians and scientists leaped up and ran out of Control Central. I guessed they went to where they could do some good.

"Come on!" said Liz, getting up.

We followed her out to the hall and down to the light-table room. There were still a couple of sandwiches, chips and drinks on the cart. And the closed bags in many colors. Dana took up the seat. Liz leaned out in the hallway. People in shirtsleeves and white coats were running in every direction. She saw Bronson and waved to him. He came in, followed by Foster and Reggie.

"We don't know what happened," said Reggie. "We have people checking on it now. As soon as we know what's what, we'll see if we can get a picture back."

Doctor Bronson cut in. "One of the guys said that the orbiter is still there, just not sending a signal. It's odd."

Foster took up the explanation. "They seem to think some sort of interference cut in on the signal and overwhelmed the system. But that's just conjecture."

"Good," said Liz. "Now, if you will all make yourselves comfortable, I would like the one who knows more about this than anyone to tell us what the hell is going on. Mister Matthews, if you will." Liz leaned back against the wall, her arms crossed and a smug smile on her face. She had complete faith in me, which was good because I had none in myself.

36
Team Reunion

All faces turned to me, questioning, disbelieving. Of all the people in the room, I was the last one they expected to know anything. "Well, Hi. I'm Tom Matthews, from Washington. I work for Senator Hughes, who heads the committee that controls the budget this place runs on. I was working on a joke about the funds running out and some clerk in D.C. pulling the plug on the Mars Express. But, it's far too close to the truth to be funny."

"Yeah, yeah, Tom. Get to it," said Liz.

"OK." I took a deep breath. "Here goes. There is just one person in this room I've never met before – that's Doctor Wright." I looked at Dana. She looked at me and her eyebrows shot up.

"The rest of you, I have known before – before today, before this life. I don't know what you believe, but for the moment, I'd like you to just go with me on this."

The faces around me appeared unchanged, waiting for a madman to rave and ready to half believe him. I pressed on.

"Reggie! I remember you as a young, eager Lieutenant. If we hung out together, I could tell you more, but that's all I have for now. Doctor Foster, Caroline! Powerful women often ruled in centuries past and you were one of them. I'm not sure if we were friends or enemies, but that doesn't matter now. Those days are gone. Doctor Strayer was at my side when my bride died in the square on the day of our wedding. We drew swords and rode after the attackers together. Those were wild days!"

Liz smiled, as if remembering, but I was sure she was just enjoying the picture I painted.

"Doctor Bronson, we were at university together. You were the professor, I was your student. You chided me often."

Bronson smiled, more at the ridiculousness of the tale than the remembrance of it.

"Only you, Dana, don't trigger a memory in me. We are making new memories, and I for one am happy for it."

Dana looked at me unchanged. It was all too much for her to concern herself with the small things. I turned to the entire group.

"Why do I remember these things and you do not? Why when we touch do you not get a twinge of memory? I am sure you have all experienced deja-vu. It's the feeling that you have been somewhere or done something before. Perhaps it is that you have met that person before or been in that place before. It happens to everyone, whether they acknowledge it or not. That's the memory seeping through."

The small collections of old friends shifted in their seats. I was touching on things they had experienced.

"I have seen True-Love and Love-at-First-Sight. I believe that when you have betrayed each other enough times in enough lives, you can't help but be madly in love. In fact, I'm convinced that some people are just stuck with each other."

Small smiles began to crack the faces of these serious doctors.

"So, why don't you remember me when we touch? Why is there no spark of recognition? I believe now that it is because there is a switch in each of us that gets thrown at birth. We get born knowing nothing of our former lives. We believe that we have one life and that's all. We hear that, reaffirmed over and over. Why is not the issue, but we're hammered with the one life idea. This is all there is: One life. And yet, you and I, Doctor Bronson, spent my university years with each other. You called me 'Ticky-Bird,' though I don't know why. It just came to me now."

Bronson made a face, like he'd just tasted something and couldn't place it. I continued.

"There is a device in each of us that allows us to start out fresh. Let's call it 'the Forgetter Switch.' We get born, the Forgetter Switch goes click and we are free to learn new things and have new ideas. We meet new people, not burdened with old animosities and old loyalties. It's a good system, as far as it goes. After all, as I told Doctor Strayer, it is not who we were that matters so much as who we *are*. It's right now that's important. Placing too much emphasis on our earlier lives would be the wrong thing to do. So please don't put too much stock in what I have said. You don't have to behave different to me or to each other. We are who we are. And who we are is the spirit of being, the spark of life. We are the glow that age and illness cannot extinguish."

I paused to take a breath. The faces before me just looked.

"So much for theory. I believe there was an actual place, a physical location, where we got this Forgetter Switch. I believe that the spirit of the being, the spark of life, became captured. It entered at one end of the processor and moved down the conveyor to the other. We got rigged with a Forgetter Switch, programmed to kick in when the doctor slaps us on the tush. I believe we were not meant to find the place where they installed the Forgetter. They buried it and abandoned it and set it with a booby-trap to go bonkers if we got too close. When Express went dark, I was as surprised as anyone else, but I knew why it happened. We weren't supposed to get that close."

"Why didn't you say something earlier?" asked Doctor

Bronson.

"This is coming to me in bits and pieces. These are things I didn't know before. There are things I don't know now that I'll know in a few minutes. When I first spoke with Dana in Washington, I didn't know there were structures on Mars. When I saw the photo, it was plain as day. She's been going with me on faith ever since."

I looked over at Dana and she was nodding. She believed in me, though I was spouting like a madman.

"If we were to find ourselves on Mars, we would find a gigantic complex designed with one purpose. The purpose is to entrance us, to send us through the procedure. And then to slap on a Forgetter Switch at the other end. We would have a hard time going there with Earth bodies. It is not meant for bodies.

We would have a hard time not getting transfixed at the front end – whichever end that is – because that is the catcher. We would have a tough time confronting what is inside because it is inside of us, what we have all been through. And we would have trouble with the Forgetter, because we all have one."

"Why?" asked Doctor Bronson. "Why go through all that?"

"Control. We must be controlled. By who? I don't know. I might know in a minute or an hour, or a week, but I don't know right now."

"But why would we put up with it?" asked Bronson.

"Good question. Why do you look at a television screen when there is someone in the room talking to you? Even if there's a commercial on, you become enchanted by the screen. It's mesmerizing. You'll sit there for hours, even with something you've seen before and you know is bad. Through fund raising pleas, commercials and public service announcements. You will watch that screen because it's hypnotic. The front end of this is a catcher. It hypnotizes you. You've all been through it. I've been through it."

"Then why do you remember?"

"I don't know. I don't remember remembering people in earlier incarnations. I think this time, my Forgetter got broken. I think it's busted. I don't know how it got broken. The memories didn't start until I was in my twenties."

"What do you think triggered it?" asked Bronson.

"I don't know. And you're going to hear that a lot from me. There's parts I don't know. I'm just putting it together. This is all new to me too!"

Another anxious pause made me wonder if I had done the right thing. Better to push on than fall back, so I did.

"Look, I've never told anyone about this. I told Liz just today and I'm not sure why I did that. Now I'm telling you and I've never done that. So I don't have it all codified and organized. Until now it's been my guarded, embarrassing secret."

Dana raised her hand, as if in school. I looked at her. "And you don't have a memory with me from before?"

"That's right. I believe you and I have just met for the first time."

The room was quiet with reflection. Reggie spoke up. "You said something about me. But we just met."

"Yes, and I believe that lifetime to lifetime, the same people show up to work together. In Washington, I have met people from all over the country and I have been working with them for centuries. We fought in battles, worked on ships and toiled in fields. We marched parade grounds and sat in classes. I am amazed at how many people have been part of my team. You are all part of my team and I am part of yours. We have all worked together before."

I looked at Dana. "Except me. I'm new," she said.

"Yes, but I'm glad we're on the same team now." I addressed the rest of the group. "And I am on your team. Happy to be aboard."

There was an uneasy silence. It went on for about a minute, but it was a minute too long.

"Or, this could just be the ramblings of a madman and you can have me shipped back to Bellevue. I'll shut up now."

"No, no." said Liz. "This is all new data, and like Doctor Wright said earlier, we're on unknown ground. It is a good idea to keep an open mind. I for one am all ears to hear Tom's theories on the subject. They do, after all, constitute one explanation for what has just happened. The only one offered. We must put what we as individuals believe on hold, in suspended animation until this plays out."

Reggie was the first to move on it. "Look! Let me go and find out what did just happen and I'll report back." Reggie looked at me. "Once an eager lieutenant, always an eager lieutenant."

He trotted off, into the throng that still filled the hall. It was as if everyone in the building was at the wrong end trying to get to the other. Bronson looked after him and then at me. "You don't disappoint, Mister Matthews."

I sat down, glad that no one was bringing tar and feathers into the room. I reached for one of the colorful paper bags. Inside I found cookies, two of them. I took a bite and looked at Dana, who was looking at me with wonder.

"Chocolate chip," I said.

37

The Oath

I walked out into the hallway and got hit with a flying tackle. Carrie had just arrived at Houston with the volunteers from Caltech. She had walked into the NASA building when she saw me. Impulse took over and she ran to hug me. It caught me off guard.

For a moment the confusion took me over. My sister used to attack me with the same running hug. It was unladylike. But then she was always a tomboy in bloomers. Once I recovered my composure, I was glad to see Carrie.

"Guess what I heard on the plane," Carrie said, doing a dance in place to display her joy at seeing me.

"Um, you heard that there was life on Mars."

"No, I heard that Doctor McClellan has been telling the press that she discovered life on Mars. She's trying to take credit for the whole thing."

"She's going to have a hard sell to NASA Houston." I began walking toward Control Central.

"She holds press briefings in front of the observatory when Doctor Cutler isn't looking." Carrie fell in step with me.

"Cutler will have her guts for garters!" I said, lowering my voice.

"I have his phone number on speed dial. You want me to ring him?"

"Oh, yes, Carrie, I do want it. Gimme, gimme, gimme!" I felt giddy with a boyish sense of revenge. McClellan was taking credit for the whole thing since the beginning. That was why we marooned her in San Diego. Besides, we didn't want her in on it at all, she was a step behind.

"Doctor Cutler? Hold for Mister Matthews." Carrie handed the phone to me.

"Hello Doctor. Actually, the news I have to relate is from Carrie. I'll let her tell you." I handed the phone back to her. "It's your newsflash, give him the 411."

"Doctor Cutler? Me again, Carrie. Yes, sir, I am, I just landed. Before I left I noticed Doctor McClellan holding a press briefing outside the observatory. Two of the volunteers told me it was her fourth briefing. She is taking credit for discovery of the markings on Mars. She said that you were doing a wonderful job – under her, that is. Did you know you got a demotion?" Carrie held the phone and I could hear yelling and cussing. She winced, tried to get a word in and winced again. She smiled a PR smile at me and turned around. "Uh, yes sir,

I will, sir. He's right here." Carrie handed me the phone.

"Yes, sir?" I said.

"I want you to call McClellan, Carrie's got the number. Tell her that you couldn't reach me. Tell her you have an important message to get to me. The message is that the lines are optical illusions, like the canals. I'll take it from there."

"Yes, sir. I will."

"And Matthews," said the Doctor.

"Yes, sir?"

"Good work. Let me have Carrie."

Carrie took the phone. She did a little curtsy. "Oh, thank you, sir. I appreciate it. Thank you." She closed the phone and put it in her purse. "He likes you."

"That's good," I said, grateful for any allies in these troubled times.

"I like you, too," said Carrie.

"And I like you back. You remind me of my little sister. We were close."

"Until you see her again, I'll be your sister. I'll take good care of you."

"I'd like that," I said, bursting inside to hug her like I used to. But we were in the middle of a large and busy hall, and I was not twelve.

"Where's your other half?" asked Carrie.

"Hmmm?"

"Doctor Wright. Where is she? I've got to take care of

her too. I took an oath."

"Uh, she's checking on something. You took an oath?"

"Yeah, I swore I'd take care of the both of you through this whole exciting adventure. They assigned me to Logistics."

"Oh, so it wasn't an official oath."

"An oath's an oath, Mister Matthews. So here I am. What do you need?"

"Stick with me, things are moving pretty fast. Is your phone charged?"

"Yup!"

"Good. Then find a place to plug mine in, it's running down."

38
The Slush Fund

"Mister Danning?" called out Pam Barkley.

Don Danning turned around looking for the source of the hail. He spotted Barkley and waved.

No one called her Pam, just like no one called him Don. He was Danning and she was Barkley. It had always been that way and will always be that way. He even called her Barkley when they woke up in bed four months earlier and decided to make it a regular thing. At the office, they had been perfecting their professional relationship.

"Yes, Barkley, what's up?"

"I have something I have to show you, could you step inside my office?"

Danning looked around, "Are you sure? We should maintain discretion," he whispered.

"No, silly," she replied. "I mean I really have something to show you. Please professionally step into my office."

"Oh. OK. Here I come." Barkley closed the door behind him.

"Look! Two days ago, when we were looking at cutting funding for NASA. I came upon a small slush fund that saw little or no activity under the Senator. April was keeping an eye on it. I didn't think anything of it. He likes to have a little spare cash around for emergencies, after all. She would handle the administrative details."

"Yes, I know that."

"But then the move to pull the plug on NASA and the slush fund goes wild, with a huge sum of money coming to it. Overnight it's $450,000."

"Really! Seriously? I knew there was petty cash around but almost half a mil? When the committee finds out, the shit's gonna hit the fan."

"Oh, but wait! Just today, the pendulum swings the other way. Life on Mars and NASA's back in the money. But the fund we're talking about isn't moving in that direction. The money is quietly transferred to an account in the Caymans."

"Cayman Islands?"

"I know! It's a rookie move. Hughes is too smart for that, but April could have done it without his knowledge. If she's moving the funds for him, it's not only illegal, it's too obvious. He'll get caught."

"Show me again. Let's make absolutely sure of the facts before we cry wolf. Take me through it."

* * *

While the two silhouettes huddled in Barkley's office, April Wills was in a conference with her boss, Jason Hughes.

"Why can't we go?" sobbed April, close to tears, putting on a show for the Senator's sake.

"You know very well why we can't go, things have changed. We have to shovel money into NASA, not take it away. The spotlight will be on me and that will mean my wife and family as well. I have to become the perfect family man again and that means you get to spend more time with your boyfriend."

"I don't know what you're talking about," she said. She knew exactly what he was talking about. She just didn't think he knew.

"Oh, come on. You think I didn't know? I knew! You're a lousy liar! It's time for a shake-up, April. You need to transfer to an office where you can keep a low profile for a while."

"I like it here," said the pouting child.

"Do you like the idea of jail? If this gets out, we'll not only get ripped up by the papers but jailed as well."

"Not me. I'll write a book," she said, raising her head.

"Don't give me that, you couldn't write a tweet."

"Fine! You want me gone? I'm going. Don't try to stop

me."

"Try to get the big picture, April. The world has changed. There's been a double earthquake, evidence of life on Mars. We can't go on with business as usual." said Hughes.

"No problem. Like I said, I'm going," said April, waving over her head as she sashayed out of the door.

Hughes sucked in a breath. "I'm going to miss her," he said to the empty room. He turned to his computer and went onto the shadow program to her computer. He saw that she had moved some funds to a bank offshore. He reversed the financial transfer and sat back.

The Senator picked up the phone and dialed. "Hello, my queen. Yes, it's me. No, I'm not working late. Not tonight. Rather than stay in town, I thought I'd come home for a change. I know work has me distracted lately, but to make it up to you, I'll take you out to The Embers for dinner. How does that sound? Wonderful! I'll see you in about an hour."

He tapped in a number. Down the hall, Danning picked up his cell and held it to his ear. "Danning?" said the Senator. "April's left early – in a huff. Can you call me up a car? I'll be going to Virginia. Thanks."

* * *

Danning turned to Barkley and made a face.

"That was him. He's going home tonight – to the wife."

"Yes? That's bold. Want to know something else? Look at this: money has just transferred back to NASA. I think April's done a bunk and Hughes is covering his tracks."

"Going back to his wife is the smart move. The limelight is going to shine around here."

The light on the phone went on. It was the Senator's office. She hit the intercom button. "Yes, sir?" responded Barkley.

"I almost forgot, we're going to need someone on the phone in the morning. Tell Danning to call up someone from the pool. Thanks, dear."

Barkley clicked off the intercom with a look to Danning. Danning dropped his face into his hand. "So much for keeping a low profile."

39
Diversion

"Doctor Megan McClellan," said the voice on the other end.

"Doctor McClellan, this is Tom Matthews, Senator Hughes' aide. I'm trying to reach Doctor Cutler on a matter of great importance. Is he there with you?"

"No. Do you not have his number?" asked McClellan, there was a tone of impatience in her voice. This was a bother. She had no time for it.

"I'm guessing he hasn't charged it. Can you tell him something for me? It's important."

"Is it long?" she asked, considering pulling out a pad and writing it down.

"No, short. Very short," I said.

"Oh, all right. What is it?"

"OK. Please tell him the pass by the Orbiter Express has shown nothing. The marks on Mars were just optical illusions. They looked like something from this distance.

Like the famous canals, they were just a trick of the light. Can you tell him that?"

"Uh, yes, Mister Matthews, I can. Are you sure?"

"Yeah. We have to get this under control. The press has gone crazy with a misconception. Unless we get it capped soon, we're going to have egg on our faces."

"All right, Mister Matthews, I'll take care of it."

"Thank you, Doctor. Good bye."

I touched the button ending the call, a little too happy with myself. I was ending a career. Well, I wasn't ending a career exactly. She could do as I ask and relay the message to Doctor Cutler, the man who suggested the subterfuge in the first place. "But she won't," I thought. "She'll run to the press. They'll check the story and she'll be hustling French fries at the local Burger Shack by morning."

Carrie appeared at my side with a coffee in a NASA mug. I was ready for coffee. I had just done a good piece of work. I was getting a taste for Washington politics.

My next call was to the Senator.

"Hughes," said the Senator.

"Matthews, sir. Answering your own phone?"

"I'm a little pressed for time, Matthews. Get right to it. What's the latest?"

"A PhD in San Diego is saying it's just an optical illusion. But here at NASA we have confirmed that there are structures on Mars made by intelligent life. It's proof positive, sir. This is the game changar we've been anticipating."

"Damn, Matthews! You're sure?"

"Absolutely, sir. No doubt about it."

"Stay there! You're my eyes and ears in this thing. I'm going to be in committee meetings pretty much from now on. History is happening and we're part of it. Keep me in the loop!"

"Will do. And, sir? Hello? Sir?" The Senator had hung up already.

"Did that go well?" asked Carrie.

"Well, he wants me to stay here, so I guess it did go well."

"What would you be doing if you were back there?" Carrie asked, climbing onto a stool next to me at the high table by the coffee bar.

"Same thing you're doing, seeing to the needs of a guest in the office, getting coffee, giving the tour."

"You're more valuable than that," said Carrie. She furrowed her eyebrows at the injustice of it all. She was glad to be there. I was glad to be there as well. I looked at Carrie.

"So are you," I replied. "Where's Doctor Wright?"

"Command Central. They're trying to figure out what happened to some satellite."

"Mmmm. The Orbiter Express. We should go."

I stood up and looked both ways. I had gotten turned

around. Carrie pointed down the hall. I nodded and began to walk in that direction, with Carrie hot on my heels.

If Hughes had said to come home and do crap work, I was ready to take the Speaker of the House up on his offer. Bob Cartwright had a better shot at the White House than the Senator did. In fact, given the few things I knew about the Senator, he was as likely to get investigated as run for President. I was keeping the Speaker's offer in my vest pocket, just in case.

40
Spent

In the converted country farm house of the Hughes family, Senator Hughes tried to sleep in bed next to his wife. He had much on his mind, but the turnings and pitches of the day exhausted him. He had survived worldwide earthquakes, funding upheavals and proof of life on Mars.

His secretary had also threatened to write a book.

Mrs. Hughes was wide awake. She hadn't seen her husband in her bed in months, maybe years. She wasn't trotted out except for an election photo op. What was up?

* * *

In a cozy Foggy Bottom apartment, Danning and Barkley slept well. They had put away double portions of pasta and a bottle of Merlot. Under discussion were all the possible ramifications of April leaving and Hughes going home to his wife. There was the movement of the

NASA funds, the double earthquake deep within the Earth and the discovery of life on Mars. Then they made love and went to sleep.

* * *

In Houston, I guided Dana down the hall of the Heritage Hotel toward the room Carrie arranged via the logistics desk.

"I am spent!" whispered Dana. "Has it only been a day? It feels like a week since we were in bed in San Diego."

"Almost there, then you can lie down."

"With you? I want to lie down with you."

"You can do that. You can lie down with me."

"My leg hurts."

"I know it does, baby. Almost there."

"Which one is it?" she asked, looking up and squinting at the doors as we passed.

"This one coming up. 1212. I have the key here." The key was like a credit card. There were holes in it. I took a moment to look at the picture on the card so I can see which way it went. Then I slipped the card in and got a green light for my prize. I opened the door and guided Dana inside.

The only light came through the window. There was the usual table with two chairs, a desk with a chair and a large console holding a television screen. And the center attraction: a bed.

The bed was large, I guessed king sized. On it was a flowered cover, turned down. There were mints on the pillows.

I found the light and turned it on.

"No, too bright," said Dana, holding her hand up to her eyes.

I turned the light off. The glow from the window would be enough; after all, we knew where everything was.

"So close! So close, and yet beyond our reach. I wanted to just grab that orbiter and hit it like my dad used to do to the old TV. He'd hit that thing and the picture would zig-zag the other way. He'd hit it until it gave him what he wanted."

"A bruised hand?" I quipped.

"No, a picture, it gave him a picture. I wanted to hit the Express like that, until it gave us a picture."

"I know, pigeon. I wanted it too."

She looked at me as if I was weird. "Did you just call me pigeon?"

I felt stupid, but I could not go back.

"Yes," I said, hoping honesty would get me points.

"Why?" she asked, blue eyes fluttering at me.

"I don't know. I suppose I thought it was cute. I've been trying to think of a cute name for you, but they all seem stupid. Snookums, Honey-bear, Sweetness."

"Call me Dana. I'll call you Tom. Call me for breakfast, I'm spent." She leaned toward me and let her blouse fall to the floor. I reached around and unsnapped the single hook in back. Her bra fell to the floor. She stepped to the side, pulling me with her onto the bed. I drew the cover back and pulled the sheet down. Then, I undid the button and zipper of her slacks and pulled them down.

In the glow of the moonlight through the window, she looked so beautiful. I wanted to kiss her from head to toe, pausing at my favorite places along the way, and then work my way back up. But more than that, I wanted to protect her, this smart, awkward, beautiful woman on the bed with me.

A soft, gentle sound came from her, then repeated. With it, thoughts of kissing and pausing vanished. Dana was asleep. I pulled the sheet up, lifted her legs into the bed and lowered the sheet. I laid my clothing over the chair at the desk and climbed in next to her. The only kiss given was on her forehead.

"Goodnight, Cuddly-bear," I whispered.

Dana stirred, sighed and drifted back to sleep. I wasn't far behind.

41
Impossible!

In the early dawn hours, a skeleton crew sat watching blank monitors. The screens at Command Central blinked, sputtered and came alive. The main screen showed a complex of structures poking out of the red sand.

Technicians woke up and started shaking their colleagues. Techs checked their machines to make sure they were on and recording. They threw switches, picked up phones and shouted orders. One tech guy ran, his white coat flying out behind him, down the hall to the lunch room. There Reggie Stanes sat with his head cradled in the crook of his arm.

"Reg! Reg! Wake up! You gotta see this!"

"Wha? What?" said Reggie, his mouth dry from breathing through it. He felt for his glasses, put them on and looked up.

"We got image, pal. Wake up," said the technician.

Reggie's eyes widened and he stood up. He looked at

the door and ran for it, kicking over the chair. He left the chair on its side and ran down the hall with the technician right behind him.

Across the room, a small bundle unfolded as a red raincoat dropped to the floor. Carrie sat up, rubbed her eyes and looked around the lunch room. There was a chair on the floor and the door was just shutting. Then she remembered where she was and jumped up. She left her coat where it was and ran to the door. She looked down the hall, but saw nothing. She reached out her ears and heard faint running far to the right. She took off in that direction, determined to find out what had happened.

At Command Central, Express displayed full, close-up pictures of the structures stretched across the surface of Mars.

"How did it come back on?" asked one of the techs.

"The question is: how did it come to be in this orbit?" said Reggie.

"I've gotta get the Doctor." Carrie continued looking at the screen.

"C'mon. I'll drive," replied Reggie. "You're recording this, right?" he asked the tech.

"You bet your sweet ass, we're recording this! Eight ways to Sunday!"

"I'll be back! Don't let anything happen!"

Reggie ran off with Carrie in tow, leaving the

technician looking at the screen muttering, "Yeah, right!"

In the corner of the room, asleep on the carpet, lay Doctor Caroline Foster. She decided to stay at NASA and check the situation. Now she sat up, her coat draped over her legs, looking at the big screen with her mouth open. Her reddish-brown hair sat up in a wave. It crested on the left side of her head like the tsunami that never happened. She opened her phone and punched in a number.

"Hi, News Room? You know that report you had about the markings on Mars being just an optical illusion? Well, guess where I'm calling from."

Doctor Bronson woke up. Something jerked him awake, and he didn't know what. He looked around. He was in a small room someone had equipped with a cot for mid-day naps and emergency stay-overs. He had been grateful. Now he was wide awake in the darkened room. Outside, there was a faint sound, then another, then a growing rumble. He heard voices. He got up, felt for his shoes and opened the door.

"What's going on?" he asked a passing tech, a young woman in khakis and lab coat.

"It's Express, it's back up and sending pictures."

"Impossible!" said Bronson, following her down the hall.

42
Express Delivery

Knock! Knock!

Deep within the pit of sleep into which I had fallen came a sound. I was in total blackness. Not even memories of my many lives played in the theater of my mind tonight. Theater was dark, closed. No one could find me here.

Knock! Knock!

"Mister Matthews," said a voice.

The picture of my sister came into my head, framed by the window in her bedroom. Outside, the sun was shining and the leaves were falling, telling me that it was my favorite time of year.

"Mister Matthews," *said my sister. No, it couldn't be her. We weren't Matthews then, we were...*

Knock! Knock!

"OK, OK, I'm up." I stumbled to the door in my boxers, opened the door and peered into the hallway. I wanted to say something about whoever it was knowing what time it was, but not as a question. I didn't get the chance to be indignant.

"It's sending! Express is sending! And it's good! It's ... it's good!" said Carrie. She stood there with Reggie, both of them dancing back and forth, unable to keep still.

"OK. I'm up. I'm coming." I closed the door and went to the bed. "Dana? Dana, darling? Dana, you have to wake up now."

Dana turned over and looked at me with one eye open, her arm up over her head. "What?" she said.

"Express is sending. Carrie and Reggie are outside."

"Oh, OK, I'm up. I'm up. where's my clothes?"

I threw Dana her clothes and reached for mine. A quick swish of mouthwash and a splash on the face were all we would get until later. Within two minutes, we were exiting the room and following Carrie down the hall.

"Reggie is bringing the car to the front," said Carrie over her shoulder as she lead the way to the elevator.

Dana kept up in spite of her leg.

I tried to put my brain in gear. We were at the car before I succeeded.

"I'm going to need a chair and a foot-rest in that room. Also some breakfast and a toothbrush. Are they recording it?" I asked from the back seat.

"Yeah," said Reggie, driving.

In the shotgun seat, Carrie sat turned around, looking at us both. She was making mental notes, adding a hair brush to the list. "You look tired," she said.

"Tired people run the world," I replied. In the rear view mirror, I saw Reggie make a mental note. He would use that later, at some appropriate time.

We stopped at a side entrance, near the main room. A volunteer stood by to open the door. We got out and followed Carrie while Reggie parked the car.

In Command Central, Bronson came up to us. "Doctor Wright, this is incredible! Come, we have a seat for you up front."

We went up to the front of the room where the chairs were still there from the night before. Carrie ran off to attend to her list of items needed. As Bronson showed us to center seats, no one else noticed that we had arrived... they were all fixated on the screen.

In the center screen, Express was moving over the line of structures. It snapped photos every second and relayed them to Earth.

"There's a delay. We're getting this later than the actual shot but the resolution is great," said Doctor Foster in the seat next to me. "I've already informed the press. They're on their way. This is big!"

"The press knows?" I asked Foster, without taking my eyes off the screen.

The tops of the structures were visible, no more than a meter above the sand. They were square and round and oblong. Some were rectangular and there were spaces where it appeared there was no building at all. I pictured a shorter structure or perhaps a courtyard down under the sand.

"Yes, I wanted it to come from us, not someone else. I was the only one up – barely up," replied Foster.

"Quite right. It should come from us." I said. "When they arrive, I want to talk to them."

"I think we should all talk to them, a united front. Let them know that there is a team on the case. There are five of us: Bronson, Dana, Liz, me and you. That's a good balance."

Now and then the screen would flicker. The assembled technicians would utter a gasp. Then the screen would return to normal and silence would again prevail.

"What is that?" Dana asked me, touching my arm.

Carrie arrived with a foot rest for Dana. She left without a word to locate the next item on her mental list. History was happening and she was not going to interrupt it.

"We're traveling the other way now, against the flow of the ... well, we talked about an assembly line. This is closer to the beginning than the end."

"Why did it stop sending?" asked Dana, still clutching my arm and watching the screen.

"Just guessing now, but I think it shorted out the camera somehow, a defense mechanism. It didn't want anyone to see, so it blocked the camera."

"Why did it come back on?"

"It could be that as we got away from that end, it couldn't interfere with the signal anymore. I'm still just guessing."

"Hmmm." She was just taking it in, not evaluating the data.

I stretched out my mind, pushed my memory for what this was, which way it went and how it worked. I kept coming up blank. My memory of the place was somehow, I knew, distorted. It was an image of an image, without the definition and detail of the original.

"Wait a minute!" I whispered, as if it was a secret – which it was. "This isn't from a memory I have. It's a memory of a memory. I remember this place because I wasn't here, not because I was."

Dana looked at me for the first time since we walked into the room. "I don't get it."

"It's a little hard for me. OK. This is where the switch goes in place, right? The Forgetter Switch. This has to do with..."

At that instant, Carrie appeared at my side. She had a cardboard tray with three cups of coffee and three donuts. She set the tray on the arms of my chair and Foster's. She smiled and turned around.

"Carrie!" I whispered.

She crouched by my chair, trying not to get in Foster's sight line to the screen.

"What do you need?" she asked.

"Just that you are the best, you're the best there is. You're wonderful and I love you. Thank you so much for everything. We'll figure out a job offer later. OK?"

Carrie's grin told it all; she nodded and then left for her next thing. She may have been running on carpet but she was also floating on air.

"Carrie is the key," I said to Dana. She looked at me, her eyes wide with wonder. "I'll explain later," I said and pointed to the screen. Dana turned her eyes to the screen, but I knew her attention was still on me.

43
Press Conference

The assembled technicians broke up into four teams. There was one team that monitored the Orbiter Express and the photos it was sending down. A second team formed to come up with preliminary planning for a Mars launch. A third team shepherded the current projects in progress so they didn't get neglected.

The fourth team was us and we were about to meet the press. A battery of students with combs and lint brushes saw to it that we were presentable to the press.

We went out to a temporary podium. Doctor Bronson stood with four representatives from NASA. The questions had already gotten crazy.

"Is there life on Mars?"

"Are you going to Mars?"

"What do these markings mean?"

"Is this a sign from God?"

"Matthews, thank God you're here. Help me, I'm over my head," said Doctor Bronson. I stepped to the podium.

"Some people see a message from God on their morning toast. If you see this as that, who am I to contradict you? But we are dealing with Mars and there is much to learn. We have our best, most qualified people on it."

"Does that include you, Mister Matthews?"

"Yes, it does," said Doctor Strayer. She turned to Bronson and whispered, "End this!"

Liz pushed me out, taking Dana by the arm on the way. "Come on! This is not where we belong. We have work to do."

Behind us, Bronson was bringing an end to the press conference. He corrected earlier false reports saying rumors of the markings on Mars being optical illusions were the ramblings of an overworked scientist who needed a rest. He hinted that she may have been smoking something.

Liz brought us to a room where lunch was laid out. Carrie was there and sparkled when we came in. I smiled back at her.

The warm place I felt for Carrie was the memory I had of her. She was the sister who had passed away early, the sibling I missed more than any I recalled. She ran and hugged me, as if she had not seen me for years. I hugged her back, feeling even closer to her.

Dana looked at me with fondness. She knew it wasn't sexual with me and Carrie. In fact, Carrie was growing tighter with Reggie by the minute. He was at the other end of the room putting out cold drinks. He was an important figure at NASA, yet was not above helping with lunch.

Liz pulled us to a table and sat us down. Doctor Foster followed, taking a place next to Liz.

"There's been a development. A question has arisen about this being a sign from God. Several here at NASA have said so, and not like a scientific observation. They are inflexible, unshakable. You dare not argue with them. A couple of people, who disagreed only a little, got called demons and witches. Fourteen people have quit and walked out, because NASA won't erect an altar to this thing. They demand we proclaim that they are now disciples of the true God."

"I was afraid of this," I said.

"You knew this would happen?" said Dana.

"Like so many things, first I don't know, then I do know and then it's obvious."

"Spill!" said Liz.

Carrie put a plate of steaming eggs and potatoes in front of me. I looked at it and picked up my fork. I arranged the potatoes as I spoke. "The assembly line starts here," I poked one end of the trough I had made of my hash browns. "and goes along here. There are things added to the process along the way. Some are pictures of things. If you get too near these things, they hit you in the face. All at once, you 'know the truth' of something and no one can shake you from it."

Three sets of eyes looked up at me. Was I knowing something they couldn't shake me from? Was this whole thing a picture instilled along the way? I sidestepped those questions and continued.

"When you come out the end, you get the Forgetter. You're going to see some strange changes in some of your workmates. Cling to what you know. If we stay together, we'll be fine."

"Good enough for me," said Liz. She had faith in me, more than in a trivia-happy god who puts distorted pictures in morning toast. She looked up, caught Reggie's eye and motioned him over.

"Listen, Reggie, the people who got religion and left?" she began.

"Yeah," he said, expecting anything.

"Temporary insanity. It's going to happen a lot. When you get into stuff like this, a major shift that changes the whole game, you're going to get a certain percentage going bonkers. Tell whoever is in charge around here that we said to just let those people go and work with who's left. Got that?"

"You bet!" said Reggie. He took off to find someone to tell.

44

How It Works

"Alone at last!" said Dana, after breakfast.

We had found ourselves in a side room decorated like a receiving lounge. It came complete with comfortable chairs and subdued lighting. She looked at me as if I had candy and wasn't sharing.

"OK, Buster! Give! What was that in the room there? What is going on? What's this 'memory of a memory' thing? And why are people going around the bend?"

"I explained the round-the-benders; that's all I know. As for the complex, yes, I have been there. I went through the wringer just like the rest, just like everyone here. Everyone you've ever known, everyone – even you. We all went through that thing.

"We became fascinated at one end. We went through the process. We shot out the other end complete with a Forgetter Switch."

"So how come yours is not working?"

"I willed it so." I looked at Dana. She wasn't buying it. "OK! Listen! What's the strongest thing in the universe?"

"I don't know!" Her voice strained.

"You didn't even try," I chided.

"No games! Tell me!" she shouted, then realized someone might hear, she lowered her voice. "Tell me or I'll twist your nose off!"

"OK! The strongest thing in the universe, whether you know it or not, whether you like it or not, is you. But you don't pick up barbells or push railroad cars; instead, you decide. The way you change the universe is by deciding to."

Dana gave me a blank look. I continued. "I used to have a friend who would say, 'if you say so.' It drove me nuts! I'd say, 'This project is going to take me weeks to finish,' and he would say, 'if you say so.' But then I'd take another look at the work in front of me and get it done in a few hours. The point he was making is that if I said it, it would happen. There are whole schools of thought that go along with the theory of 'what you say is what you get.'"

Dana looked like she was taking it in, so I kept going.

"Now, expand that out to the concept that you are the most powerful thing in the universe. You make things happen by words."

"Like, 'Let there be light,'" said Dana.

"Exactly. Heinlein said 'Thou art God,'"

"*Stranger in a Strange Land.*"

"Exactly!"

"That's science fiction." Dana was on the defensive now.

"So were cell phones and computers at the time, and until a few decades ago, the Internet. Please, don't close down, open back up. Let it in. Trust me; I know what I'm talking about."

"You said Carrie is the key."

"Yes, she is, or was. She was my sister, my sister in a former life. It was a long time ago. I don't know the years, it doesn't work that way. I see a room, that's all. Outside there were horses and carriages. She was dying and I couldn't save her."

Dana put a hand on mine. I realized that I had misted up. "I loved my sister. With a love most people don't understand. And she loved me. Today people would call that perverted. It wasn't sexual and it wasn't perverted, it was beautiful and pure. She said she wanted me to remember her and I said I would. I swore to her that I would always remember. I made that decision and I have always remembered her. I have always remembered everyone. That decision broke my Forgetter."

I looked at Dana as if seeing her for the first time, remembering that just two days ago, I *had* seen her for the first time.

"You!" I said, not knowing what I was going to say next.

"What about me?" asked Dana, fearful that something

bad might follow. Luckily, the rest of the sentence came to me.

"You are the first person I have ever met, that I know of, whom I have never known before. Everyone else, even Doctor Bronson, Doctor Foster and Liz. Everyone who I have just met on this trip, I have been with them before. I have worked alongside them, loved them, fought and died with them. They are what I call 'my team.' When I meet someone, I wait for that memory that will tell me who they are, what part they played on my past team. Then I forget it and get to know them all over again."

"But not with me?" she said, looking at me as if she didn't quite believe me.

"No, not with you. You're new."

"And is that a good thing?"

"Yes. That's a good thing. Dana, I've known you two days that have been like two years. We have traveled across the country and back and looked into the heavens together. I want you as part of my team, the main member of my team."

There, I stopped. I was at a loss for words. I closed my mouth and looked at Dana. I held her by the shoulders and the words came to me.

"Look! Take all the old, hackneyed phrases that you hate and string them together. All those things people say to each other and later go back on them. I now say those to you and I mean it."

"So, you love me, want to be with me forever and I am your everything?"

"Yeah, all that."

We stared at each other for a minute that seemed longer. Dana blinked.

"OK! Now what about this decision? You mean you just decided to remember your sister? Way back in the days of crinolines and carriages, and after that your switch didn't work?"

"Exactly! It took a while before I realized what was happening. The revelations of these past two days have been the most forward movement I have known, but yes."

Dana looked at me as if she was ready to ask me for the proof. I hated that. I beat her to it.

"Dana! In my world, you don't prove what is or is not. You know it. I can't bring out an eye witness to swear that on such-and-so a date, the being to be later known as Tom Matthews did make a decision to always remember his sister. There wasn't a loud crash as my Forgetter Switch broke, falling into pieces on the floor for the butler to sweep up. I decided to remember. Now I do. You're going to just have to believe me. Liz does."

"She knows? Yes, of course, she knows. You told her yesterday. But she already knew, didn't she?"

"Yes, I told her earlier yesterday. That's what made it possible to tell the rest of you."

"Why did you pick her?" asked Dana.

"We have a long history, not the least of which, she was my best friend and classmate at the academy. We fought together later in the Crimean War. We died with the Light Brigade. It was a heroic time."

"She was a man?"

"Yeah."

"So, the man-woman thing..."

"Not so important. It's like you change clothes and then you look down and see that you are wearing a tutu and you begin to dance. Later, you look down and see that you're dressed like a clown, so you act funny."

"You decide," said Dana.

She was beginning to work with the data. To Dana, it wasn't a matter of believing, it was a matter of workable theories. If she had a workable theory, she could use it. If it turned out to work, then it became fact for her. If it didn't work, she would discard it without a second thought. This was a theory that I was expounding. If she thought about it and made it a workable theory, she could put it to the test. If it proved to be true, so much the better.

"Yes, we decide." I looked at her waiting for the next sentence.

"And it is so."

"Yes, it is so."

"More examples." The scientist was in the room with me now, not the snuggle-bunny.

"Why does a baby get born blind?" I asked.

"German measles," replied Dana. She was ready for me. I was ready too.

"Why does that life choose a body with German measles?"

"A decision?"

"Yes! A decision. What decision? I don't know. Only the person knows. But let us suppose that a person goes to war. War is horrible. The sights are unbearable, impossible to confront, to even conceive. So he decides, as he is dying in the muddy trench, to not see it anymore. He goes to the ward and chooses a baby who will not see and slips inside."

"Why does he find a baby?"

"Because he has a programmed command to do so."

Dana looked at me. The concept was working in her mind. She took a breath. "So, it's all psychosomatic."

"More than you know."

We stared at each other for another minute.

"Who is Carrie?"

"Currently? She is an undergraduate assigned to me as a volunteer and has gone beyond the call to serve us both well. She arranged for that room we were in." Dana took it in and I continued. "Beyond that, she was my sister and I loved her. I said I would remember her and I have."

"She doesn't know?"

"No. What good would that do? Telling someone who they were in their former lives can prove upsetting. It's not something I go around doing."

"You told them," she said, indicating the rest of the group.

"I was talking to scientists, I needed examples."

"Are you keeping my former life from me?" she asked, looking at me askew.

"No. I already said: no memories."

Dana sucked in a large volume of air, stretched and scratched her head with both hands.

"OK! Here it is. You tell your baby sister that you will remember her. It is such a statement that your memory kicks into high gear. It overrides the whatever-it-is that makes you start off each new life with a clean slate. At some time in this life, you begin to remember people. You hone that talent until one day you touch a California grad student and find your sister."

"Yes."

"So now you have no Forgetter Switch and the place where you got it is in your far distant memory vaults."

"Yeah, keep going. You're on the right track."

"So when we found this place on Mars, it was not only out of business. It's abandoned and covered up for centuries. Yet you still recognize it."

"Yes."

Dana thought for a minute. Then came the

unanswered questions.

"Where are they now, the people who ran this place?"

"I don't know." It was true.

"The population is growing. How did new arrivals go through this thing if it's closed?"

"I don't know."

"How come no one else has overcome this memory canceler?"

"Maybe some have, but they haven't told anyone. Maybe some have and told someone, and they got put away and drugged into oblivion. Maybe some remembered and couldn't deal with it, so they said it was something else and forgot about it. Maybe I'm not so unique."

"Oh, you're unique, all right. You are the most unique person I know."

Dana got up, stretched and grabbed me by the shirt. She pulled me to my feet and kissed me hard and long. Then she pushed me away.

"Come on, we've got to take a look at those photographs. We've got to figure out how to get someone up there to look around."

"That might not be the best idea," I said, pulling back.

"Why not?"

"You remember when I said that everyone here has been through those structures, has gone through that process?"

Dana nodded. "Uh-huh."

"There are things that some people will remember when they get too near that thing. And some things they will forget, most likely. This discovery could affect people in a bad way."

"Like the people who got religion the moment they saw it."

"Exactly! We should approach this discovery with caution. It's dangerous!"

Dana looked at me. My workable theory was becoming complex and hard to handle.

45

Report to the Senator

"Fill me in. Tell me about Mars," said Senator Hughes. He was trying to catch up, to cover everything in a few minutes.

It had been just two days, but two days that felt like a year. I had been gathering data for Senator Hughes. Congress found money for Mars exploration. Much of the money was for tsunami aid. By some miracle, the expected tsunamis hadn't occurred. So here I was filling in the Senator via Skype.

"Mars is the fourth planet from the sun," I began. "It's one of Earth's next-door neighbors, the fourth planet, and Jupiter is the fifth. Like Earth, Jupiter, the sun, and the rest of the solar system, Mars is about 4.6 billion years old."

"Did you get this from the Discovery Channel?" asked the Senator.

"Do you want to talk or learn? Mars got itself named

for the ancient Roman God of War because its color resembles the color of blood. Viewed from Earth, Mars is a bright reddish-orange. It owes its color to iron-rich minerals in its soil. This color is also like the color of rust, as it's composed of iron and oxygen."

"So the planet is rusting?" asked the Senator, being snide. Being snide was his way of being on top. If he was snider than you, he won.

"It's old and poorly maintained. Scientists have viewed Mars through telescopes based on Earth and in space. In recent times, space probes carrying telescopes and other instruments looked at Mars. NASA designed early probes to observe the planet as they flew past it. Later, spacecraft orbited Mars and even landed there. But no human being has ever walked on Mars."

"Until now," said the Senator.

"No, not yet."

"But soon! The committee is meeting now to vote a trainload of money for Operation Mars Quest."

"Mars Quest?" I asked, though I knew. Some marketing person came up with the name. The whole thing was redesigned to fulfill that promise.

"Yes, Mars Quest. Already leaked to the media. Pretty soon the NASA boys will find out about it. They'll be on board."

"Do you still want to know about Mars?"

"No, that's enough. There will be endless specials

about it. Already they're coming up with Mars Discovery Day. They're deciding if it will be cards, candy or gifts – or all three. It could be as big as Christmas."

"Great! Then we'll get nothing done year 'round."

"Don't be a gloomy-Gus. You're in the catbird seat, right where the action is. The committee said we should send someone out there and I told them we had a man out there. Do you want to go to Mars?"

"No, thank you. There's dust storms. In fact, if we get a big one, it could re-cover our discovery."

"Doesn't sound inviting. Maybe I'll rethink my trip."

"If you do go, bring a coat, it's minus 195 degrees, though the average is about minus 80 degrees."

"So, it's cold," said the Senator.

"Yeah, cold."

"OK! Good thing to keep in mind. So if these guys who built this thing are still alive, they're different from us. They'd have to operate in sub-zero weather."

"Yes, roughly minus-sixty degrees, Celsius."

"Good to know. How long will it take to get to Mars?"

"To get there, about seven months. Then you have about nine months of orbiting and breaking."

"Breaking?"

"Yeah, you have to slow down so when you enter the atmosphere you don't pull a MRO."

"What's an MRO?"

"Mars Reconnaissance Orbiter. In 2006, it entered the

upper atmosphere wrong and disintegrated."

"Yes," said the Senator. "That would be a bad thing."

"Yes, it would."

"OK. Anything else you might need?" he asked. It was, I believe, the first time he had concerned himself with my needs.

"No, Senator, I think I have everything I need. Thanks much."

"Then I'll leave you to it."

The Senator hung up and I went in to check email. I had more than the day before, but that was a common occurrence; there was always more than the day before. I scanned the email.

My school wanted me to speak at commencement. There were more than a dozen job offers in the private sector and several proposals of marriage from complete strangers. My popularity was growing as I was now the voice of Congress at NASA Houston.

46
The Working Press

Knock! Knock!

April Wills stirred. It was too early for visitors. She lifted her head and looked at the clock. It was 10:15 in the morning.

Beside her, another body stirred. Albert Montgomery, known as Rocko to his friends and band members, rolled over and dropped his size thirteens onto the floor. He smacked his lips twice and stood up.

Knock! Knock! went the front door again.

"Comin'!" he grunted. "Hold yer friggin' horses already!"

Rocko stumbled to the door in his boxers, red and covered in Fender Stratocasters. He played bass, but they didn't have any boxers with Fender bass guitars on them.

"Yeah?" he said, peering out of the door with one eye.

"April Wills?" said a woman in a medium gray business suit. She wore her blond hair up in a French roll. Behind her was a man with a camera on his shoulder. He didn't appear to be taking a picture of anything.

"Uh, no, I'm Rocko, her boyfriend. What cha want?"

"Is she here? We have it on good authority that she lives here with her lover, Senator Jason Hughes. Is that true?"

Shandra Tyler was following a hunch, less than a lead, little more than a rumor. The good authority she had it on was a weak whisper on Capitol Hill, nothing more. Following those could run your career right into the ground; not following them was worse.

"Uh, no, babe. She lives here with me, Rocko. I'm her boyfriend. I got a rock band, House of Whacks. We were at the Brickskellar last week. Did you see us?"

"Is April Wills here?" asked Shandra. Interviewing the boyfriend was going to get her nowhere.

"Well, uh,"

"Let me handle this, Rocko," said April, slipping under his arm and around in front of him. April placed a hand in the center of Rocko's chest. She pushed him into the apartment and turned back to the people standing in the hall.

"Hi, I'm April. How can I help you?" She had taken a minute to put on a cute nightie with matching robe. She had pulled her hair together and swished out her mouth. The effect was not lost on Shandra Tyler. Shandra had done this before. She was one of the working press, the ones who went out and got the story.

"Are you the April Wills who is secretary to Senator Jason Hughes?"

April knew that the woman knew that she was. She didn't answer. She leaned out from the apartment, casting glances in both directions down the hall. "What would an exclusive be worth?" she whispered.

"Just what would that entail, Miss Wills?"

"Inside information on how Senator Hughes is trying to rip off NASA for their Mars money. What would that be worth to you?"

"I'm not in a position to negotiate for the network. I only have a few questions. Perhaps we can do a short, preliminary interview, just to get things rolling."

"Me first; I'll talk when I have a deal." April closed the door. She stood for a moment looking at the closed door, then turned and went into the bathroom.

At the rear door to the apartment, Rocko leaned out. He was still in his boxers, but with a lime green House of Whacks t-shirt. "Hey!" he called out in a whisper, waving Shandra and her cameraman, Kamil, to come down and talk to him. "She's gonna bullshit ya. You wanna know the real scoop, I got it. How much your people gonna pay for the down-low?"

"As I told your friend, I'm not in a position to negotiate, but if we were to make you a deal, what would you be able to give us?"

Shandra tapped her foot against Kamil's boot. Kamil swung the camera up and turned it on without looking through the eyepiece. He had done this before and was good at not changing expressions.

"OK. For starters, this ain't her place. It's in her name and all, but the checks come from the slush fund of the Senator's. She writes her own bonuses and gives herself raises. But they're not gonna be here long. They're going on a trip."

"Oh? Where are they going?"

"Bahamas. She bought a one-way ticket for two days from now. I think they're planning to run away together. How's that?"

"That's great!" said Shandra. "One more time, tell me who you are and about your band."

"Rocko. I play bass for House of Whacks and we were at Brickskeller last week." He paused to point at the tee shirt. "It was a great gig. You want me to let you know when we're playin' next?"

"I'll watch for it. Thank you, Mister Rocko."

"Yeah, babe. Call me." Rocko wiggled his hand next to his ear.

Shandra and Kamil walked down the hallway.

"Got it?" she asked in a whisper.

"Yup," whispered Kamil.

"Yeah, call him. In his dreams!"

They shared a laugh and continued to walk down the

hallway.

Back in the apartment, Rocko sat at the breakfast table as April walked out of the bathroom.

"What were you gonna tell 'em? Were you gonna tell 'em about the trip to the Bahamas you and the Senator are gonna take?"

"Climb down off your platform, Albert. You've been enjoying the Senator's money as much as me. Or isn't this place better than the Southwest loft you share with the rest of the band?"

"But, you only have one ticket and it's one way. What am I gonna do when you go off to vacationland? You gonna gimme a key?"

"Don't be ridiculous! Anyway, it's not going to happen. He gave me the boot. I'd cash the ticket in, but it turns out they don't do that anymore. Just enjoy the apartment til the end of the month. I don't think he's going to continue paying for it after that. The son-of-a-bitch is developing a conscience."

"Don't you have the checkbook?" asked Rocko.

"Not anymore. He made it clear, or rather his lackey, Danning made it clear, that I was no longer needed by the Senator."

"So what're ya gonna do?"

"I'm going to make a deal with that lady. If she doesn't bite, I'll sell the story to the highest bidder. He's going to regret the day he chose Mars over me." April turned and walked into the bedroom.

"Yes, well, just don't forget who's stuck by you all the way, even while you were seeing another man." He said it to the back of April's head. "And don't call me Albert. I'm Rocko!"

Rocko sat at the table, pondering whether to have breakfast or go back to bed. "Yeah," he said to himself. "Rocko!"

47
Dodging Bullets

"Hughes," yelled Speaker of the House Cartwright. The Senator turned around, trying not to wince at the voice of the man who told him what to do at every turn.

"Speaker Cartwright. How nice to see you again."

"Cut the bullshit, Senator. What's with the Mars shot? Are we going to Mars or not?"

"We're still ironing out a few wrinkles. It's not just the money; there are the months it would take to make the trip. This is not the moon we're talking about. Mars is further away. And then there's the problem of keeping our people alive to arrive on the planet and getting them back later."

"OK, we're still working out logistics. Are we going or not?"

"Yes, Mister Speaker, we're going. You have to let me do my job here. This is a process."

The Speaker looked at the Senator as if trying to look through his veneer. "Well, then get on with it," said

Cartwright. He turned and walked down the hall, leaving Senator Hughes with the feeling that he had just dodged a bullet.

The Senator walked back to his office, pausing at the desk that Tom Matthews had sat at just a few days earlier. It was a few days that seemed like a month. Down the hall, Don Danning sat keeping a suspicious eye on the Senator. Behind him, Pam Barkley tapped away at the computer.

"Danning. Will you have someone for Miss Wills' desk today?"

"Yes, sir. I'll have someone today."

"That's good. Miss Barkley, have we found all the missing NASA fund money?"

"Yes, sir. It was somehow transferred to a slush fund that April Wills oversaw. We've corrected that error and the money is back, except for an airline ticket to the Bahamas. I have the airline on the phone trying to cancel the ticket and get a refund."

"What's the hold-up on that?" asked the Senator.

"They don't believe that it was purchased by mistake. I'm making headway, though."

"I'll be in today, so if you need to, transfer them to me."

"Thank you, sir."

The Senator went into his office and closed the door. Barkley looked at Danning with surprise on her face. The

Senator had never been so accommodating. He was acting funny – almost normal.

"Hello, Don," said a woman's voice, deep and serious. Danning turned around to see his boss's wife standing behind him. Her face looked as if she had been there all day, waiting for him to notice her.

She was stunning, in matching skirt and jacket over a sheer silk blouse. She wore her hair pulled back into a tight bun that gave her the look of a female SS Officer.

"Hello, Mrs Hughes. How nice. We don't often get to see you in these halls." Danning tried to sound sincere in his pleasure at seeing her. Her plastic smile told him he was failing in that attempt.

"Where's my husband's little secretary?" she asked, laying her purse on Danning's desk and dropping into the chair in front of it.

Mrs. Hughes crossed her legs and Danning could see that she was not wearing stockings. He was careful not to notice anything else, but kept his eyes on hers. It was an effort, but one he had practiced in the past. He was getting good at it.

"She was making a little too free with the petty cash. We had to let her go. I was just about to choose a replacement."

"Really! Let me see." Mrs. Hughes leaned forward. She cast an experienced eye over four résumés on the edge of Danning's desk. Each came complete with a snapshot.

Three were what one would expect: young and pretty with dubious skills. The fresh faces that made Washington the only city in the U.S. where the women outnumber the men. They were easy to profile. Each had aspirations to rise in government. Each shared an apartment with three or four other girls. Each stretched their paychecks to buy new clothes every season. And each had a boyfriend, but it was not serious. Each was a potential for late night projects in close quarters with the Senator.

The fourth was 45, married and had children who were grown and on their own. Mrs. Hughes smiled. "This one! This is the one you have just discovered to have the best résumé. She's experienced and knowledgeable. She will best serve the Senator. See that she's able to start immediately, would you?"

"Right away, Mrs. Hughes."

"Thank you, Don." Mrs. Hughes stood up, picked up her purse and walked out, knowing that every eye in the office was on her. Knowing they wondered how she got away with wearing that skirt without a panty line.

"How is it that the Senator takes a chance at a fling with April when he's got that tigress at home?" asked Barkley.

"There's an old proverb that says for every beautiful woman there's a man who's tired of putting up with her crap," replied Danning.

Barkley nodded, still watching the retreating rear end of Mrs. Hughes as it sashayed down the hall toward the double doors.

48
On the Head of a Pin

We spent a full day of watching the pictures sent back from Mars. We then went over the images with a magnifying glass. At last, we took a break.

We had some food brought in. NASA warned the local restaurants that everyone was on high alert and there would be a demand for meals. We had overwhelmed the in-house kitchen.

Dana sat in a wheelchair with her leg raised and an ice pack. Carrie had discovered the chair in the guest accommodations area. She was becoming invaluable. She was also becoming fond of Reggie. Everyone saw it coming; no one tried to stop it. It was as inevitable as the Mars orbit. If I had more power and a budget, I would have hired them both on the spot.

Carrie got Dana a tray that fit to the wheelchair, making it easier for her to eat. Dana chewed, but her eyes were thoughtful. Her attention wasn't on food, it was on those pictures. "We've got to get closer. We've got to get inside," she said to no one in particular.

"That'll be interesting," I said. Even I wasn't sure if I was being sarcastic or not. I knew what was in there when it was operational. I didn't know how I knew, but I knew. Now that it was no longer functional, I couldn't predict what we was on the inside of those structures. Where the beings had gone who had built it, what they looked like and where they are now was also a mystery to me. I didn't dwell on what I didn't know, I had enough on my hands.

"What do you think we'll find?" asked Dana.

"My guess is that it will be like walking through an abandoned warehouse, one that used to be active and productive. The power will be off, the machines will be dusty and broken, if they are there at all. Several successive groups would strip the place, each in order. The workers will have taken everything of value. The first looters strip everything of questionable value. Later the scavengers will have taken everything else, everything not nailed down."

"So, empty," said Dana.

"Yeah, empty. Another sad commentary on life, only on Mars."

"If it is a people-programmer, and if it's closed, then who's programming people?" she asked. We had covered it a dozen times, but the question still came up. I was not providing answers fast enough or complete enough. I knew that without even thinking hard. I didn't have all the answers. Still, I seemed to be the only one who had any.

"Near as I can figure," I mused. "it was set on auto-pilot. When it closed, everyone was already programmed. Some people, I guess, went into storage, to bring out later."

"Millions? Billions?"

"Yeah, well, look at that place, it's huge."

Dana continued to eat; not looking at me or anyone else. She was completely absorbed. There was a lot of that going around.

"Where would they keep people until they are born?"

"On the head of a pin, I guess. I mean, we're talking about something with no space, no weight, no need for sustenance and no need for locks. Doors and walls are irrelevant."

"So how were they held captive?" asked Liz, sitting just on the other side of Dana. She had been listening in.

Liz considered me the expert on such things. She had parked anything that contradicted what I said off to one side. She would consider it at a later date. I challenged everything her parents spoon-fed her as a child. I challenged her early schooling, Sunday school and Bible studies. All this by a man she had just met, and I wasn't even a doctor. Yet, she was putting complete faith in me. Whatever I said was the way it was, for now. Like Dana, she was working with the data. As long as it worked, that was good enough for her.

"Fascinated! Captured by an image from which they could not turn away. There would be a TV there and the souls in the waiting room would get fixated on that screen. they would stay there watching the pretty pictures for eternity if need be."

"Deer in the headlights syndrome," said Liz.

"That's my theory."

"What's playing on that TV?" said Reggie, sitting on the other side of Liz. Just beyond him, Carrie leaned in, following the conversation.

"Doesn't matter. As long as it keeps them transfixed, it's workable."

"I have an aunt who'll watch anything. She has that thing on 24-7," said Carrie.

"That's what it's like," I continued. "They're about to go out the door but they see the screen and just sit down and watch it instead. Nothing will move them until you stand in front of the screen and give them an order."

Across the table, one of the junior technicians who worked there looked up at me. "Mister Matthews. You're here as a representative of the Congressional Committee who oversees our budget. Is that right?"

"That's right," I replied.

"So, you're not a PhD or even schooled in the subjects we deal with here. You are a politician. Is that right?"

"No, not a politician, but I am not a doctor, you're right there."

"So what are you doing telling us what's up there?" The junior technician got a smug look, narrowing his eyes. The table got quiet. All eyes focused on me, all ears trained on me, anticipating my impending answer.

Liz Strayer interjected.

"Because, you young pup, he's been right so far. And he's the only one, including you, who is coming up with answers. So until you grow up and start contributing to the flow, shut the hell up!"

The silence continued, but all eyes were now on the junior technician. He turned beet red and returned without comment to his plate of food. He took two bites, decided he was no longer hungry and got up. We watched him take his tray out to the trash can and drop it, cup, flatware, plate and all, into the trash. The rest of us returned to our meals.

"Someone's going to have to fish out his plate," said Dana.

"That's why the cost of space exploration is so damned high: the waste," added Liz. There were chuckles all around the table.

49

A Look Inside

Over the sounds of dinner, we heard footsteps coming up the hall, fast and growing louder. Doctor Bronson burst into the room, followed by Doctor Foster.

"A break! There's a break!" shouted Bronson. He then doubled over, trying to catch his breath

Doctor Foster continued the news. "The Express is still going over the line of structures. Some of them have been broken, ruins. The camera has, in some cases, been able to see inside through the collapsed parts."

"Get me out of this contraption," said Dana, handing me her tray. Scientists laid their forks and spoons down as the entire room stood up, leaving their meals on the table. I helped Dana up and got her cane. We moved to the main room. The giant screen was still showing pictures snapped by the Orbiter Express.

No one knew why, but the satellite was somehow sending us images of the entire length of the complex. This after having changed its orbit and trajectory. The giant complex went almost from horizon to horizon. Pictures showed different designs of structures along the way. Breaks in the buildings could be roads, courtyards or undeveloped land. The material of the buildings was the same as the sand around them. Either made to be that way, or stained by years of burial in oxidized dirt.

Buildings with jagged edges and vast openings in their tops and sides suggested ruins. Technicians transferred these photos to the light table and studied them. Doctor Bronson and Doctor Foster came in, panting for breath. They joined the conversation at one of the light tables. Dana and I sat looking up at the big screen in wonder.

"It's too bad we don't have a shuttle that'll make the trip," said Liz, sitting next to Dana.

"Who says we don't?" said a voice behind us. It was Reggie. All heads turned to regard Reggie. Out of politeness, no one brought up that the Shuttle Program had been all but closed down due to lack of funding. Of course, that was going to change any minute.

"Spill, Reggie!" said Liz.

"Mars Explorer Nine, sitting in a hangar not a mile from here. It's fueled up and equipped for a trip to the Red Planet. We have space suits and a geodesic dome ready for transport and setup. Five astronauts trained up for the mission. They're ready to go."

"Why didn't we know about this?" I asked.

"You know why," replied Reggie, his arms waving in

the air. "Congress pulled the plug. We couldn't exactly say that we were all dressed up for a party and so they should buy a cake. It was a big blow when the space program closed down. After all, that's what we do around here. So we just said, 'Fine, we'll take our toys and go home.' That's what a lot of people did: they closed their laptops and went home to play *Modern Warfare.*"

"We've been here for days," said Dana. "You should have mentioned something about having a plane waiting outside."

"Look," replied Reggie. "There's still a lot to know before we saddle up and hit the trail. We don't know what we're up against. For all we know, the next thing we'll see is little green men sitting on an anti-aircraft gun. But don't worry, we've got you covered. This is NASA. We know what we're doing." Reggie looked up at the screen, ignoring us. I turned back around as well. Dana and Liz decided to put their attention on the question at hand rather than the secret shuttle and crew. But all our heads were working overtime.

There was a shuttle: Mars Explorer IX. There was a crew, recently let go but still sharp. I pictured them sitting in ranch style houses with their wives and kids. They watched the news anchors go back and forth with stories about lines, then strange writing, then optical illusions and now structures. They were no doubt wondering when the media would get it right. Then they would get a call in the middle of the night saying, "Report! We're going to Mars!"

Before they get that call, NASA will get a call from the Capitol that their funding is back in place. Not just the pittance that they had been getting to keep the lights on, but all their funding. Currently, we had the lights dimmed, so the screen was that much more visible.

A gasp rippled through the room and heads that had turned away from the big screen turned back. Lost in thought, my eyes were looking but didn't see. Now I focused.

A major structure in the line had collapsed and was open for all to see. A jagged edge showed the near wall and the camera clicked away at the inside of the building. At the top of the screen, we could see the broken edge of the side of the structure. It looked like age and weight of the sand on top of it had taken their toll. The camera focused on the surface; the inside was dark, impossible to see. We all stretched our eyes, trying to get a look at what was inside.

Then the collapsed structure opened up enough to let light inside. We leaned forward in our seats, as if that would get us closer. We peered into the chasm, the great gap in our knowledge. Something appeared to be on the walls, something on the floor below, something unsure. Something!

But there was nothing. The space was empty. There

was no floor, only the darkness deeper in the depths. There was nothing written on the walls. No prophesy or warning, no graffiti by some delinquent space teen. The far wall came into view and soon the open building was behind us. We watched the screen for the next revelation.

What came was the other end of the line of structures. The last one, or the first one according to my theory, was coming into view. Beyond that, the plains of Mars and nothing more.

Of course, we didn't know that. A few days ago, we knew for sure that there was no sign of life on Mars. Nothing but a few scant whispers of the possibility of moisture. Now we know there are these strange structures. Like Tommy Lee Jones said in the movie, *Men in Black*, "What will you know tomorrow?"

"You were right," whispered Dana. Liz Strayer leaned forward in her seat, hoping to hear what I had been right about. I wanted to hear it myself.

"Just like an abandoned warehouse, stripped of everything."

Liz nodded and leaned back. Dana reached out and took my hand. She gripped it, watching the final building in the line come closer.

"Now that's something that's pretty amazing!" I said. "A woman just told a man that he's right."

50
The Beginning and the End

The final building in the line of gigantic structures was funnel-shaped. It began narrow and widened out at the far end. Of course, I knew that it was backwards. This was, in fact, the first structure in the line. We approached it from the back end and it actually started out wide and narrowed to a pinpoint. How I knew that was still a mystery. The revelations were coming as fast to me as anyone at Houston Command Central.

Something deep inside me was saying, "Good, we're coming at it from this angle. It's safer this way." Like everything else, I didn't know why but that was true. That is when the fear worsened.

Earlier in the course of this project, I was afraid of whatever it was that we were finding. Now that fear magnified a hundred times. It was not just fear for me or for Dana or our group, I was afraid for the whole world, everyone on planet Earth.

"Shut it down," I said, low and soft.

"What?" said Dana, not completely sure what she had heard.

I held my hands up, hoping she would see it as a sign that I needed a moment to collect my thoughts. I had to know if what I was feeling was real or false. Was it my picture or did it belong to someone else? Was it a memory, knowledge or something planted deep within my mind? Was it real or imagined? I looked at Dana. Here was something real, something I could depend on. Dana was real. My feelings for her were real. I had a stable datum. She was one. But I needed another one.

"Liz," I called in a loud whisper. She leaned forward, looking at me with concern. I tilted my head toward the door and stood up. I whispered to Dana, "I'm going to go and have a little chat with Liz. I want you to wait here for me and save my seat. I want you to think about last night and the night before. Think about how we feel when we're together and about how we communicate. Know that I'll be back."

Out in the hall, people were running back and forth from this project to that, as the priorities came up. If there was nothing pressing they would go into the big room and look at the screen, keeping up with latest developments.

Liz followed me out, catching up with me in the hall. "This way," I said. We went into the lunch room. No one had cleared out the meals abandoned earlier. Liz pulled up a couple of chairs and we sat down in the corner, away from everything.

"What's up?" asked Liz.

"You're someone I can count on. You're special. In the past we have been fast friends and I still feel the bond. You are someone I trust. Do you agree?"

Liz nodded, wondering what was coming next.

"I need you now as a sounding board. Tell me if I'm crazy or not."

"OK, Tiger. If I can," said Liz, mentally rolling up her sleeves.

"In this device," I held my hands to emulate the funnel. "Beings, life-forces, spirits or souls, if you will, get fed into the end we just saw. We saw it from the back, the part that looks like a funnel."

"OK, I'm with ya," said Liz.

"Throughout the process, they are in limbo, held fascinated, in a sort of trance. It's much like the crew in there, looking at that screen. They can't look away. The consequences would be horrible!"

"Yeah, I noticed that."

"As these spirits go along, they see pictures. They are not their own pictures. They are pictures given to them. You with me?"

"Let's say I'm following."

"Close enough. Now, these pictures aren't theirs, but they think they are. They perceive them as truth. Now, I don't think the pictures are there in the structures anymore. I think, like the abandoned warehouse story, they got removed when the factory closed."

"Seems right," nodded Liz.

"We've had, what, about fifteen cases of people looking at this thing and getting religion? Not religion, more like obsession. You can't talk them out of it. They're convinced, though there's nothing to back them up, no proof whatsoever. No one and nothing will dissuade them. Is that right?"

"Yes, that is correct." Liz looked at me, ready for what came next. I was laying a foundation of something and she could hardly wait to see what it was.

"I think those people saw this and remembered, but below their level of consciousness." I hoped she would get it.

"Subconscious, below the level of thought?" Liz was tracking with me now.

"Yes! What they saw, what they heard, in those structures, the memories are old and buried deep. But when they saw it on the screen, they remembered a tip of that memory and suddenly saw it as undeniable truth."

"Uh-huh!" said Liz, waiting for what was next.

"Yeah. So, that's what happened. But here's the thing. There's about a hundred and fifty people in that room off and on. That's ten percent who have gone off the deep end."

Liz furrowed her eyebrows, what could I be getting at? Somehow, I knew that if I kept talking, I would get to it and know for myself.

"Not that I'm against someone finding God or becoming a good person. But it should be their own idea, their own choice. If I'm right, these people are not behaving according to their own decision. They are responding to an idea given them by someone else, someone who is no longer around to argue with them. The ones who gave them those pictures, real or imagined, are no longer here."

"Not that we have been able to find," agreed Liz.

"As we get further into these structures, more and more people will remember. They'll begin acting in strange new ways. They'll start believing in angels or devils or groundhogs and behaving weird. We won't have a way to handle it."

"Uh-huh!" Liz looked at me, digesting.

"Liz, I think if a thousand people see those pictures and remember, at least a hundred of them will experience being under the influence of something planted in their memories, something that will make them behave different than we expect. And if a million people see them, then a hundred thousand or more will have reactions – reactions they will believe to be the only truth there is."

I looked around the room, then at Liz.

"We were looking at that funnel backwards, from the back. If we look at it from the front, I believe we will never look away. We will become fascinated and transfixed and will be under the spell of it. Sooner or later, we will figure out how to turn Express around, how to look at that building from the other angle. When we do, we're sunk."

We sat there looking at each other. She knew I was saying what I believed and I knew that she believed I was saying the truth as I saw it.

"So you think sooner or later we'll look at this thing straight on. And when we do, more people will become affected."

"Yes!" I said in a cautious whisper. She was getting it.

"Greater numbers, more people start to sing about the Gospel Train a-comin'. You know, these people didn't just get religion, they went nuts! They turned within a second into wide-eyed fanatics. I'm not just being colorful when I talk about the Gospel Train, all fifteen of them have mentioned it by name. They talk about a Gospel Train that will actually come down a track, stop and pick them up and carry them to Glory. They'll be waiting at the Glory Depot and the conductor will come out and punch their ticket. Now, how can fifteen strangers talk about the same thing and in the same context overnight?"

I nodded. That was exactly right. I put the concept into words.

"Either it's the truth – and we have yet to define that –

or they are all sharing the same truth. Maybe they believe it so hard that they will not consider argument or proof otherwise."

"Right!" said Liz.

"Now, imagine ten percent of the population doing that. Imagine they leave their jobs as doctors, judges or air traffic controllers to sit at abandoned railway depots."

"So you think we should shut it down."

"It's a frightening thing to consider saying out loud. What if I'm wrong? What if fifteen people just decided that God is coming for them and he's coming by rail? What if no other cases develop?"

"That's something to consider," said Liz. There were other sides of the argument. But there were also arguments still evolving.

"Mind you," I continued. "there are other viewpoints. There is a faction that still believes this is an optical illusion. Others are saying it's the work of the Devil. Still others are saying witchcraft is to blame. There are more crazy schools of thought about this than there are level-headed scientists trying to figure it out."

"You got that right. There's just a handful of us," said Liz.

"Liz, I don't care if there is a shuttle in a hangar just down the street. Hell, I don't care if we ever go in there and find out what it is. We should shut this down! We should shut this down now! There is too much riding on it."

Liz got up, she had to walk now, wave her arms. She did. "We can't just leave it up there, not investigated."

I stood up as well; the conversation was taking up more room. "Sure we can! We do it all the time! We just decide that it's not worth our while to do further research into this or that and we leave it alone. Nobody cares. There are diseases that have no cure because not enough people die each year to bother about them. The people who die will argue the point with you, but it does no good. Science doesn't care about them. Science shouldn't care about this, either."

"How sure are you about this?" asked Liz.

"Aw! Come on, Liz!" I yelled. "How sure are those people that the Gospel Train is coming, track or not? I think what I'm saying is true. So sure, in fact, that here I am, saying so to one of the top experts in the field. I'm standing in NASA Houston, less than a mile from the Shuttle Mars Explorer IX and I'm saying it should stay in the hangar. I'm sure! I'm as sure as a heart attack!"

"We've got to have a meeting, a briefing," said Liz. "We've got to get people in here. I'll be back."

51
An Unpopular Act

"Senator Hughes office," said an unfamiliar voice.

"Let me speak to the Senator, please. This is Tom Matthews and it is important."

"One moment, please." I danced back and forth waiting for him to pick up. What if he doesn't take it? What if he's in a meeting? What if...

"Matthews, you just caught me," said the Senator.

"Sir, how would you like to save the world by doing something really, really unpopular?"

The Senator was about to have a new experience. Someone was going to propose that he do something guaranteed to shoot his reelection in the foot. It was something that no one wants, that no one agrees with, but to do it with bold strokes, for the sake of all. It will be the most unselfish thing he has ever done. History may name him a hero, but not right away. It sounded crazy to me, too. I took a deep breath.

"What are you talking about?" he asked.

"Pull the NASA funding." There was a long pause on the other end of the phone. I was breathing heavy and I could feel my heart pumping in my neck.

"Are you insane, Matthews? I just moved heaven and earth to make it happen."

"I know, Senator, but it's important. There's a shuttle in the next hangar, there are astronauts ready to go to Mars and it can't happen. It must not happen. It's not a good idea."

"No, no, no! The idea was for you to go there and keep me informed, not decide to close it down. What the hell is going on?"

"It's too complex to explain over the phone. Just take my word, there are people here responding badly to the events and structures on Mars. If more people see them, more will act crazy. If men go to Mars and reveal what is there before we have a way to deal with it, the adverse effects could be worldwide. We could be dealing with a global epidemic and no way to handle it."

"You're raving, Matthews. Get hold of yourself. It can't be that bad."

I looked up to see Liz coming with Dana. I knew the rest were close behind. "I'm about to go into a meeting, sir. I believe the end result of that meeting will be an announcement to close this investigation into the structures on Mars. But it is important enough that if they don't shut it down on this end, you have to do so on that end."

"You don't know what you're asking. With public opinion like it is, this could be the last act of my career. In fact, just bringing up the subject would be political suicide. Like it or not, son, we're going to Mars."

"Yes, sir. Uh, I have a meeting. Have to go." I closed the phone. I didn't want them to know I had already been stabbing them and the project in the back.

52
Alienating the Team

The meeting was one I had called. After telling my thoughts to Liz, it would be easy to reveal them to the rest. You'd think so, anyway.

Liz and Dana sat down, followed by Bronson, Foster, Carrie and Reggie. Liz looked perplexed. Carrie looked worried. Reggie, who took everything in stride, was anxious to get back to the ongoing planning sessions for the Mars launch. It was now a "go," whether anyone gave the OK or not.

I was looking at my team, my crew. They had been with me through thick and thin. We had lived together, loved together, cried together and died together. They were my long-term allies, save for Dana, the new arrival.

As my team looked at me wide-eyed I explained how the funnel building held a device. The device would hold anyone who looked at it in a trance for an indeterminate length of time. I explained how the hardcore scientists who had left their posts to join a new cult were just the tip of the iceberg. I went over the concept that where there is danger or just not enough interest, one abandons investigation. One then relegates whole areas of knowledge to ignorant darkness due to lack of interest. I told them that if Mars Explorer IX takes off, it will be a disastrous flight. I told them that I had asked Senator Hughes to stop the funding. That got 'em!

"Matthews, are you insane?" yelled Bronson.

"Tom, you can't be serious!" said Dana.

Everyone had something to say, but at that point, it was all said together. I held up my hands.

"Please. You've already seen some pretty insane behavior. I believe that if we continue on this line that we will see more and worse."

"Thank you, Mister Matthews," said Doctor Bronson. "You have been an invaluable help in this project, but we're done now. This is too big to just turn our back on it."

"No! You can't go on with this..." I began. Liz stepped up and put a hand on my chest.

"Geez, Tom. If you had been there when we invented fire, we'd be all sitting in the cold now. You have to let science take its course."

"But you believed me."

"No, Tom. I believed that you believed it. I have always been my own man. Well, my own woman. The point is, you've done your job here. Mine is just beginning. It's been great, pal." Liz walked out of the lunch room shaking her head, following Bronson and the rest.

Only Dana and Carrie remained. Dana looked me in the eye. "Tom, you know how I feel about you. We never needed all the old, overused phrases. But our paths diverge here." She turned and hobbled out, favoring her left leg more than she had been lately. It was my guess that events weighed heavy on her and she reflected the strain in her leg.

Carrie looked at me, tears in her eyes. "I love you so much! But you know Bronson is on the phone right now having you reassigned elsewhere. You know I have to stay here. I mean, you know that, don't you?"

"Yes, Carrie. I know that."

Carrie took one last look and walked out of the lunch room after Reggie.

Tears began to form in my eyes and I felt a hole in my heart. It took that long for my team to turn against me. One moment we were all on the same page and the next, we were in different libraries, on different planets, in different solar systems.

The call came within the hour; I was reassigned back to the Senator's office. Don Danning would be coming out to take my place as the eyes and ears of the Senator. I was to catch the next transport back to D.C.

I needed to think. I took the train.

53
Slow News Day

Shandra Tyler sat at the conference table at Channel Eight Action News, going through her notes. It was thin, downright thin. Still, she might be able to sell it. If not, she had another ready to go. Around the room sat a dozen other reporters, doubling as segment producers. Each was vying for a spot on the evening's broadcast.

Her boss and program director, Ed Fillmore, walked in and pulled a chair out. He sat down and looked around, taking mental attendance. "OK! Let's get this started. Tyler, whatcha got?"

"The secretary for Senator Hughes, she wants to blow the whistle on him keeping funds from NASA. She says she'll sell the exclusive. Meanwhile the boyfriend says the Senator pays for the apartment, via the NASA petty cash. Also that she has a ticket to the Bahamas, one way."

"Two tickets?"

"No, one."

"What does the committee to fund NASA say?"

"They report no money missing and say that she no longer works for the Senator. Could be a case of disgruntled employee syndrome."

"The boyfriend, is he a viable source?"

"Bass player in a rock band."

"No story there, drop it. What else you got?"

"Rumors of the man Senator Hughes sent to Houston to be his eyes and ears is saying it's not a good idea to go to Mars. He says it will be dangerous."

"Well, of course, it will be dangerous. It's Mars! Go with that one, the man who OKs the money has someone in his office trying to put on the brakes? That's the story."

* * *

Across town, Doctor Megan McClellan stood in the doorway of an up-and-coming tabloid named the Foggy Bottom Snoop. The man she came to meet claimed to be the nephew of the editor. He looked too young to work on a paper.

"I don't know," said the young fellow. "It seems like not much of a story to me. Do you have pictures? It's always better with pictures."

"No, no pictures. But it's true. They told me the markings on Mars were writing. They they said structures, then a complete town, then an optical illusion. When it came out that they were actually buildings made by intelligent life, they put me off the project. My own university wouldn't take me back, and I was in the inner circle, where the data flowed."

"So, you're not there anymore?"

"It's a conspiracy to get me out, to take the credit. I deserve to be the one interviewed on this Mars thing. I was the first to discover the markings on Mars."

"I thought you said your name was McClellan," said the young man at the desk. He glanced at his ham and cheese sandwich, hoping he could get back to it soon.

"Yes, Doctor McClellan."

"So, not Wright. Not Dana Wright?" He looked down to see if there was a cane anywhere. He had heard that Dana Wright used a cane.

Doctor McClellan looked at him and made a decision. "Thank you for your time. This was a mistake. Uh, when exactly is your uncle, the editor, coming in?"

* * *

In a television studio just outside D.C., a producer with a headset stood in front of a camera. He held up four fingers, then three, then two. He took his hand away and the music played. Behind the commentator, stills of the Martian surface showed straight lines and curved lines. Then a close-up of a building with part of the roof caved in appeared. It was covered with sand up to its height.

"Breaking news this hour: The first photos released by NASA taken by the Mars Orbiter Express show a long line of structures, some intact and some partially or completely collapsed. For the first time, signs that intelligent life was at one time present on the Red Planet. Though there is no indication of life at this time. Quoted on the scene was Doctor Dana Wright, the first to see the structures."

A recorded image of Doctor Wright showed up on the screen. She looked bigger on TV. "This is a significant find. The question of are we alone in the universe is no longer moot. We are not. There is intelligent life out there. Intelligent life built this." She waved a hand at the picture behind her, indicating the large, funnel shaped building at the end of the complex.

The commentator returned, looking serious. "A spokesman for NASA is quoted as saying they are preparing to launch a manned ship to Mars within the month. Meanwhile, in other news..."

* * *

In the underdeveloped southwest portion of D.C., Rocko was walking into an empty store that had been rented that very afternoon by a newly formed group seeking recognition as a church. Over the door was a large, orange banner announcing, "The Glory Depot."

"Albert Montgomery, sister. How do I join?"

The teenage girl covered in bright orange paint smiled and handed him a brush. "Don't need a ticket, you just get on board."

* * *

Meanwhile, I was on a train heading back to Washington. It was the slow train, pausing at every whistle-stop and jerkwater town along the way. I took it on purpose. I needed the time to think.

Each time the train pulled into a station, I stepped out for a newspaper. I had my computer open with the network sites feeding me the news on the hour.

Each time I saw my name in the paper or heard it on air, I cringed. The news about Mars was so big, with so many heroes, that there was a shortage of people to hate. I was one of the few "bad guys" around and so received the bulk of the negative media. I hoped the shouting would die down sooner or later.

In other news, all over the country, people walked off their jobs to join strange cults. Sometimes they left in the middle of a shift with no explanation. The biggest was the Gospel Train, which you caught at the Glory Depot. Members painted The Glory Depots bright orange. They decorated the buildings in Day-Glo orange banners and the attendees wore matching t-shirts. They called it Golden, but it was orange.

The cult members were a cross section of people, not of any one age or color or sex, they were just people. Like the first fifteen at NASA Houston, there was no pattern. The bizarre effects created by seeing the pictures from Mars appeared to be influencing a random selection of people. "I hate it when I'm right!" I said to my self aloud.

In the bar, I ordered a double.

"Hi, I'm Patty," said a candy-cane voice next to me. A pretty coed with a red ribbon in her sandy blond hair was smiling up at me.

"Tom," I said, wondering whether to buy her a drink or a lollipop. I was being careful. All I needed to make my downfall complete was to get caught by the press with an underage girl.

"Tom what?" said the girl, bending over just enough to throw me off my game.

"Tom Matthews," I said. Then I wished for all the world that I could have sucked the words back in, never to let them out again.

"What? The guy who tried to stop the Mars Mission? Really? No way! Bonnie!" she called out, waving to her girlfriend who had just cornered a jock at the other end of the bar. "This is the guy who tried to get the Mars program defunded."

"Shut up!" cried Bonnie.

"No way! What a dork!" added the jock.

With no dignity whatsoever, I poured the rest of my drink down my throat and walked out of the bar. I hoped nobody was reading the paper in the observation car.

54
Reassignment

Barkley glared at me as I sat down at Danning's desk. He was in Houston, I was here. It was a step down for me, a step up for Danning but it meant Barkley was sleeping alone.

Where April used to sit was an older woman with the face of a drill sergeant. She looked at me as if I were a naughty ten-year-old waiting for the principal.

Before I she admitted me to the Senator, the conversation played our in my mind. I would say I'm sorry but that I still believe I was right. He would say I was wrong and I am not to speak to the press ever again. I would offer my resignation. He would take it and give me a non-disclosure agreement that would have me going to prison forever if broke it. In my head, it was a short meeting.

The actual meeting was even shorter.

"Back, Matthews?" asked Senator Hughes, standing up and offering me a hand.

The memory flicker from the Senator was so familiar that I didn't even notice it. I lead with my prepared apology. "Senator, I just want to say that while I am sorry..."

"Yes, yes. I know, but that's water under the bridge, bygones. Don't think of it again. Just stay away from the press, OK? Take Dannings desk. I've pared his responsibilities down so it won't be too much at first. You might as well ease into it after your ordeal: tough days, running all over the country. Glad to have you back."

"You want me to stay?"

"Absolutely! Did you think I'd fire you? No, no, not at all. You're fine. Throw yourself into work. That's what I always do after a setback."

"Of course. What would you like me to do?"

"Like I said, ease into it, keep away from the press. I'm sure Barkley has some things."

"Of course, sir. Well, I'll just get started."

"Glad to have you back, Tom," said the Senator, waving as I headed for the door.

Yes, he was glad to have me back. Better here, under his thumb than out there where the press can enjoy picking off the rest of me. He didn't need me being the loose cannon. He needed me quiet.

Walking down the halls, I got the feeling that everyone was staring. Also pointing and whispering. It was overwhelming. I looked in vain for a friendly face. Finally,

I saw one, Speaker of the House Cartwright.

"Speaker Cartwright," I said. "How nice to see you." I didn't reach out a hand, as is standard for these halls. I didn't want to know who had once been on my team anymore. It was enough to know people now without also knowing who they had been in the past.

"Matthews. Back from your adventure?" the Speaker didn't offer a hand either. In fact he seemed to have an edge to him.

"Yes, sir. It's good to be home."

"What will you be doing?"

"Just a little follow-up work from the Senator's office. Nothing long term. In fact, you said at one time that there might be a place for me in your organization."

"Oh! Did I say that? Don't know what I was thinking. No, I don't have an opening right now. Check with me, well, in a couple of ... no, more like, well, if anything opens up, I'll let you know. Gotta go, Matthews. Good to see you. Welcome back."

The Speaker of the House walked on, a little quick it seemed.

So there it was. I had become the joke of Washington, D.C. I was the man who, when the entire world was putting a shoulder behind NASA, wanted to cut the budget. When everyone and his brother was in favor of the Mars Project, I was against it. All Washington wanted the flight to Mars to happen as fast as possible. I was the only one with his heels dug into the dirt. It was a new personal low for me.

On the way home I went to a liquor store. I bought large bottles of tequila, vodka, bourbon and some schnapps for good measure. I also bought several movies from the dollar bin at the local discount store and a stack of frozen pizzas. Then I went home, closed the door and disconnected the phone. I wished I had a do-not-disturb sign for the door.

As the smell of cheese and pepperoni filled the small apartment, I couldn't help but watch the news. It held a fascination for me akin to a bad accident. I dared not look away. I was transfixed as if I was looking into the funnel.

On the screen, NASA engineers were describing the path of the Explorer IX. There had been more than 75 Explorer craft, but the idea of going to Mars was new. Explorer Nine was not even known to exist, but there she was, shining, smoking and ready to go.

As the press interviewed the professionals associated with the launch, I poured a drink. Dana came on the screen. She was walking without her cane and dressed to the nines, in a stunning pants suit with silk blouse. Someone had done her makeup and hair, rather well, I thought.

It was forty-five minutes before the news gave way to the ball scores. The OJ trial hadn't raised as much interest. The whole world was watching us charge off to Mars after just a few weeks. We couldn't leave fast enough.

"And now for the lighter side of the news. What do kids want to be these days? You guessed it, an astronaut! We're here at the Falls Church Elementary School talking with..."

I turned the sound back down. Nothing like peace and quiet to sooth the soul.

"Ding!" went the timer. Time for my pizza.

The little tyke on the television was talking to the announcer. In my mind, I imagined him saying, "I want to be an astronaut when I grow up – or a doctor or a lawyer. Anything but assistant to a Senator who wants to stop the NASA funding."

I finished the drink. The bag of movies I had bought without looking for a dollar apiece was on the couch. I grabbed the bottom of the bag and dumped them out onto the floor, hoping one would catch my eye. One did. There in the middle of the pile, facing me, was an old classic: *Mission to Mars.*

I refilled my drink.

55
Landing on Mars

Mars Explorer IX took six months to get to Mars, not seven as first thought. The two planets were enjoying a rare proximity. They were just 55 million kilometers apart.

In Washington, snow was falling and stores were having sales. The most popular toy for Christmas was the Martian Explorer Action Figure with real voice commands at the push of a button.

There were five movies about Mars released. Seven television shows filled the small screen, ranging from documentaries to sitcoms. One was a soap opera with Martian vampires who would fall in love with human girls and then break their hearts.

At the office, the Senator was polite but distant. His new Gal Friday was downright chilly. Barkley hated me for four months, but then became indifferent.

The job had come down to a nine-to-five for the first time in my life. I was kept where I couldn't make any trouble. I stayed because I knew it was the only job I could get – anywhere. Half of the world was in on the trip to Mars, and the whole world knew about it. There was only one person who was against it so it was not a time to be looking for a new job.

In the weeks before Christmas, I considered trolling the bars in search for a lost soul. To find someone as lonely as me to share the holiday. Then I would imagine our hands or our lips touching. The thought of seeing an image of a battleground or monastery, and me reuniting with an old army buddy or aging priest, gave me chills. In the end, spending Christmas alone didn't seem that bad.

* * *

On Mars, the astronauts were being picturesque.

"Houston, the Eagle has landed," announced Astronaut Christine Blain to Command Central at NASA. They had landed in the primary craft, the HAB, short for Habitat. It was a lander. A separate craft, the Earth Return Vehicle, ERV for short, landed a short distance away. They would use it for the return trip. The HAB would remain on the surface. It would become living quarters for future mission personnel.

The craft also held Astronauts Roger Hanson, Freddy Rodriguez, Elaine Metcalf and Arnie Chin. They sat back in their flight suits, still strapped in. They waited the minutes it would take for the message to travel on the light beam to Earth and the response to return. When the response came, it was an excited voice with screaming technicians in the background.

"Roger, Niner. We have you as secured. Prepare for Program One, Collection of Immediate Environmental Samples. This is Houston, out."

The slow process of equalizing air pressure within the vessel began. Removing the flight suits and acclimatizing themselves to the Martian gravity took several hours. It was all part of the program, including taking air and soil samples. They took photos of the giant funnel, the reason they chose this site. They were less than a football field from the opening, the part they named "The Amphitheater." The section of the funnel visible from the ship was the left, rear quarter. Whatever was inside the structure was not visible from that angle.

On the second day, the schedule had the astronauts going to actually look at the structure up close. They observed safety precautions at every step. The dust can be treacherous, sharp and jagged. It can wear away at the fabric of a space suit and, in some instances, create a tear.

The Rover vehicle was nicknamed "Insect." they lowered it onto the planet's surface. The astronauts entered for the short drive to the mouth of the funnel. Shaped like a VW bus with three axles, six outboard wheels chugged through the sand. After six minutes of travel, the rover came to a stop at a small ridge of rock. Rather than go around, the crew decided to investigate the Amphitheater on the ground.

This was a momentous occasion. The honor of being the first human being to walk on the Red Planet fell to a woman: Christine Blain.

"Ladies first," said Roger Hanson, extending a hand toward Insect's exit.

"Why, thank you, sir," responded Blain, with a small bow. It occurred to her to curtsy but the cumbersome suit made that unworkable. Such politeness seemed strange on a foreign planet. This was farther from Earth than mortal man had ever ventured.

Astronaut Blain's foot touched the crunchy Martian soil. A thrill of excitement went through her. She was the first astronaut to set foot on Mars. Astronaut Rodriguez followed with Hanson bringing up the rear. Arnie Chin closed the hatch behind them. Chin turned to Elaine Metcalf, seated at the console.

"Alone at last," he quipped.

"Sit down, Arnie. There's work to do," smiled Metcalf without looking up from her screens.

The climb over the rocks to the front of the funnel was difficult and awkward. The Martian atmosphere is one percent that of Earth and the gravity about a third. Still, the suits were cumbersome and the rocks were sharp.

Astronaut Blain, though fit, stopped to catch her breath several times on the way. Both Rodriguez and Hanson passed her on the red trail.

To call it a funnel would be to diminish both the size and importance of the edifice. This was the entry to a complex of structures that stretched across the face of the planet. It was the start, the beginning, the entrance. It was not some small plastic item for pouring salad oil into a decorative container. It was the access to the biggest find in the history of space travel.

The trio of adventurers stepped off the rocky ridge and onto the flat, red plain. They stood before the Amphitheater. Rodriguez was the first to behold it from the front. He preceded the rest by several steps and raised his head to view the spectacle in all its radiance. Then he froze solid, still as a statue at a Greek temple.

Seeing him stop, Hanson came around him to see what had him so captivated. He too stopped cold, transfixed on what he saw.

"Rodriguez? Hanson? What is it?" asked Blain, bringing up the rear. She stepped up beside Rodriguez, looking into his facemask. His eyes were focused on something far away, his breath was even and his mouth hung loose as if he had seen a ghost.

Blain turned to regard the sight that held the two astronauts so mesmerized. Her furrowed brow, set for battle if need be, softened as her eyes widened and her jaw fell. She stood glued to the sight before her, a swirling vortex of lines and colors that held her captive. Deep in her soul, an ancient command, one that told her that she must look, that she dare not look away, took hold. She complied.

"Mars Explorer team, come in. Come in, Explorer team," said Elaine Metcalf, from the rover module. She was not getting a response. "I'm going out there," she said, and she geared up for a walk on the Red Planet.

Arnie Chin sat at the console watching the fourth astronaut descend the stair at the back of the Insect. He watched her drop a foot onto the red soil. He worried about his team. He had trained with these people, flown to Mars with them. They were family. Now they were in trouble.

On the console was the button to activate the communication system. It would connect him with the Command Center on Earth. Arnie looked at the button. "Not yet!" he thought.

Metcalf didn't feel the thrill of history as her foot touched the Martian soil. Her mind was on the other three members of her team.

As she came up to the three frozen astronauts, she reported back. "I'm coming around to see what they're..."

That was the last transmission from the away team. In the rover, sitting at the console, the remaining astronaut, Arnie Chin, broke out in a sweat. He was at a loss with no one to turn to. Something held his entire team captive out on the plain of red dust in front of the giant funnel. He reached for the switch and in a shaky voice uttered a famous phrase: "Houston, we have a problem."

56

Houston, We Have a Problem

The words traveled on a laser beam to the HASA Command Center and stilled a jubilant crowd. Dana Wright turned her head, as did Reggie, Carrie and Doctor Bronson. The entire complex in Houston went silent as they waited for the next transmission.

"They're just standing there, like statues. They're frozen in place. I can't get a response," said the crackling voice of Astronaut Chin.

The room hung in suspended animation for a moment before breaking into utter bedlam. Senior scientists shouted orders over headphones while technicians tapped keypads. Experts in their fields put their heads together.

"Oh, crap!" said Dana, her face falling with a new realization.

"Are you thinking...?" asked Dr. Bronson. His question was rhetorical. He knew what Dana Wright was thinking.

"He was right," said Dana, turning toward him. "The

son of a bitch was right. Damn it! I hate when he's right!"

Liz came up to the two of them, ignoring Reggie and Carrie.

"We've got to get him back," she said, her brows furrowed, ready to repel a negative response.

"How do you suggest we do that?" asked Bronson.

Liz and Bronson both turned and looked at Dana.

"Oh, no!" she said. "Not going to happen! After I shut him down, I'm the last person he'll listen to. There has to be another way!"

* * *

Arnie Chin sat at the console waiting for a solution from Houston. He knew, because it always happened that way. A knowledgeable, father-like voice would come across, sounding bored. "All you have to do is to plug the singular matrix coupler into the channel relay selector and throw the auxiliary pump switch. That should handle the problem." That's how it worked. It always worked that way.

Seven minutes passed. He knew his communication was just getting to Command Central. At one minute intervals Arnie sent out a call to the away team, hoping for a response. There was none.

The cameras mounted on the astronaut's suits went dark. At the same time, the voice transmissions went silent. He thought the sound was out, that they could be yelling at him without success. But he could see them in the long-range camera, just standing there. He could hear their breathing; see their life signs in the monitors. They were alive, but they were not responding. It was both strange and yet familiar. Arnie could not place it, but he had seen this before.

They had come with three questions: Who made it in the first place? Where are they now? And the most important: Why? So far, Arnie had not a single answer.

Whoever made the gigantic structures, it now held his four friends captivated. Alien beings were not coming out to save them or to take them into further custody. There was no sign of other life dashing to the rescue or running to attack. That was both good and bad. He saw it as a piece of information and he needed to communicate it; that nothing was happening was also news. He waited for a response before relaying that bit of data.

"Ahhhhh!" said a crackling voice through the console speaker, trying to sound calm. "Niner, we're calling in an expert and will get back to you with a solution as soon as possible. In the meantime, take no action and whatever you do, do not walk up to the Amphitheater. You are not to step out of that module. Do you understand?"

Arnie nodded, to let them know he understood. He opened his mouth to voice his acknowledgement but it caught in his throat. He looked at the upper monitor screen.

"Uh... Roger that, Houston. I'll stay with the vehicle, but be advised there is a dust storm coming this way."

57
Eggnog

That night, I stopped by the market on the corner and picked up eggnog and a bottle of rum. It was Christmas Eve, after all.

My apartment was in one of the many brownstone conversions on Capitol Hill. It was a close walk to work and picturesque to boot.

Being winter in Washington, it was dark early. The gate to my building was noisy as I kicked it open. There was movement on the steps that made me look up. I had not noticed until that moment that someone was sitting on the front steps to my building.

"Merry Christmas," said Dana. She was all bundled up, with a scarf around her head and face, with only eyes showing. There were mittens on her hands and her coat wrapped around her as if to save her life. Her booted feet were pigeon-toed on the metal steps. Her butt must have been freezing, sitting on the wrought-iron stairs.

"I didn't get you anything," I said.

"That's all right. I didn't get you anything either."

"I do have some eggnog in here."

"Any rum?"

"Yeah! Want some?"

"Sure," she said, getting up. She had been sitting on a folded sweater to give an extra layer between her rear end and the ice-cold step.

"Come on in, I'll get a fire going," I said, leading the way up the stairs. Once inside, I did actually light a fire: gas under a fake log. I mixed the eggnog with the rum and poured two. I didn't know why she was there, and the truth was I didn't care. She was there and that was all that counted.

I was glad I had not scared up a date. It would have been awkward, to say the least. For her to find me alone on Christmas was pitiful. Still, it was better than introducing her to some random girl from the local ale house.

Dana found the plug that lit the holiday lights over the mantle and there was color in the room. With the blinking colors, the light through the window and the fire, we didn't need more. She sat down on the couch, slipped off her boots and pulled her feet under her. "So, we landed on Mars."

"Yes, it was on the news." I handed her the drink.

"Yeah. It was cool. We were all stoked when 'Niner' lifted off. Every day was a new adventure, always something to solve – like personnel."

"Personnel?" I queried.

"Yeah, we lost a lot of them, sometimes overnight. One day they're there on the job, normal as pie. The next they come to work in an orange t-shirt trying to convert the rest of us to 'get on the train to Glory.' Then they'd completely go off the deep end and we'd have to get someone else to do the job. We're beginning to run out of qualified graduate students. We're promoting undergrads who have an interest in space travel."

"Yeah, I hate it when that happens," I said, being very careful not to say anything that sounded like I-told-you-so.

"Carrie misses you," said Dana, staring into the fire.

"Yeah, I miss her as well." There was a lot I missed, but if I started naming them all, I'd either be crying or ripping her clothes off. Neither response would be good.

"We all kind of miss you."

"Oh, yeah? Even you?" I turned to Dana.

"Especially me," she said, lifting her face to me. We kissed, and it was a kiss to make up for the six months of not kissing. I spilled part of my eggnog down her back, which made it OK that she did the same thing. We laughed, set down our glasses and kissed again.

"Tom," said Dana between kisses.

"Yes," I replied, hoping she was going to suggest we take this into the bedroom.

"Tom, we have to talk." This was new.

"Talk? We never talk," I said, continuing to kiss her neck, hoping to get her back on track.

"No, no! I mean we really have to talk." Dana held me at arm's length. Her eyes were waiting for me to get on board another, yet undisclosed, train of thought.

I dropped my arms and looked into the air at nothing. I considered several short, angry words, but held my tongue. Things had been going so well! But now...

"We need to get you back to Houston, ASAP!" she said.

"Huh! Oooh, no!" I said, standing up, picking up my drink and walking over to the counter, just for something to do.

"Hear me out," said Dana, turning on the couch.

"Oh! Am I interrupting you after you have gotten started? Well, here's a flash: You got me started. It took me months to stop wishing I had died in my sleep. Now you're here and a moment ago, I was glad. You got me started; now you stop me mid-flight – again?"

"The Mars Mission has come to a halt," said Dana.

58
You Were Right

Dana looked at me, her lip trembling and her eyes about to break into tears. She was completely without defenses.

"Oh! Oh, great!" I threw at her. "So, you came out here in the middle of the night on Christmas Eve. Not because you miss me, not because you can't stand to spend Christmas without me. And not because you want to have a drink and make out on the couch, which seems like a great idea to me! No, you came because your Mars Mission has hit a snag."

"Come to a halt. You were right."

"Eh? How's that again? I didn't quite hear. I was what?"

"Please, Tom. There are lives at stake. You were right. We were wrong to send you away. I know it couldn't have been easy for you."

"Oh, no, it was a dream. No problem at all. I'm the

man no one wants to know!"

"I know, I know..."

"Oh, and they sent you on Christmas Eve. You knew I wouldn't open the door for Bronson or Reggie, maybe even for Carrie, but for you – oh, yeah! I'm the number one sucker! Was it a tremendous sacrifice, what happened between us just a minute ago?"

"Tom, don't do this!"

"Well, you put on the brakes pretty quick, so I'm guessing – yes!"

"No, Tom. You're not..."

"I can hear Bronson now: 'You're the only one who can turn him. Thanks for taking one for the team, Dana.'"

"Would you shut up?" yelled Dana. "There's more at stake than your feelings!"

At that moment, I didn't want Dana in my apartment. I didn't want a fire and twinkling holiday lights. Even the rum and eggnog seemed bitter.

Standing by the counter, I trembled with anger. My face was hot. I couldn't find the words to express the flip side of what I couldn't find the words to express to Dana earlier. I gripped the edge of the counter and vibrated with rage. Dana sat forward on the couch, speaking to the night, not looking at me. Her voice was close to a whisper.

"You were right! And I realized you were right. Everything that happened came back to me like a giant rock sitting on my chest, crushing the breath out of me. Bronson, Reggie, Carrie and I all just looked at each other unable to form a cogent thought. Carrie cried. Even Reggie couldn't console her. Liz felt terrible, like she had betrayed her best friend. Both Foster and Liz volunteered for this trip. Bronson knew you'd punch him if he showed up. In the end, I had to be the one to come. I want you to know that this isn't easy for me."

She turned toward me, her eyes imploring me for mercy. "I wanted to kiss you. I still want to kiss you. I want to kiss you naked and all night and all over. I want to hold you and pull the cover over us, blocking the whole world out. I want to put a sign on the door saying 'Do not disturb ever!' But I can't. Not now. Soon! Soon, I promise."

I opened my mouth to speak, but nothing came out.

Dana hung her head. She shook it as she continued. "Love me, Tom. And make love to me, lots and lots, until I wear out, but please, listen to me. You were right, we were wrong and now they're in danger and you have to LISTEN TO ME!" she screamed.

Dana was shaking now. She was crying and shaking and looking at me with angry eyes. I could be her savior and I was ignoring her. I gulped hard.

"OK!" I said, climbing up on one of the stools by the counter and trying not to be an asshole. "I'm listening."

Dana took a deep breath and composed herself. This is

what she came here to say. All the way here, she had overcome what had happened between us. At the same time, formulating in her mind how to deliver this message.

My mind went into overdrive in that moment, considering what I already knew. NASA had what seemed to be an endless supply of experts, each smarter than the one before. Yet, here was one of them begging me to listen to the problem they couldn't solve. The problem about which I was right and they were all wrong. But NASA was fast running out of experts. They left, one by one or in droves, to join cults. They left to wear colored t-shirts and wait for the train, airplane or taxicab to Glory.

It must be important, I thought. They sent Dana. She was maybe the one person in the world I still wanted to talk to. She was the one person in the world who didn't share a personal history with me before this lifetime.

"They landed about eighty yards from the mouth of the funnel-shape at the far end of the line of structures."

"A bad start! Go on."

"They went out in a closed rover, took readings and so on and so forth. They drove as close as they could to the funnel. Then three of them, two men and a woman, went out to see what was inside, around at the front."

I rolled my eyes, marveling at the stupidity. "Why didn't you listen to me?" I moaned.

"Then they stopped. That was six-and-a-half hours

ago. They have about five-and-a-half hours of air left in their suits."

"They stopped," I said. I shook my head.

"Like kids in front of an animated holiday window, they just stood there. When the fourth astronaut..."

"Oh my God, Dana!"

"When the fourth astronaut went out, she saw them standing there staring into the funnel. She went around..."

"Oh! Don't tell me!"

"...and she looked in to see what had them so captivated."

"And now you have four astronauts standing in front of the funnel."

"Yes! What do we do?"

"You have every expert in NASA to figure this out. Doesn't anyone have a solution?"

"No! No one has a solution."

There it was: a game changar. I reached over and flipped on the counter light. It showed a teary Dana curled on the couch, looking at me like I was her last hope. It was time for me to step up. I took a deep breath and made the decision to do exactly that.

"We've got to get Bronson on the line," I said, walking around the counter and into the kitchen. I turned on the light in the kitchen. I took out my designated pancake mixing bowl and proceeded to add the ingredients. I had to stay busy or I would explode.

Dana took out a phone and punched in a number.

"He's here," she said, standing up and walking over to the counter. She handed me the phone and walked around into the kitchen.

"Who's this?" I asked into the phone.

Dana looked around the kitchen, took a pan and began opening up cupboards. She found the spray oil and sprayed the pan. She had taken over that task, so I walked back to the stool.

"This is Bronson. Has Dana told you what we're up against?"

"Yeah. OK. So the rover is not in the sight line of the funnel?"

"Right," replied Bronson.

"And you have one astronaut left on board?"

"Yes."

"Does he have a space suit?"

"Yes."

"Good. The first thing you tell him is that he is not to look into the funnel under any circumstances. It's the head of Medusa! He'll turn to stone if he looks! Got it?"

"Yes." There was the sound of a hand covering the mouthpiece. Either Bronson was relaying that instruction or he was telling someone that I was off my rocker. "Now what?" asked Bronson.

"Is there a tether on the four astronauts?"

"Three of them have tethers to each other. The fourth isn't tethered."

"Can the vehicle get to them?"

A brief pause told me Bronson was conferring with someone. "It will have to go around a pile of rocks, but it can get to them."

"But he can't look into the mouth of the funnel. That's imperative. We have to distract them, get their attention shifted. Can you cut off their air?"

"Yes, we could. It's controlled from within the module. Would that do it?"

I pondered that. It was insane, but this was a comedy of insanity as it was. There was only one thing to do, the unthinkable.

"OK. This is going to be hairy! Go ahead. Cut off their air."

The smell of pancakes began to fill the kitchen. They smelled good. It seemed right to have the smell of pancakes on Christmas Eve. And the woman I love—and hate—cooking in my kitchen. What didn't fit was me telling NASA to cut the oxygen on four astronauts on Mars.

"There's something else," said Bronson.

"What else could there possibly...?" I asked.

"There's a Martian dust storm coming at them."

Differences in pressure in the Martian atmosphere caused the wind and dust to swirl. Dust devils miles high, filled with tiny particles of sand, result. Not like Earth sand, worn smooth by wind or water. No, these were sharp, jagged weapons that could wear away the fabric of a space suit and sooner or later, tear it.

"How long until it gets to the rover?"

"Minutes," came the anxious reply.

"Good," I said, thinking fast.

"Good?" shouted Bronson.

"Yes, we'll use it as cover. Get the rover moving. Have him go around to the astronauts and get as near as possible to them. Have him in a space suit and he'll pull them into the door of the rover. Then he has to get the hell out of there before the storm passes."

"So the storm will give him a limited visibility factor?"

"That's the idea. As he gets to them, he'll cut their air, when they fall, he'll drag them into the rover, away from the funnel. Make sure that if the storm makes viewing of the funnel possible, that he doesn't look, no matter what."

"OK. Then what?"

"Turn on the air and let them revive. They need a shock. That could work. Otherwise they'll stand there transfixed until the end of time."

"OK. Then what?"

"Revive them, but don't let them talk about it. Get them onto any other subject."

"OK. Then what?" asked Bronson.

"Then take off for Earth; you're done there."

"I'll get back to you. How soon can you leave? Dana has a plane."

"What do you need me for?"

"You're the only expert we've got. We need you! Get here!"

Dana was putting pancakes on a plate.

"Within minutes," I said.

"See you when you get here." Bronson hung up before I could change my mind. I closed the phone.

Dana put a plate with pancakes and syrup on the counter. She walked around and slipped up beside me, with two knives and two forks in her hand. "We'll get a cup of coffee on the way," she said, diving into the pancakes.

59
Return to Houston

Dana was full of surprises. The first was that there was a car sitting outside. The driver was waiting inside the car running the heater. Meanwhile, we were inside the apartment "catching up." We got into the car, a Town Car rented from one of the dozens of limousine companies in Washington.

Dana talked about personal things in the car. I assumed she didn't want the driver running to the tabloids looking for a last minute gift.

She talked about her leg. She said the facility had a gym complete with a therapist and how she hardly ever uses the cane anymore. She spoke about Carrie and how she had gotten close to Reggie, so that you rarely saw them apart. There was talk that when the project completed, she would stay on with him. Foster had a husband. About a month into the project, she had him transfer to Houston to be with her. Bronson had divorced his wife, but still flew back to San Diego every few weeks to see his kids.

Dana and Liz were rooming together and had grown close. They got assigned a nice suite with two bedrooms and a shared living room. There was a kitchenette, though she admitted neither of them did much cooking.

We took the Town Car to the airport, the private side, where there were no lines and traffic jams. There we saw the second surprise: she had her own airplane. Bronson mentioned that she had an airplane. With everything else, the information went right by me without impact.

There on the tarmac sat a two-engine jet warming up. We went from the car to the plane without fanfare. Once in the plane, the pilot disappeared into the cockpit and closed the door. We were alone.

"I didn't want to talk in front of the driver. He might go to the press. If he does, all he'll have is that Liz and I live together and Carrie has a boyfriend."

The plane began to taxi. Outside it was freezing cold, but clear. We would have a good flight. I had to admit, I did not regret leaving Washington behind me.

"I hope we don't run into Santa Claus," I said, looking out the window. Dana smiled.

The hole in my heart was beginning to heal. I missed her. The love we felt between us was real. We didn't have the opportunity in previous lives to make promises and break them. We hadn't hurt each other and left angry. We had done all that this lifetime. At least we remembered all the twists and changes. They weren't buried under a command to forget it all.

It had been fifty-five minutes to the airport. Bronson must have gotten something done by now.

"We should call him," I said.

"He'll call us," said Dana.

"Why am I going again? I mean, outside of the fact that you're going."

"Because you're the only expert we have on this subject. When we want answers, we turn to you. Just because we don't believe you most of the time doesn't mean you're wrong. It means you're right and we have a lot to learn."

The plane lifted up off the runway. Dana and I sat back in our seats. I was glad for the lack of vibration that usually accompanied large jets on takeoff. I relaxed my grip on the arms of the seat.

"Have you been following the Gospel Train movement?" she asked. The dreamy-eyed converts had of late turned ugly. They took anyone not accepting their viewpoint to task, often with violent results.

At first it was only fistfights breaking out here or there. Then gangs of orange-shirted thugs roaming the streets pressing their point. The movement proclaiming the Direct Track to Glory had much to answer for. They clashed with other groups with a different message. When they did, emergency rooms overflowed with true believers.

"Following? In the press, yes. Otherwise, no, I stay away from all the cults that are forming – like I said they would."

"Yes, yes! Would you please let it go? I said you were right. I'm sorry! I apologize! We all do! Please drop it!"

"OK," I said, turning my head away. "But I was right."

"You were right," admitted Dana.

"I want that in writing," I added.

"Will you settle for 'in sickness as in health, for better or worse, 'til death do us part?'"

"Yeah, I'll settle for that." The woman who didn't want to talk about our relationship just suggested marriage and I agreed. It was as romantic as we were going to get.

60
Old Pictures

We sat with our own thoughts for a moment. Then Dana spoke, quiet and back on subject.

"I'm surprised, we all are, at the variety of crazy groups coming into existence. They seem to latch onto something familiar and comfy. Then they stretch it into something bizarre and ugly."

"They're just old pictures. They don't even belong to the people who see them as truth. They received those images in this machine. Each stop along the corridor shoots in a different picture. Imagine a car moving down the assembly line and there are different nozzles. One coats the chrome. Then the car moves along and the next shoots a primer, then a color, then a second color, then something else. Each one has a different function."

"Only they're pictures of these nutty cults," said Dana.

"Something like that. They're meant to give us something else to look at instead of the truth, to keep us docile and controllable. It's all about control."

"So what's the truth?"

"Heck if I know. This stuff is coming to me a little at a time. If truth pops up, I promise, you'll be the first to know."

"OK, go on."

"So, the guy gets shuttled along the assembly line, injected with pictures. There's 'this' and 'that', one thing and another, all being equal in value to the others. If he tries to look at the truth, this picture pops up and says, 'Here it is!' and he says, 'Aha! I knew it!' and he's still stuck. Anyone not stuck with him on the same thing, he presses the point. After all, his picture tells him he's got the truth. Everyone else must be wrong!"

"Why does one thing jump out and become his 'truth' and not another?" asked Dana.

"It depends on what he gets stuck in. You get one of these guys having a serious shock and he could snap out of it. He won't know what he saw in that thing. He'll open his closet one day, see a row of orange t-shirts and wonder what the hell is going on."

"OK, but why did our astronauts just stand there?" She asked.

"They get fixed onto this thing and then they move along down the corridor. But this one isn't moving at all, so they just hang up at that step."

"They'd still be there if some outside force didn't act on them?" asked Dana, her eyes wide, head to one side like a curious puppy.

"Now you're getting it," I said. Having someone start to understand even a small corner of what I had been saying was gratifying.

"So he goes along, receiving these pictures…" Dana was ready for the next thing.

"Right, and then they get to the end and meet up with the final step, the Forgetter Switch. They get the switch attached and they're sent on their way. When they start a life, the switch goes 'click' and they wake up knowing nothing."

"No memory of the assembly line," said Dana.

"Right," I replied.

"No memory of former lives."

"Right."

"No memory of what they had learned earlier."

"Yes, but it's faulty."

"What do you mean?" she asked, furrowing her brow. This was complex enough without being faulty to boot.

"It's flawed, broken. It has leaks. Stuff leaks through. How do you get some kid living in the backwoods of Tennessee who becomes a piano virtuoso at the age of six?"

"I don't know," said Dana. It was Dana-ese for "Tell me."

"Deep down they remember being a piano virtuoso. Once they get their hands on a piano, they have this magical knowledge no one can understand. Remember, I said it's a decision, that people make decisions."

"Yeah," urged Dana.

"I think there are geniuses who decide not to know anything. They're tired of being the smartest kid in the room, tired of everyone taking advantage of them. So, they make a decision. Next lifetime they're an idiot and have to have someone dress them every morning. But they are also a savant and can tell you the periodic tables frontward and backward."

"So they decide and that's that."

"Yup! That's what I think."

The plane hummed in the background as we spoke back and forth. Dana plied me for details and I told her what I knew, what I thought I knew and what I didn't know, until I ran dry.

I wanted to lean over and kiss her, but I didn't know if that would be acceptable here and now. Instead, I broached the subject that I thought we had decided back in my apartment.

"I'm staying with you tonight," I said. It was not a question.

"Yes, when we finally get to bed at all," she confirmed.

"And waking up with you in the morning," I said, just to be sure.

"Yes, or whatever time it is when we wake up," reconfirmed Dana.

"OK. Just making sure," I said, leaning back.

It didn't matter to me if we were upside down in our schedules, as long as we were upside down together. As an astronomer, Dana was upside down most of the time, up all night and sleeping during the daylight hours.

I tried that schedule once, working nights when it was quiet. The problem was that the noise level and frequency of visitors was higher in the day. Trucks drove by, kids yelled and sirens wailed during the day. Less so at night. During the day, evangelists visited, delivery men knocked and door-to-door salesmen plied their trade. Trying to get a good night's sleep in the daylight hours was a challenge, but I was willing to face it with Dana. I had it bad!

"And I want everyone to know," I added.

"What do you want everyone to know?" asked Dana, not following the train of thought.

"That we're a couple. I don't want anyone whispering that we might be together. I want it out in the open and known."

"I'll introduce you as my husband. That'll clarify matters," said Dana. The statement just hung there in the air, not acknowledged further.

61
The Insect

At the console of the rover, Insect, Arnie Chin wiped the perspiration from his forehead. He set his jaw and turned the wheel toward the end of the line of jagged rocks. Arnie wasn't using sight. He steered from the monitors, radar and sonar readings. He guided Insect over the uncertain ground at a riveting seventeen kilometers per hour. It felt like he was driving in slow motion.

The storm hit him from the rear. It jolted the rover forward and to the left. He steered to compensate, hoping he wouldn't flip.

The edge of the rock chain came up before him; he could see it, with visibility a mere twenty yards. Arnie gauged the angle of the rocks below the surface of the softer sand. He gave it ten feet extra before turning right, toward the stranded astronauts. He was driving with the storm to his right now, threatening to push him off course. The Insect's wheels dug into the sand, reaching for traction.

As the storm picked up, he drove more and more by instruments. The four dots on his screen were before him, with nothing showing in the way – so far. He hoped it would continue that way.

Outside the Insect, there was a familiar sound of wind howling. The normal mild winds of Mars were furious inside a dust storm. The sharp granules of Martian sand could slice through a compromised suit. Arnie knew that if they stood there for too long, he might not be rescuing them so much as collecting their bodies.

A rise in the terrain tilted the rover, threatening to overturn it. Arnie steered left, then right again, back on course. It seemed to be taking forever to get to the stranded astronauts, and Arnie did not have forever.

At last, he reached them, still standing, in spite of the dust storm. Visibility was down to ten feet and Arnie was on full instrument navigation. He put on his helmet and opened the air lock at Insect's rear hatch. On the remote console, he cut the oxygen to Blain's suit.

Arnie opened the hatch to see one body lying on the ground. It didn't even register that he had just become the fifth person to ever set foot on Mars. He stepped out and walked toward Blain. He lifted Blain and carried her to the rover, closing the air lock behind him. It would be a slow and tedious rescue.

He sat her against the bulkhead in the airlock and

turned on the oxygen in her suit. Then he turned off Rodriguez and stepped out to retrieve the fallen astronaut. He repeated the process for Hanson.

Arnie was two steps from the rover with Metcalf in his arms when disaster struck. He fell, tumbling Metcalf onto the ground. He saw the thin, worn suit tear.

Arnie turned her over and pushed hard on her chest, expelling all the air from her lungs. He had to do that before they would expand and rupture. He dragged her into the airlock, knowing the he had less than ninety seconds to revive her. He shut the air lock and turned on her oxygen.

In the airlock sat the other three astronauts, looking dazed but breathing. It was close quarters, as they designed the airlock for two, not the entire crew at once.

Arnie opened the hatch and pulled the crew into the Insect one at a time.

"What happened?" asked Blain, once Arnie had helped her with her helmet.

"No time for that now, I've got to get us out of here. Can you help me with these suits?" replied Arnie.

"Yeah, I think so." She reached over to help Elaine Metcalf with her helmet. She looked into the faceplate to see Elaine's deep brown eyes looking off at some distant point. She wondered what had happened to put her into such a state.

"She had a tear. She lost pressure," said Arnie Chin.

"Did you catch her in time?" asked Blain.

"I think so." Arnie was helping Hanson out of his helmet as Rodriguez sat coughing next to him.

Arnie stood up, surveying his crew. Elaine was recovering slower than the rest, but she was breathing and that was a good thing for the present. He got into the pilot's seat and turned the rover around, heading back to the landing module. He hoped the storm would hold until he got out of the sight line of the Amphitheater.

Arnie pushed the button on the console, sending a message to Earth.

"Houston? This is Insect. We're loaded and turning around for the return trip to the landing module."

It was several minutes before the response would come back to him, enough time to get to the turn in the rock ridge. The storm was coming in from the port side. Arnie was doing his best to navigate terrain never before seen by man. When the response came, it was not what he expected.

"Ahhh, negative, Insect. Readings confirm that the landing module was overturned by the storm. It is no longer in its former position. It is non-functional. Suggest you continue on to the ERV, which is in a protected location and still functional."

Arnie gulped hard and turned the rover around. He knew that he would have to cross in front of a structure that would turn them to stone if he were to look into its face.

The Earth Return Vehicle had landed in a spot that was outside the storm, so it was still there. The landing module was not. The storm was worst at the landing site.

If the ERV was not there, if it was out of commission as well, there were no other contingencies. The rover had about twenty hours of air left.

"Affirmative, Houston, we will precede to the ERV," said Arnie. Tiredness and resolve both sounded in his voice. This was not the screaming success they had planned, but they might just get home to talk about it.

The original idea was to land, look at the thing and take readings. They would spend several days gathering data and return with proof that life was once or is now on Mars. If there were intelligent creatures found, this might well be First Contact.

62
Back in the Game

Bronson was standing in the rain at the airport as the plane rolled in. He was in a trench coat right out of a 1940s Bogart movie.

"You know, my boss isn't going to like this," I said as I stepped down from the plane.

"I'm your boss. You just quit the Senator. You answer to me now and you have a raise in pay, a serious raise."

"That's good to know, because I haven't gotten Dana anything for Christmas yet."

"The holidays are going to be late this year, at least for us. The car's this way."

We began walking to the car together, with Bronson at my elbow, making sure I didn't slip away. Dana brought up the rear, blocking my exit. Not that I had plans to bolt, but they were making sure.

Bronson opened the door. I saw Reggie at the wheel.

"Hi, Reggie."

"Hi, Mister Matthews. Glad to have you back."

"Thanks, Reggie."

"We have to get back to see how many astronauts we can count," said Reggie, starting the engine.

"Right," said Bronson.

As soon as Dana was in and the door closed, Reggie drove us out the gate and into the night.

"How much of a raise?" I asked.

"You're going to negotiate with me on Christmas Eve?" Bronson shot at me.

"Can't think of a better time," I replied.

"An impressive raise. I'm assuming you were making crap."

"In public service? Why would you assume such a thing?" I joked. In truth, I was making crap. I had a feeling that I would save a lot now that I would no longer be drinking to cure loneliness.

"Let's just say that the private sector pays better and that you've already proven your value. Holding my feet to the fire isn't going to get you anything but a boss with burnt feet."

The subject of my raise, of my hiring at all, went onto a back burner. Like spending the night with Dana, I assumed it was a given. If later a job was not realized, I would pitch a fit. Right now, I was content to be in the thick of things and surrounded by friends once more.

As we stepped out of the car at the side entrance closest to Command Central, a technician ran up to us.

"Sir?" said the technician to Reggie.

"What is it?" he replied.

"Solar flares. There have been solar flares reported, big and headed for Mars. They have to get to the ERV in a matter of minutes."

"Is the colonel notified?" asked Reggie.

"Yes, sir," snapped the technician. It seemed Reggie was a bigger cheese than we knew.

"What's up?" I asked him.

"Solar flares," he explained as we walked into Command Central. "Earth has a magnetic field that protects us from the charged particles of a solar flare. Mars doesn't, it lost its magnetic field four million years ago. Those particles will go right through a space suit, right through a vehicle or lander. A special section of the ERV will protect them from the charged particles of radiation. Like x-rays, they go right through most things."

All heads turned to the large screen. It showed the picture taken from the on-board camera in the rover, Insect.

The dust storm blew its fury at the little craft and threatened to stick it in the sand several times. Each time, Arnie Chin drove as if his life, and that of his entire crew, depended on it. He was the astronaut who stayed behind and ended up saving the day. Now he was driving them to safety.

At the ERV, the crew abandoned the Insect and climbed into the hatch. They settled in and closed the hatch, hoping that it would be for the last time. They reported their status and awaited instructions.

"What now?" asked Reggie. Doctor Bronson turned his head to see as well as hear my answer. Behind him, the technician also froze in place, as if he had looked into the funnel. They were waiting for my edict, the words that would guide NASA's next move.

"Bring them home. You're done," I said, without looking at them.

63
In the Interest of National Security

Caroline Foster came up to me, grinning. She looked at the screen and then turned to me. "The astronauts are aboard the ERV. A little disoriented but alive and recovering in the solar flare locker. Glad you're back, Tom. It's been tough going without you."

"Thanks, Caroline. Good to be back." It felt both strange and familiar, meant to be and yet unexpected. I was standing in the middle of Command Central telling astronauts what they should do next.

That's when the screen went black and the sound vanished. A protest rose up in the room and assistants scrambled to see what was going on. Reggie slipped out to the hallway, following a hunch.

"All right, people. Quiet down," said a stern voice over the public address system. We all got still, waiting for the god-like voice to explain. "We've cut the sound and picture in the interest of National Security. Please await further instructions." The voice clicked off.

Reggie reappeared, wide eyed, tapping my arm. "Come here! You've got to see this!" he said.

We followed Reggie to the lunch room, which had two uniformed guards on the door, armed. They each held up a hand as we approached. Bronson stepped forward, his chin set ready for a fight.

"I'm Doctor Bronson. These are my colleagues and we are vital to this mission. I demand you let us in."

"OK," came the same barking voice we had heard on the Command Central loudspeaker. "Let 'em in." The doors opened.

Someone rearranged the tables in a horseshoe. Around the tables were a dozen uniformed men and women, from all branches of the Services. At the open end, in front of a curtain flanked by American flags, was a large gentleman. By the stars on his collar, he was a general.

"If you're going to come in, you're going to sit down and shut up. There are some seats at the end there," said the general, pointing to a few empty chairs.

All the uniformed personnel watched us as we found our way to the seats.

"Let me in there!" came a yell from the hall. It was Liz. The general waved a hand and Liz scurried in. She found a seat next to me, grumbling. "Glad to see you, boy," she whispered, patting my arm.

"If I may begin," growled the general. All became silent as he looked around, as if deciding who to eat first.

"Ladies and gentlemen, the President of the United States."

The general turned to the side as a man in a dark suit stepped from the curtain. It was President Statler. The closest I had ever been to him was a campaign poster. I hadn't even seen him on television during the debates. And now here he was standing in the Mission Central lunch room.

"All right!" he began. His soft admonishing voice was reminiscent of times he had put Congress in its place.

"We sat back when you fired off a mission to Mars, though someone warned against it. We stood by when people from all walks of life wandered off and joined cults too crazy to imagine. We watched as you lost four out of five of your own team. Then you brought in the expert from Washington, the one with no credentials whatsoever."

President Statler looked over at me, overwhelmed by the stupidity of it all. He took a long, deep breath and continued, looking a little too pleased with himself. "But now it's our turn. There is a news blackout as of now and until further notice. We're briefing the press about a technical malfunction. We're keeping them away while we repair the damage."

Our little group exchanged glances. There was no malfunction. There was a switch and someone threw it.

"We have to follow the situation so the screens will

come back up. The room, of course, is empty now, we'll have limited attendance. You in this room can come in, but you will sit down and be quiet. You will not interfere or we'll kick you out. Under normal circumstances, I would ask if you got that, but I don't care if you got it or not. If you interfere you will get the boot. If you get the boot, it will be with force and permanent. Now, let's get in there, we don't have time to waste."

The dozen officers got up and left with haste. We followed them out, not asking questions.

In the hall, Dana looked up at me, questioning what was happening.

"There's always a contingency plan," I whispered.

Only a few vital technicians were evident in Command Central. The rest were a handful of Secret Service Agents and a few uniformed personnel, all armed. We sat down and watched the screen. A colonel came over and sat in an empty chair near us. He spoke to us without introduction.

"As you can see, they are preparing for liftoff. We have made the decision to return this discovery to the dust of Mars, where wiser minds once put it. As you know, all the astronauts aboard are military officers. They are under orders should the mission encounter anything like it encountered earlier tonight."

The colonel looked at the screen. There was an image of the funnel from the side. A vibration shook the camera. Within minutes, a blast of red dust shot out into the picture. They had engaged the thrusters.

"The ERV is equipped with an array of explosive warheads. These air-to-surface missiles will distribute the payload along the length of the discovery. As they blast off over the area to be re-buried, these rockets will fire. They are timed to reach their targeted areas in sequence. There will be many blasts. This will once again be a wasteland, uninterrupted by signs of intelligent life."

The screen showed the ERV launching. We sat transfixed as it took off. Minutes went by and still we watched. NASA engineers removed earlier attended a briefing. They were told about the malfunction prohibiting them from viewing the takeoff.

The camera shook.

"There go the first missiles," said the colonel. In the corner of the screen and on other screens, we could see rockets speed toward the surface of the planet. I sat as in a trance, staring at the screen. Dana's hand found mine and squeezed. The camera shook again.

"There go the next."

On the surface, explosions flanked the amphitheater. Soon, the funnel-shaped structure on the end of the long line of buildings disappeared.

I knew it to be the entrance. I chuckled inside, "That's because the astronauts were entranced," I said to myself. "Entranced at the entrance. Ha!" But now was not the time for jokes. I reflected that there would never come a time for that joke.

The sequence repeated: the camera shook; rockets fired. On the surface explosions brought up huge clouds of red dust.

"It will take ten days to two weeks for the dust to settle over that area. When it does, we expect that the entire site will disappear below the dust." The colonel glowered at the crowd. He slipped out of his chair and crept up the stairs to the side in such a way that no one would notice him.

President Statler stepped to the center as more rockets went off. More explosions raised giant clouds of dust. He spoke in his soft voice, so that everyone had to strain to hear him, but strain they did.

"During the technical malfunction, the Mars Mission Explorer Nine ERV took off. It sent up large amounts of red dust, as you can imagine. As the cameras looked back, the takeoff triggered a chain reaction on the surface of the planet."

President Statler didn't look at the screen. He took in a large breath and continued. "The clouds took days, perhaps even weeks to dissipate." He was talking now about the future as if it was the past. "The clouds dissipated. The structures once discovered in the dust of Mars were no longer visible. The buildings were once more claimed by the sands of time—which is as it should be."

We soaked this in as we watched the last of the rockets from the ERV. A minute later, the last of the explosions took place on the surface. Immediately, red dust rose to cloud the picture.

President Statler nodded to someone in the back of the room. The picture changed to inside the shuttle. The astronauts had their headgear off and were piloting the craft.

"Houston, we have liftoff. The birds are away and we have one hundred percent saturation," said the voice over the com-system.

"There will be no more Mars flights," said the President. "Mister Matthews will warn against them and people will listen this time. Or there will be other things that need the money more. Or the next popular fad to sweep the country will be the anti-space race. Other countries will follow suit. The concept of coming up with their own space programs will become unpopular. They'll find interest in other things. Perhaps in other planets, the space station or just staying on the ground. Something! But never again will we entertain a trip to Mars to dig up that—whatever the hell it is up there. Is that clear to everyone here?"

We all nodded like school children.

"It had better be. I'm not losing any more of my people to that damned train cult. Now, if you don't mind, Doctor

Bronson, I'm going back to Washington. I've got real work to do."

President Statler left. He was followed by two lines of Secret Service agents and a collection of uniformed officers. Armed soldiers stayed behind to stand at doors and generally look intimidating. It worked on us. We were intimidated.

"The next time you open your mouth, Tom, I'm going to listen," said Liz.

"Yeah, me too," added Dana, sneaking her arm into the crook of my elbow.

"Well, people," said Doctor Bronson. "They'll take six months for them to get back. It's Christmas Eve. I suggest we all go home and go to bed or Santa won't come."

"Sounds good to me," I said to Dana.

"Do you think there's a place where we can get some eggnog and rum?" asked Dana.

Liz answered her. "Got to be. After all, it's Christmas."

64
A Second Mars Quake

The headlines on Christmas Day told of tremors on Mars. These warned the astronauts that another Mars quake was about to happen. They took off to avoid a disaster. Sure enough, there was a quake. It buried the discovery uncovered earlier on the surface of the planet.

In the breakfast nook, Liz had waffles in progress. The coffee was already made and filled the apartment with a wonderful aroma.

A knock on the door said we'd have to make more coffee. Liz opened the door and Carrie came in, bearing gifts.

"Are you still talking to me?" she asked me.

"Sure, kid. You're like a sister to me. Come here!" I gave her a big hug and a familiar feeling came over me, one that I had always enjoyed from centuries before.

It was Carrie, the spirit that was Carrie, who started this. Her love for me, my love for her, a brothers love for his sister, prompted me to say that I would always remember. The feather-lite decision changed my life, for lifetimes gone and lifetimes to come. It changed the course of history for the whole planet. If it hadn't been for her, I wouldn't be here. And if not for me, those astronauts would still be standing in front of the funnel until their air ran out.

"I got you a present," said Carrie.

"I didn't get you anything," I said, caught unawares as I was.

"That's all right. You just got here. I got a birthday coming up. See you then." Carrie laughed and handed me a package wrapped in cheesy holiday wrapping. I tore it off and saw a t-shirt. It was light blue and said, "Explorer IX went to Mars and all I got was this lousy t-shirt."

"I got 'em for you all," said Carrie. She gave the other two packages to Liz and Dana.

There was a red one for Dana, Liz's was green. Carrie took off her jacket to reveal the same shirt in light blue. She had seen them on the side of the road and couldn't resist.

We put on our t-shirts and sat down for waffles on Christmas morning.

"I don't get it," said Carrie, as she reached for the syrup. "The quake on Mars uncovered that thing on Mars, but there were quakes here too. What did they do?"

"Oh, my God!" said Dana, "I'd forgotten. There were

quakes on Earth, in the Bermuda Triangle and the Dragon's Triangle. The expected tsunamis were a footnote next to the discovery on Mars. But the quakes were simultaneous."

She looked at me, hoping I would come up with an explanation. I could feel my face go white as I realized that I in fact did have an explanation.

"They were here, too!" I said, almost in a whisper, but emphatic. "There was a complex in the Bermuda Triangle and one in the Devil's Triangle. There are remnants of them still beneath the ocean. They lie in waters too deep or too dangerous to investigate."

A film I had seen taken underwater by a graduate student came into my mind. The student later disappeared in the Bermuda Triangle. I remembered seeing massive stones. Intelligent life had to make them, deep under the water. Speculation was that this was the lost city of Atlantis. There were similar films of similar stones, said to be ancient temples. Believed swallowed by the sea, they disappeared before history could account for them.

These two areas on Earth were the centers of strange and unexplained activity. All the activity was deadly. Ships and planes were lost, divers vanished and those who go searching are never heard from again. The facility on Mars was only one. There were two more on Earth, buried long ago where man could never go, under the water.

I looked up and into the eyes of Carrie and Dana, their faces also pale and bloodless. It was as if I had been speaking out loud. They understood.

"There's something under the water off China and off Florida. Something that's like what we found up there, isn't there?" said Carrie.

"Yes, I believe there is," said Dana. "We didn't have to go all the way to Mars to investigate this occurrence. We could have done so right here at home, under the sea."

"Good thing we didn't," I added. The color was returning to my face, but the realization lingered. The ramifications rolled through my brain.

"Who do we tell?" asked Dana.

"We don't tell anyone," I said. I reached out to take her hand in mine and at the same time reached for Carrie. Her little hand took mine and we all nodded. We decided, we had made a pact. No one would ever know about the connection we had just made. If someone were to make the synaptic jump, we would squelch it. If anyone put together an expedition, we would jump on it and bury it before it could gain momentum. We were our own little conspiracy.

65
Heroes and Lovers

The Mars Explorer IX crew were welcomed home as heroes. There was lots of fanfare and parades in every city. Kids still wanted to be astronauts and people still dreamed of going to Mars and digging up the ruins that lay beneath the surface, though no further missions were planned.

Three days after the crew took off from Mars, people started to wake up. The Depots were abandoned and you couldn't give away an orange t-shirt. People went back to their jobs and tried to explain what happened to them. Things that made perfect sense one day sounded like the ravings of a lunatic the next. Support groups were formed and a general policy of forgive and forget was pushed on television and radio.

Doctor Bronson made good on his job offer and I became a Special Congressional Adviser to NASA, at a considerable increase in pay. The Senator let me go without a fight; not even a whimper.

Carrie and Reggie have a standing invitation for dinner and Liz is a regular fixture at our place.

Weekend nights find Dana and me in our vintage pickup truck a few miles out in the desert, looking up at the stars. I get a kick out of asking, "Where's Mars?" and Dana delights in saying, "There," pointing to the sky. I reply "Oh."

"You know all those trite, hackneyed phrases people say to each other to try and communicate that they love the other person?" Dana asks.

"You mean, like 'you're my everything, I'll love you forever and you mean the world to me?'"

"Yes, them."

"Yeah, what about 'em?" I ask.

"Well, me, you, all that," Dana says, snuggling into my chest.

"Mm!" I tell her. "You are so romantic!"

End

About the author...

Born in Washington D. C. to artistic parents, Jon Batson is a writer, entertainer and the driving force behind Midnight Whistler Publishers (MWP), an independent press located in Raleigh, NC. Originally established as a music publishing house in 1979, MWP expanded in 2006, to include all forms of book publication including e-books, which are an agreed-upon game changer in publishing today.

Jon takes great pride in the choice of manuscripts he publishes. He looks for well-written, insightful, and thought-provoking non-fiction that focuses on education, politics and government. The fact-based fiction works, in addition to being entertaining, awaken readers and throw a light on relevant situations happening in the world.

An award-winning author, Batson's stories are told from a place of truth and enlightenment. His gritty, often irreverent style strikes a chord of contemplation and demands your attention with subtle innuendo and carefully scattered satire. His signature is intentionally provocative and refreshingly entertaining. He is a four time winner of the Lower Cape Fear Short Story Contest and twice awarded Honorable Mention in the internationally known Writers of The Future Contest for science fiction writers. Jon has successfully participated in National Novel Writing Month seven years.

Jon lives with his wife, Eileen, in Raleigh, North Carolina where he is no doubt working on his next novel.

Visit www.TheRealJonBatson.com

Fiction by Jon Batson

Deadly Research

When author Jack Richmond researches his next novel, he uncovers the biggest conspiracy in history, happening under our noses and in plain sight. Now Jack and his girlfriend are running for their lives. *Deadly Research* is the first novel in the Jack Richmond series.

Research Triangle

Jack Richmond discovers a building on the edge of the Research Triangle where school children were being remotely monitored at a distance for medication reactions. The monitoring room was joyous at the killing of 32 students until the discovery that they were being recorded. Jack Richmond wakes with no memory at all.

Terminal Research

The story continues as Jack Richmond returns home on Halloween to find that his fiance, Teri, has been abducted. Finding her becomes his first objective, but along the way he has to deal with new assassins, old friends gone bad and members of the organization that is really running things.

Murder at Thompson Bog

A collection of short stories that tend to be on the darker side. If you like curling up with a scary story, this may be your ticket to insomnia.

Encounter in a Small Café

A light-hearted collection of short stories including some prize winners from The Lower Cape Fear Historical Fiction Contest.

Doll Bodies

Out-of-this-world tales including other possible futures, space stories, and excerpts from two future full-length projects. If you are craving a little Sci-Fi in your day, here you are. Enjoy!

Nina Knows the Night

Nina Richardson, a mild-mannered law school dropout, is tired of the criminals in her neighborhood. She dresses in black and ventures into the night to become a kick-butt crime-fighter. She discovers her superpowers to be her own inner-strength and purpose.

What they're saying about Jon Batson:

"Jon Batson is not just a writer, but a storyteller. His gift is making you experience what his characters feel and see while he slings irony and witty asides that make others wonder why you're laughing so hard. He looks closer at the ordinary world and determines what extraordinary things a person can do given the right circumstances. The result is a story that won't be put down."

Alice Osborn,
author, editor and teacher of *"Write from the Inside Out."*

"Colorful, engrossing, and highly entertaining! Jon Batson has produced an evocative collection of engaging characters whose lives unfold in amusing, tragic and, often, unexpected ways that send the imagination gliding over each one's winding paths, hairpin curves and jarring potholes with the artistic finesse of a truly masterful storyteller."

Karen Michelle Raines, poet/author

"Batson's stories are contemporary yet reminiscent of an earlier time – O'Henry, Raymond Carver and Edgar Allen Poe come to mind. Luckily for us although the aforementioned have gone onto their last edit, Jon will be with us for a long time."

Steven Elliot, Falls River Books

"I could hear you in every sentence. Easy reading, nice payoff, and a few surprises."

Gary Young, Author

"Thanks for writing and sharing your short stories with me. Your characters in these creative adventures come alive with the action and your clean concise writing keep the tales moving at a fun pace! I enjoyed reading them and look forward to more."

J. K. Gildersleeve, Writer and Illustrator

'A good book is one you think about all day and wonder what is happening with the characters, cannot wait to get back to them and hope you haven't missed much while you're away. I found myself emotionally connected all the way through as the story unfolded.'

Susan Henson, Avid Reader

Mars Quake was edited by Alice Osborn. About the book, Alice says: *Jon's images and characterizations are in my head. In fact, I'm using him as what to do right in my fiction editing class!*
Thank you, Alice.

www.ingramcontent.com/pod-product-compliance
Lightning Source LLC
Chambersburg PA
CBHW062012170626
46813CB00001B/134